PUPPET
POLITICS

To BARBARA CALDWELL—

Puppet Politics

HARRY HAINES

Harry Haines

10/11/13

Colonial Publishing, Inc.

This novel does not depict any actual person or event.

Colonial Publishing, Inc.
2576 Oak Valley Drive
Vienna, VA 22181

COPYRIGHT © 2013: Harry Haines
COVER DESIGN: Steven L. Mayes
Library of Congress Control Number: 2013902067
First Edition—First Printing 2013
ISBN: 978-0-9834537-3-4
Printed in Canada

To Steven Lee Mayes
. . . the world's best book-cover designer
. . . the guy who came up with the title for this novel
. . . and, most of all, a truly great friend.

Novels by Harry Haines:

Orphan

Texas Panic!

Collusion

The Cover-up at Ann Arbor

Offshore

Puppet Politics

1

The horse barn, six miles north of Midland, Texas

The first clue I had was a big "whoosh," a sound like that of someone lighting a huge hot water heater—a gigantic gas burner.

"What was that?" asked Tim, my ten-year-old son, his eyes wide, his face filled with fear.

Our two horses, Midnight and Champ, skittishly backed away from me and their feed buckets.

"Let's check it out." I dropped a sack of feed and sprinted toward the barn door. Tim ran with me. As we neared the large open doorway, I felt heat.

"Careful," I said, grabbing Tim's shoulder, pulling him close, trying to use my body to shield him as I peered around the corner of the barn. One quick look told me.

An oil well was afire.

HARRY HAINES

The well, located less than a hundred yards west of our barn, normally faded into the landscape, and I sometimes forgot it was there. Now, it raged with red-orange-yellow flames that leapt hundreds of feet into the air and produced an enormous black plume of smoke.

I took off my Stetson, held it in front of my face, and tried to analyze the danger. The intense heat and pungent smell of burning oil caused my brain to lapse into lockdown mode—I literally couldn't think. So I stood like a zombie, petrified with fear, maneuvering my hat to catch quick glances of the inferno, knowing something had to be done.

"Dad. What is it?"

I pulled back, gave my hat to Tim, and said. "Just a quick look, no more than a second." He stretched his head out and immediately pulled back.

"Wow," he said. "What're we going to do?"

The pause for Tim's quick look gave me a second to think. My first reaction was to save Tim and myself. But instantly I had another thought. "We can't leave the horses," I said.

As if in response, Champ and Midnight panicked, their whinny-screams filling the barn with sounds of imminent disaster.

"Should we turn 'em loose?" Tim asked.

Again I peeked out the door, only to see a dangerous situation growing worse. A huge grass fire—one that had started from the spewing oil—raged in all directions from the well's platform. In a matter of minutes, maybe only seconds, flames would be at our barn door. I made a decision.

"We can't," I said. "Our only hope is to load them into the trailer and make a run for it. You get the hitch ready while I back the pickup into the barn."

Luckily, my fifteen-year-old pickup was parked only a few steps from

8

the barn entrance. Not so fortunate was its dependability factor. I ran to it and hoped it would start. Just that morning I had stopped at the Ford dealer to inquire about trading it for a new vehicle. His offer of fifteen hundred dollars had halted negotiations. If only I'd made the trade.

But when I needed it most, the dilapidated old rust bucket started, and in less than a minute I had it backed up to the horse trailer. Tim slipped on the hitch, and in record time we had it coupled and ready.

Then came the tough job.

Our two horses, normally gentle, selected for children, now bucked and kicked like wild animals. I pulled a lead rope off the wall and ran toward the first stall. Champ, Tim's three-year-old chestnut quarter horse, stared at me with fire-crazed eyes. As I approached the door to his stall, he reared up, hooves pawing the air, his frantic motions accompanied with loud screams of panic. I didn't see how I could get in the same stall with this fear-stricken, thousand-pound horse.

But Tim did.

He opened the door, snapped the lead rope on Champ's halter, and talked to him in quiet, soothing tones.

I've heard a lot of stories about "horse sense." And I guess Champ's sense of trust in his youthful rider momentarily overcame his fear of fire. Tim led. I grabbed the other side of Champ's halter with my bare hand, and together we got him into the trailer and securely tied.

Next came Midnight, my daughter's five-year-old black mare, who had almost kicked the stall door off its hinges and was about to escape. I arrived just in time and made a lucky stab with my lead rope. The snap caught on Midnight's halter, and I pulled her close.

"It's all right, girl, we're gonna go see Emily," I said as I walked her to the trailer. "That's a good girl. We're almost there." Seeing another horse already loaded helped calm Midnight.

The grassfire had reached the door to our barn, and flames now threatened the building. Hay bales in the corner loomed as an unthinkable disaster. If the dry hay caught, the resulting conflagration would trap us. With Tim by my side, I floor boarded the old Ford and we blasted out of the barn. Barreling through the blazing pasture, the next thirty seconds seemed like an eternity.

But we made it.

Driving onto the nearby blacktop, an indescribable feeling of euphoria came over me—one I will remember for a lifetime. I reached over and put my arm around Tim.

"Son, I'm mighty proud of you," I said.

"Dad, I was really scared."

I gave him my best smile and pulled him tight. "Me, too."

As we headed away from the fire, the road began to fill with fire trucks, ambulances, and rubberneckers by the dozen. We were safe, but I wondered about others—especially those who might have been working on the well. Looking back at that huge inferno, at the charred remains of the tower and its equipment, I couldn't see any chance of survival.

2

I pulled out a chair at our kitchen table, sat, sipped coffee that burned my tongue, and unfolded the morning paper. A huge photo, right under the masthead of the *Midland Reporter Telegram*, dominated the front page. The strange photograph—solid black around the perimeter and stark white in the center, with jagged edges separating the two—reminded me of an ink spot used in a Rorschach test. I stared at the image for several seconds trying to figure out what it depicted. Finally I gave up and read the caption:

OILFIELD FIRE KILLS STATE SENATOR

Then it made sense. Once I knew what to look for, I recognized the huge flame—a picture taken at night, from a distance—fanned by our typical West Texas wind. I turned my attention to the accompanying story.

HARRY HAINES

"Abner Stone, longtime state senator from Odessa, was killed late yesterday afternoon while visiting a wildcat drilling rig, located north of Midland."

The article went on to describe the fiery incident. The rig was destroyed. Three oilfield workers were taken to the hospital with second-degree burns. A preliminary report from the Midland County Sheriff's Office called it an accident.

My wife Suzanne scooted a plate of sausage and scrambled eggs in front of me. "What's the photo?" she asked. She took the chair opposite me.

"The fire out by our barn. It killed Abner Stone."

"Murder?"

"Why would you think that?"

"Everyone I know is after his scalp."

"Poor old Abner," I answered, my voice dripping with sarcasm. "Can't even die without being accused of skullduggery."

"I wasn't accusing him," Suzie replied. "I'm thinking of him as the victim."

I smiled and tried to decide whether or not to push her buttons—to escalate this morning's headline into a fight. I'm a Republican. She's a Democrat. I sorta liked old Senator Stone and usually voted for him. Suzie hated his guts, his politics, and everything he stood for.

For a brief moment I silently considered the opportunity that lay before me. If I extolled Abner's political record, she'd lash out with a diatribe about his many shortcomings, and we'd be into it like cats and dogs.

"Don't say it," she cautioned.

"Say what?"

"You're about to bait me with lies about what a sterling character

Abner Stone was."

"Was not."

"Was too."

I smiled, shaking my head, innocence oozing from every pore. "Why on earth would you think that?"

"Because," she answered," I could see it in your eyes."

"In my eyes?"

She came over, sat on my lap, put her arms around my neck, and kissed me. "You have the cutest, 'the devil made me do it' look that telegraphs your intention when you're thinking about goading someone into an argument."

I pulled her close—so close I could feel her breasts pushing against me—and kissed her. She kissed me back, and my thoughts changed from devilish confrontation to lustful accord.

Then our ten-year-old ball of energy burst into the room.

"What's for breakfast?" Tim asked.

I smiled at my wife and released my grip.

"Later," she said as she stood. "Sausage, eggs, toast, and milk. You have to make your own toast."

"What about the fire?" Tim asked. "Have they put it out yet?"

"Yes," I replied. "One man died, three taken to the hospital."

Emily, our seven-year-old blonde, always laconic in the morning, came into the room and plopped down in her chair, her hair a mess, a sleepy frown on her face. "What's for breakfast?"

"The usual," Tim answered. "You pour the milk, and I'll make the toast."

"I don't like it when you burn the toast," Emily grumbled.

"Okay, you get the milk *and* make the toast."

"Mom, Tim won't do his share."

Then I made a mistake—I joined the conversation. "Tim, you need to help with breakfast. Why don't you pour the milk?"

"Dad, I offered to make the toast. She's being her usual bossy self, ordering me around."

"He's the one who's bossy," Emily shouted, her sleepy manner now transformed into open conflict. "And he always burns the toast."

Tim rolled his eyes. "See?"

The phone rang.

A law degree hadn't been enough preparation to handle breakfast fights. I left Suzie to referee and walked down the hall to the phone in our computer room. "Hello." The caller ID read McComas and Davis, Attorneys. I looked at my watch—6:45 a.m.

"Sam, this is Art." The familiar voice rushed at me with an edge of excitement.

"What are you doing at the office at this ungodly hour?" I asked.

"Getting ready for court and taking your calls."

"I think that's why I have an answering machine."

"Okay, you're right. I should have let the voice mail pick up."

"But you didn't," I said. "And now you're calling me. So what's up?"

"The lieutenant governor called a minute ago. I thought I should give you a heads up. He's going to call back after eight o'clock."

"Who?"

"Homer 'Whiskey' Williams, Lieutenant Governor of the State of Texas."

"Damn, what does he want with me at this time of the morning?"

"It's a long story. First he talked about your work for the Texas Republican Party. Then he asked about your interest in the environment, ecology, and greenhouse gases."

Art paused, and I could tell there was a zinger coming. For the ten years we'd been partners in our law firm, I'd learned to wait, to be quiet, and to let him form his words for dramatic effect.

"I think he wants to appoint you state senator," Art finally said, "to fill Abner Stone's unexpired term."

I wasn't sure I had heard what I thought I heard. "Art, say again that last part, slower."

3

Driving to the office

Art's early morning phone call had me worried. Of course, he probably had it wrong. Whiskey Williams didn't even know me, and I couldn't think of any reason he'd be interested in a little-known Midland lawyer for an important political appointment. It wouldn't be the first time Art had gotten something wrong.

But suppose he didn't. If the lieutenant governor called about appointing me to the post of state senator, the big question was, "Why?" And if he offered the appointment, an even bigger question followed— "Should I?"

I came to the intersection of Wadley Street and Big Spring Road, the corner where I always turned left, and headed south toward downtown Midland. In so doing I had to use my right hand to turn the wheel. It caused me to reflect seriously about my misshapen hand.

A birth defect, my right hand had come with only a thumb and forefinger. My mom tried to teach me to accept it, and over the years

I'd found ways to compensate, to grasp things like a car's steering wheel using just a thumb and finger, and in general, to live an almost normal, everyday life. Mainly, I'd learned to hide my hand, to keep it lower—out of sight as much as possible. And I was good at it. Many people who'd known me for years remained unaware of my deformity.

Until we had to shake hands.

That was something I had learned in the first grade. People abhorred the touch of a deformed hand. So since childhood, I'd used my left for handshaking. Like Senator Bob Dole and others with abnormal limbs, it became a customary response. Life goes on.

But politicians shake hands—a lot.

Bob Dole was a war hero. His right hand was an injury, a badge of honor, the result of service to his country during World War II. My ugly hand was simply a birth defect and branded me as a less-than-normal person. No honor in that.

I made a decision.

If Whiskey Williams, or anyone else, should offer me the appointment of state senator for District 31, I'd turn it down. No reason to subject myself to the embarrassment of explaining my birth defect—of awkward social occasions and endless reminders about my handicap. I wanted to hide my hand, not focus a spotlight on it.

I relaxed, exhaled a long slow breath, and felt better. The process of making a decision allowed me to forget it and move on to the affairs of the day. I parked my car and walked the short distance to my office building with renewed determination.

Rebecca Harris, our sixty-ish, gray-haired secretary gave me her usual formal greeting. "Good morning, Mr. Davis."

"Good morning, Mrs. Harris," I replied as I hung my coat on the corner hall tree.

HARRY HAINES

Not once since I'd joined the firm ten years ago had we ever addressed each other by first names. Which was fine by me. She ruled the office with an impersonal air that crackled with efficiency. She had coffee ready. I poured myself a cup and headed into my office.

Much to my annoyance, Mrs. Harris had once again straightened up my desk. Everything was in perfect square piles. My problem? I didn't know what was in which pile. I had spoken to her many times about my wish to have my desk off-limits to her neatness compulsion. It did no good. So I sipped my coffee and started going through the stacks when Art wandered in.

"Morning, Sam," he said, a grin running across his face like an insider who knows secret information.

I hate it when someone gives me that *I know something you don't* expression. "Good morning Art," I groused.

"What'd you tell him?"

"Tell whom?"

"Goddamn it, Sam, you know who I'm talking about."

"My son, Tim?" I grinned back. "He and I had words this morning."

"Sam Davis, why did I ever pick you for a partner? You can be the most infuriating, argumentative, exasperating, confrontational, quarrelsome, obstreperous human being on the planet."

"All qualities of a good lawyer. Maybe that's why you chose me?"

Arthur McComas turned beet red. I could almost picture steam coming out of his ears.

"Better ease up," I said. "Remember your high blood pressure."

"Whiskey Williams," he blurted out. "You know damned well who I'm talking about."

"No, I've not heard from our beloved lieutenant governor." I smiled. "Have you?"

Art gave me a nonplused look, as though unable to decide what to say next.

I chose to wait him out. In the courtroom—when I held the upper hand with a confused adversary, a lawyer whom I had verbally outmaneuvered—it usually worked to my advantage to force him or her to speak first.

"Whiskey promised me he was going to offer—"

The light bulb came on. "Art, you sonofabitch."

4

The McComas and Davis Law Office

Art shook his head.

"You're behind this," I yelled. "You're pushing Whiskey to name me?"

"Not just me," Art replied, his voice softer, like a kid caught with his hand in the cookie jar. "Think what it would mean to the firm to have one of its members named a state senator."

"Fine with me to have someone in the firm in political office as long as it's you," I replied, "or Mrs. Harris."

Art didn't register any response to my attempt at humor. In his same low voice he said, "They didn't ask me."

"Who's *they*?"

"The executive committee of the Midland County Republicans. They met last night and asked me to call Whiskey, so I did."

"How come no one thought to ask me?

"Because I told them your knee-jerk reaction would be to turn it down."

"And you would have been 100 percent right."

"So this way, you have a chance to think it over." He looked at his watch. "Maybe it's a moot point, and he's decided to call someone else."

"Good. Let's forget it."

Art stood. He frowned, shook his head, and said, "Sam, you're a helluva lawyer, probably the best in West Texas. But sometimes I don't understand you."

I held out my left hand.

He grasped it with his right, an awkward gesture, but one we were both used to.

"Thanks, partner," I said. "I know you mean well."

He turned to leave. "Let me know if you change your mind." He closed the door behind him.

Nothing happened for the next hour. I fired up the coffee pot on my credenza, poured myself a cup. I like it stronger than the weak stuff brewed by Mrs. Harris. Art popped his head in for a second and told me he'd be in court for the rest of the morning.

A few minutes later the intercom buzzed.

"Yes?" I answered.

"Mr. Williams is here to see you," Mrs. Harris said.

"Who?"

"Lieutenant Governor Williams—from Austin, Texas."

"I'll be right out."

I opened the door and recognized him from the many times I'd seen him on television news. Tall, gray-headed, and folksy, he cultivated the image of a Lyndon Johnson politician. "Governor Williams," I said. "What an honor, Sir."

"Mr. Davis—soon to be *Senator* Davis, I hope—the honor's all mine." He extended his right hand.

HARRY HAINES

I took it with my left. "Come in, please." With my right hand I gestured to the open door to my office. I checked his eyes. He frowned as he looked at my deformity.

5

"I've been hearing lots of good things about you," Whiskey Williams said.

"In the world of politics, you believe everything people tell you?" I asked.

"Why, of course." He laughed, a big robust sound, one that I would expect to hear in response to Jay Leno's, or Dave Letterman's, best joke.

Because he laughed, I did, too. And for a moment we shared a feeling of camaraderie. "Know any other good jokes?" I asked.

"Sure. You heard about the two Texas Aggie engineers who went out to the bicycle rack to get their bikes? One of them asked the other, 'Where'd you get such a great bike?' The second Aggie replied, 'Well I was walking along yesterday, minding my own business, when a beautiful woman rode up on this bike. She threw the bike to the ground, took off all her clothes, and said, take what you want.' The second Aggie nodded approvingly. 'Good choice. The clothes probably wouldn't have fit.'."

It was an old joke, one I'd heard fifteen years ago when I was a student at the UT School of Law. But I laughed because of the way Whiskey Williams delivered the punch line. Two minutes with him and I had the feeling that life around the lieutenant governor would be a barrel of laughs. He knew how to win favor—I couldn't help liking him.

But then, as our laughter subsided and as I thought about what was happening, it seemed like a shadow of something hidden came over our conversation. I realized he was manipulating me to his point of view.

"Coffee?" I held up my cup and gestured to the pot on my credenza.

"Thank you," he said. "And a little sugar if you have it."

I filled a cup, placed a spoon and a packet of sugar on the saucer, and handed it to him. "Would you like two?"

He smiled. "Three if you can spare them."

I shook my head as I piled on a handful—at least a half-dozen packets. "You sure you have enough coffee to go with your sugar?"

He made a production of peering into his cup, of squinting with narrowed eyes. "Yep," he said, "just right." Then with exaggerated gestures, he ripped open the packets two at a time and dumped six of them into his cup. Stirring with his spoon, he looked at me with a condescending grin. "Ah've got a heck of a sweet tooth."

"Really?" I chuckled and took a sip of my strong—some would say bitter—coffee.

"So how about it?" he asked. "You like the sound of *Senator* Davis?"

"I'm flattered, of course. But no, you'll have to find a more qualified person."

"Now hold on, Sam." He chuckled at my answer. "There ain't a more qualified person." His laughter was laced with insidious elegance. It mirrored my ridicule over his outlandish sugar usage and, by implication, made fun of me and my negative answer. I'd heard that Whiskey Williams was a masterful politician. I hadn't been in the same room with him for ten minutes before I could see he was about to change my "no" into "yes."

"And you're a big flatterer. You know there are hundreds, probably thousands, of eminently qualified citizens in the Thirty-first District."

He paused, slurped his sugary coffee.

I, too, sipped my coffee. It seemed for a brief moment we might reverse course—to acknowledge my negative response.

But only for a moment.

Then he said, "Hurried answers are not good for you, for me, nor for the State of Texas." His smile faded, and a look of pensive reflection came over his face. "Why don't you think it over for a few days?"

I didn't want to. I had my mind made up. But he had just given me a way to avoid confrontation. So I said, "Okay, I'll give it a couple of days. How can I contact you?"

He gave me his card.

The pressure off, we shifted to pleasantries for the next thirty minutes. Our coffee finished, he looked at his watch, and asked about calling a taxi to the airport. I offered to drive him in my old pickup. He accepted. On the fifteen-minute drive, conversation turned to his Lear Jet.

"If you accept this appointment, I'll make it available to you for trips to Austin," he said.

"Whiskey, that's very generous, but I couldn't do that."

"Promise me just one thing?" he asked.

"Sure."

"When you discuss this appointment with your wife, mention the Lear."

I shook my head.

"Promise?" he asked again, pushing.

I caved. "Okay."

HARRY HAINES

I'd driven to the Midland-Odessa Airpark thousands of times. But on this trip, Whiskey directed me away from the terminal to a gate that I'd never seen before. He showed his credentials to a security guard, the gate opened, and we drove out onto the tarmac to a gleaming white corporate jet.

"Want to take a peek inside?" he asked.

Honestly, I didn't. But I said, "Sure."

As we walked up to the plane, the door opened electronically. Whiskey introduced me to the pilot, and I climbed inside. It was beautiful—much larger than I had expected. I counted six seats and a small bar in the back.

"This a state plane?" I asked.

He smiled, shook his head with a very small gesture, and gave me a one-word answer. "No."

I expected him to continue—to explain. He didn't, so I asked, "Whose is it?"

"You don't know much about politics, do you?"

I chuckled, smiled, and asked, "What does my knowledge of politics have to do with a question about who owns this airplane?"

He gave me another one word answer. "Contacts."

For a moment I tried to analyze his answer, to decide what to say next.

"Have a seat," Whiskey said. "We need to have a little 'father-to-son' talk." He gestured to two of the big, plush seats that faced each other.

I sat.

He took the other.

"Sam, I've been in politics for forty-two years. Started after law school working as a flunky for a representative named Thomas Henderson and eventually became his chief of staff. He showed me the ropes and helped me win the senate seat from the Austin district. After twelve years in the senate, I ran for lieutenant governor and . . . well, you know the story from there."

"An impressive political record," I said. "Going for governor?"

"Why? The lieutenant governor has all the power in Texas politics."

I nodded. I knew what he said was true. "I read *Texas Monthly's* feature article on you last year," I continued. "They called you 'A Legend'."

He laughed. "Usually that sobriquet is reserved for the deceased."

I laughed, too. "All the more of an honor."

His face turned serious, and he leaned towards me. "Son, politics is all about power. And if you have it for a decade or more, that's when they start using words like *legend*."

"Still, a compliment."

"Politics has made me a wealthy man." He relaxed back into the big, plush seat. "This little plane cost me fourteen mil."

"Wow." I didn't know small jets were so expensive.

"You gonna talk to your wife about this appointment?"

I nodded. "Of course."

We both stood, and I followed him down the little stairway onto the tarmac. We walked over to my pickup where he grabbed my left hand with both of his and said, "I'll expect you to get back to me next week."

Then we parted company—he in his 14-million dollar Lear Jet and me in my 15-hundred dollar Ford pickup.

6

At the dinner table I told my family about my day with the lieutenant governor, his offer, and his fourteen-million-dollar jet.

Suzie got up out of her chair, came over, and threw her arms around me. "Oh, honey, this is so exciting." She kissed me and went to get me another cup of coffee.

"Daddy, what's a senator?" Emily asked.

Before I could answer, Tim interceded. "Dummy, that's a politician who makes the laws," he answered.

"Do they make a lot of money?" she asked.

"Crooked ones do," Tim replied." And it sounds like this guy must be the king of crooked politicians."

I marveled at the moxie of our ten-year-old son. Suzie looked at me and rolled her eyes. Then she turned to him and said, "Tim, that's not a nice thing to say about a man we don't even know."

"How much do state senators and lieutenant governors earn?" Tim asked. "I'll bet it's not enough to pay for a fourteen-million-dollar jet."

I laughed. "How do you know so much about money?"

"Dad, I'm in the fifth grade. We study current events and read about companies like Brown and Root, Halliburton, and others who make gazillions off the war."

"Where'd you read this?" I asked.

"*Newsweek,*" he said. "They had an article about a company in Ohio that sold a toilet to the army for ten million dollars."

"Really?"

"And a senator who supervises the Pentagon—I've forgotten his name—was on the board of directors for the toilet company. If he sells very many toilets to the army, he can buy himself a fourteen-million-dollar jet."

I chuckled. "Just like the lieutenant governor of Texas."

"Daddy, why don't you make toilets and sell them to the army?" Emily asked.

Suzie laughed. "Yeah, Daddy, why don't you?"

"Well, one thing for sure," I replied, "I'm not going to accept this appointment to be a state senator."

Suzie's face turned serious. "Can we talk about it?"

"There's nothing to talk about," I said. "I'm *not* going to do it."

"All this talk about money and politics is boring," Emily said. "May I go watch television?"

"May I be excused?" Tim asked. "I've got homework."

"You're both excused," Suzie replied.

The children left the room.

I helped Suzie load the dishwasher.

"Surely you're not serious about turning down the appointment?"

"Oh, but I am. Very serious."

"When do you have to tell him?"

"Next week."

"Could we talk about it before you decide?"

I had heard those words before. Suzanne has the most cleverly indirect and delicate way of confronting me. She never argues. No angry words or open hostility. In soft tones she *suggests* we "talk about it." And in our twelve years of marriage, I couldn't remember a single case where we had "talked about it" and the result failed to go her way.

I'm a lawyer. I make my living winning arguments. Other attorneys, even judges, tell me how good I am at winning arguments. It's a good thing they never had to watch Suzanne and me "talk about it."

That night the sex was not just good, it was memorable.

Every night for the next week, Suzie prepared my favorites for dinner. Even the kids noticed.

"Apple pie again?" Emily asked. "That's Daddy's favorite."

A week later I called Whiskey Williams and told him I'd take the appointment.

7

Two weeks later, Austin, Texas

They scheduled my "swearing-in" ceremony for Wednesday morning in the senate chamber of the Texas Capitol Building.

On Tuesday afternoon, the day before, Whiskey Williams had sent his Lear for me and my family. I thought the flight, my first in a private jet, was fantastic. Suzie went into ecstasy. Tim and Emily couldn't find a single thing to argue about. In less than an hour the little plane had whisked us from Midland to Austin in supreme comfort and luxury. We booked adjoining rooms at the Omni, a beautiful, futuristic hotel with dazzling all-glass front, soaring lobby, and magnificent restaurant.

On Wednesday morning, a chauffeured limousine took us to the Capitol. For the occasion, Suzie wore a new dress. She also purchased new "Sunday best" clothes for the children. I wore my one-and-only Brooks Brothers suit, a black pinstripe. The Davis family never looked better.

Someone had worked overtime to make sure my ceremony was a

media event. Television and newspaper crews from home, as well as Austin, filled the room with enough lights to illuminate a stadium. And I learned a valuable political lesson—the media made Tim and Emily into the news of the day. Nothing is more photogenic, it seems, than a politician's young children. But our kids took it in stride, and I was really proud of Tim and Emily.

Finally, the Chief Justice of the Texas Supreme Court called me to the microphone. With Suzie standing next to me, I took the oath. And then we ran head on into the part I dreaded most— shaking hands with hundreds of people.

At first it was awkward, but gradually people caught on with a "their-right, my-left" exchange that became the norm. Eventually we got through it, and all of this was followed by a luncheon at the governor's mansion. Then the limo took Suzie and the kids to the Austin airport where they caught Southwest Airlines back to Midland. A big day, one our family will never forget.

I planned to stay in Austin for the next two days for orientation and legislative committee meetings. Whiskey gave me a list of what to expect:

Thursday: 9:00 - Office staff meeting; Noon - Lunch with senate leaders; 2:00 - Senate agriculture committee; 7:00 - Dinner with Lieutenant Governor Williams

Friday: 9:00 - Senate/House Joint Committee on Oil and Gas Legislation; Noon - Lunch with Republican Finance Committee; 4:10 - Southwest Airlines, Flight #34 to Midland; 7:00 - Arrive Midland

It looked formidable. Wednesday night I had trouble sleeping, and when I did doze off, I had nightmares about the mistakes I was about to make in my legislative duties. Finally, at 6:00 a.m., I gave up, showered, shaved, dressed, and went down to the coffee shop.

PUPPET POLITICS

It's not often one can have breakfast in a room with spacious outdoor ambiance. The Omni's restaurant, with its huge glass front, ceiling ten stories high, and especially its forest of trees and other indoor plants, provided an atmosphere that lifted my spirits. The food was excellent. I lingered at my table for two hours, read the *Austin Statesman* cover to cover, and drank enough coffee to saturate my brain with caffeine. The Omni Hotel sent me off to my first day at work, representing the citizens of senate district thirty-one, with an upbeat attitude.

I took a taxi to the Capitol, where I found my three District 31 employees waiting: Sylvia Newsom, chief of staff; Louis Jordan, her assistant; and Madison Martin, the secretary. Sylvia had been Abner Stone's aide since the first day he took office, a stretch of over eleven years. It didn't take long to discover two important facts—she knew the job, and she could be a tremendous help to me.

Later that morning, Sylvia handed me two manila file folders: "Noon luncheon with senate majority leader" and "Senate agriculture committee meeting." Each folder listed the date and location of the meeting. Sylvia led me through the material, and I found her briefings specific and comprehensive. She gave me background, what to expect, and possible conflicts. On my first day in the office, Sylvia had me up to speed and ready to attend two important meetings.

The luncheon went well, and I picked up a new job—membership on the Committee for Equine Standards and Activities. The majority leader wanted me to help draft new rules and regulations for the private ownership and care of horses in Texas. I looked forward to it.

The Agriculture Committee was exactly the opposite. The chairman, an elderly senator from College Station, hadn't even prepared an agenda. So for three-and-a-half hours, we meandered through a minefield of multi-million-dollar requests for next year's budget. Since my term of office was only ten months and the calendar dictated the choosing of a new senator at the next election, I thought the whole afternoon a wasted effort. It was a relief when the meeting adjourned at 5:30 p.m. I hurried back to my room to get ready for dinner with Whiskey Williams.

Getting ready meant changing clothes. Whiskey had sent an e-mail with specifics—jeans and cowboy boots. He didn't specify a Stetson, but I brought it. In the elevator on the way down to the lobby, two couples gave me a hard time. The guys sported tuxes, and the ladies wore strapless dresses with lots of rhinestones. Obviously, they were attending a dress-up event.

"Where 'ya headed this evening, cowboy?" one of the ladies drawled.

I put on my hat, gave them my biggest cowboy smile, and replied, "The OK Corral." Which, incidentally, was the name of the restaurant that Whiskey had selected.

"Looks like yore ready for the big shoot-out," she replied.

"Shore nuff," the other lady added.

The elevator opened, and we laughed as we walked to the front door together. Once outside we parted company—they hailed a cab to their formal affair. Whiskey had sent a limo for me. It seemed incongruous transportation for a cowboy headed to the OK Corral, a fact that appeared not lost to the group heading off in the taxi.

I found Whiskey seated at a table in the middle of the restaurant. He too wore jeans and boots. "What'll you have to drink?" he asked.

I noticed he had a bottle of Lone Star beer. "The same," I replied.

He ordered the sixteen-ounce T-bone, medium-rare, baked potato loaded, and salad with ranch dressing.

"The same," I said.

The waitress left. Whiskey and I swigged our beer.

"How'd it go today?" he asked.

"It had its ups and downs," I replied.

"Tell me about the uppers."

"The staff . . . and the luncheon with the majority leader."

"Sylvia's great, ain't she?"

"Impressed the heck out of me." I gave him a summary of our morning, of the briefing folders and how much she had helped.

"Let me guess about the downside," he said. "The ag committee."

"Bingo," I answered.

"We need a new chairman next year."

"Obviously."

"How about Senator Sam Davis?"

"No way," I said. "And you know damn well I'm only here to fill the unexpired term. Ten months from now I'm history."

"We had a meeting of the State Republican Party's executive committee this morning, and—" He left the thought dangling, and took a long draw of Lone Star.

"And what?" I asked.

"And they want you to run for a full term."

8

The next evening, dinner at home with Suzanne

"They want me to run for a full term," I said.

"Oh, honey, that's wonderful," Suzy said.

"I told Whiskey I wasn't interested."

She looked down, used her fork to move the food around on her plate, and, after a tension-filled minute, took a small bite. Finally she broke the silence with a question. "He wanted an immediate answer?"

"No, he said to think it over for a month or so. But I don't want a career in politics, so I told him."

"Why are you so negative about this?"

I started to rattle off an answer, but a small, still voice in my subconscious warned me. "You want to 'talk it over,' don't you?"

"Well, that's what normal, intelligent people usually do when faced with important decisions," she said.

"Art told me about how he and Linda do it."

"Okay," she replied with a frown and an edge in her voice, "tell me about the McComas's approach."

"Art said, that when they were first married, Linda suggested he handle all the big decisions, and she would take responsibility for the little ones."

"And Linda agreed to that?"

"Hey, it was her idea."

Suzie shook her head and exhaled a long slow breath, a sigh of resentment.

I continued, "So he gets to decide what to do about the war, about the national debt, about immigration—the big things."

"And what does she get to decide?"

"The little things, like vacations, the family budget, or choosing names for the children."

She laughed, "You sorry, unethical, underhanded scoundrel. You had me going there for a minute."

"Come here," I said as I stood.

She did, and I pulled her to me. We kissed—long, slow, passionate exchanges. "I really don't want to 'talk it over' this time."

She backed away. "Okay," she said. "But—"

"But, what?"

"But would you do what Whiskey suggested?"

I thought back through our words, trying to recall exactly what she was asking. "About waiting a month to decide?"

She nodded. "Please?"

I could argue. I could tell her again about having my mind made up. I could give her a dozen reasons why I didn't want to wait and didn't want to have anything more to do with Texas politics. Instead I kissed her and said, "Okay."

She leaned in, rubbed up against me, touched her lips to mine, and said, "You're the sexiest man in West Texas."

Then Tim and Emily rushed into the kitchen. Emily held the remote control for the television.

"He won't let me watch *Tom and Jerry*," Emily complained. "It's my favorite program."

"It's so old I have the lines memorized," Tim answered. "Why can't we watch something new?" He grabbed her arm, trying to force her to release the remote.

"He wants to watch *Wheel of Fortune*," Emily said. "I hate spelling games. They're boring, boring, boring."

"She—" Tim started.

"Stop it," Suzanne said, her voice ringing with such steely command that she reminded me of an army drill sergeant. "Give me the remote." She held out her hand.

Slowly, with great reluctance, Emily gave up her prize.

Tim smiled, a smirk of satisfaction radiating from his face. It didn't last long.

"No television tonight," Suzanne decreed. "Go find something to read. Both of you, go."

9

Nicknamed "The Tall City," Midland has a remarkable skyline for a town its size. For many years, the Wilco Building in downtown Midland was the tallest building between Fort Worth and Phoenix. It made little or no sense to spend money on staircases and elevators in West Texas, where we have such an abundance of wide-open spaces. But, back in the 60s, during the West Texas oil boom, no one cared about practicalities.

Today, the Bank of America Building—with thirty-two stories— holds the title of Midland's tallest. And though it still seems wasteful to have a tall slender building in this part of the world, Art and I chose to lease a suite of rooms on the twenty-seventh floor for our law offices. I like my corner office with an almost endless view. And the ride up in the elevator gives me a feeling of working in a big, important city.

I glanced at my watch as I came off the elevator—8:20 a.m. And I braced myself for criticism. Mrs. Harris always had a caustic remark if I arrived later than eight o'clock. Surprise. This morning I opened the door to find a smile and a greeting gushing with homage that bordered on allegiance to a feudal lord.

"*Senator* Davis," she said, "this is Lieutenant Charles Fuller of the Texas Rangers," nodding her head toward the man sitting in one of the guest chairs by the east window. He stood and held out his right hand.

"Charlie Fuller," he said.

I continued to hold my briefcase in my right hand, offered him my left, and said, "Sam Davis." We joined hands awkwardly for a second. "What brings a Texas Ranger to Midland this morning?" I asked.

He was a big man. I guessed him at six foot four and probably close to three hundred pounds. His uniform looked a bit too tight, like maybe he'd been eating more than his share of doughnuts.

"We're investigating the death of Senator Abner Stone," he said. "I understand you were out near the fire the night he died?"

I nodded, opened the door to my office, and gestured inside, "Won't you come in?"

He did and took a chair in front of my desk. It's a sturdy chair, but I heard it creak when he put his full weight in it.

I closed the door, plopped down in my desk chair, and pulled out a legal pad to make notes. I handed him one of my cards.

Without a word, he took my card and exchanged it with one of his. I scanned it for an address and, as expected, found it located in Austin.

"How can I help you?" I asked.

He pulled out a small tape recorder. "Mind if I record this?"

I placed mine beside his. They looked identical. "Not if you'll allow me to do the same."

He nodded, flashed a little smile, and said, "Sure, why not?" He

40

produced a legal pad that appeared to have a list of questions. "This is just a routine follow-up to the death of a state official."

For the next few minutes it really was routine, mostly a recitation of the date, time, place, his name, and mine. Then he asked about the details of the fire.

"You see anyone or anything that looked suspicious?" he asked.

I shook my head. "My son and I had come to feed and water our horses. We were inside our barn when the fire started." I related how we heard the sound, ran out and found the blaze, rushed back inside to load the horse trailer, and then drove away to safety.

"Didn't see anyone?"

"Well, of course, we saw all the fire trucks, police cars, ambulances—and the rubberneckers."

"The well. Didn't you study and observe the fire?"

"For a few seconds, when it first started, I tried to look, to see what danger it represented to me and my son, to my barn, to my horses."

"Where were you?"

"Tim and I were standing at the entrance to our barn. Hey, we were scared. The fire was so hot we had to turn away. We couldn't really look for more than a few seconds."

"So, tell me what happened, what you did," he said. "Try to give me a minute-by-minute description."

I did.

And the result was of little or no help to him or his investigation. Tim and I had been so focused on our personal safety—on our efforts to save the horses—that a dozen arsonists could have walked by carrying gasoline cans and we would not have noticed.

Ranger Charlie Fuller packed his tape recorder and his legal pad, shook my hand a little less awkwardly the second time, and left.

41

Mrs. Harris came in with her steno pad and sat in the chair Fuller had just vacated. Pencil in hand, she looked at me expectantly.

"Yes?" I said.

"I assume you'll want to follow up with a letter to the Texas Rangers."

"No."

She opened her mouth to speak, but nothing came out. It was one of those priceless moments when she was speechless. The awkwardness of the situation could have been finessed with a few words from me. She waited for it.

I waited her out.

"Er, eh, the Texas Rangers—"

I continued to wait, silently.

"Surely you'll want to acknowledge their visit to our firm. To pledge our support for their investigation." She looked at me, her face one of amazement. "It's our duty. We must join forces with the legend, one of the premiere law enforcement agencies in America."

I smiled, a gesture of supreme confidence.

She squirmed in her seat.

In our test of wills, I stood my ground.

She closed her steno pad, exhaled a rush of air—clearly a sigh of exasperation—and asked, "Will that be all?"

"Yes."

She stood to leave.

"Thank you, Mrs. Harris."

She gave me a look that conveyed incredulity. Silently it said *Sam Davis, you stupid nincompoop.* Then she stomped out of the room.

It was the only time in the last ten years that I could remember a clear win in my on-going battle with my secretary.

10

Art came in and closed the door. Normally we left it open when no one else was in the office. Closing the door infuriated Mrs. Harris because it made her feel left out.

"A door-closer?" I asked. "What's up?"

"Stripper wells," he said. "We're buying a few, and I wanted to see if you're interested. Read this." He plopped down a newspaper clipping. I read the article he had circled. It was titled "Stripper Wells."

> *Stripper wells are old oil and gas wells that no longer produce at a rate to make them profitable. The Permian Basin—the huge oil field that made West Texas famous—has thousands of strippers. In fact, as the years have passed and petroleum levels have become depleted, most of the wells in the Permian Basin have gradually shifted in classification to be known as*

stripper wells.

"Who's 'we'?" I asked, handing back his article.

Art named a half-dozen local oil investors. Some were our clients. A couple were members of Rotary Club with me.

"Art, I think that investing in stripper wells would be like throwing money into a black hole."

"Conventional thinking," he said. "But that could change." Art grinned at me like he'd just come from a smoke-filled room at the Petroleum Club.

"I don't see how."

"Price of oil," he said. "If a well produces two barrels a day and oil sells for $50 a barrel, the $100 income may not be enough to cover expenses. However, if the market rises to $75 a barrel, the increase in income may reverse circumstances and return the well to profitability."

"Doesn't change the fact that you still have an old well that's only producing two barrels a day."

"Texas may change the laws that affect spacing. I've heard talk that the legislature may double the spacing—allow twice as many wells per section," he said.

"Twice as many strippers that may or may not be profitable?"

"The oil depletion allowance, the ODA, may change. If the government gets desperate, they may increase the ODA to give oil investors a tax break, to increase the incentives to produce more oil and gas."

I shook my head. "It would have to be a hell of an increase to have any effect. Stripper wells don't produce that much."

"And there's a biggie," Art said. "Texas may change the laws that affect fracking."

"Fracking? I've heard about it, but I don't really understand the technology."

"Induced Hydraulic Fracturing, or fracking, is a new process that can extract hydrocarbons from shale," Art said. "It may have great potential for the Permian Basin."

I stood, reached for the coffee pot on my credenza, and held up an empty cup.

He nodded, "Just half a cup."

I poured a little for him, more for me.

He continued, "As you know, the law now allows only four wells per section. If the Texas Railroad Commission changed the regulations to allow sixteen per section, we'd have a new playing field for oil and gas exploration."

"Remember the 1920s, Spindletop, and wells that were spaced a hundred feet apart?"

"That was then. This is now."

"Hey, there's a reason for spacing. Knowing what a mess we had in East Texas, the Railroad Commission would never consider such a change."

"Maybe the Commission wouldn't, but the legislature might."

I laughed out loud. "Where do you get these crazy ideas?"

"From Whiskey."

"No way," I said. "He's smart enough to know that . . ."

"Whiskey's the biggest of our investors," Art said. "He's already bought over a hundred strippers."

I stared at him in disbelief.

"You want in?" he asked.

I shook my head. "I think I smell a termite in the woodpile."

11

At home, 3648 Everglade

"It's a black tie affair," Suzie said. "I'll need a new dress."

"We could skip it," I said.

Sometimes my wife just tunes me out. This was one of those occasions. To test her, I said, "You know Mickey Mouse has filed for my senate seat."

She rattled on without hearing my attempt to pique her attention. "Linda and Art went last year. She remembers every dress. Linda said she wouldn't *think* of wearing the same dress two years in a row."

"Earth to Suzanne Davis." I held my left hand up to my ear in a telephone gesture. "Hello?"

She stopped, her eyes narrow, lips pursed. "What?"

"We could just skip it," I said. "And then you wouldn't have to worry about my tux or your dress."

Her expression changed from a look of annoyance to one of sheer astonishment.

"It's the Governor's Ball—*the* social event of the year in Austin."

I nodded. "Yes."

"You're the state senator from District Thirty-one."

I exaggerated my nodding, my attempt to gesture condescension. "Yes, yes, we both know that."

"You *have* to go."

I held my head steady and smiled. "I don't think the voters give a flip about whether or not their senator attends the Governor's Ball."

"What about Art and Linda?" she asked.

"What about them?

"They go every year." Suzie gave me her "Mother look," the facial expression she uses with our children when they're slow to catch on. "Linda says it's important for Art to take a leadership role in the Texas Republican Party, and that's how he builds political connections for the firm."

I thought about where this argument was going. It reminded me of some poor soul facing a hurricane with an umbrella, trying to keep the rain out of his face. My position looked just as hopeless. I caved.

"It's okay with me if you buy a new dress."

She threw her arms around me. "You're such a sweetie."

"I think the word is conciliation, or one who knows when he's licked."

She kissed me. A long, slow meeting of the lips, filled with sexual overtones.

I loved it.

"And is it okay if I invite Art and Linda to fly with us to Austin in Whiskey's jet?"

"I don't know if we'll get to ride in the jet."

"I do," she said. "Whiskey called me today."

"Really?"

"You and the kids had gone to feed the horses. He called, said he was working on the schedule for his plane, and that if we didn't want it, he'd offer it to someone else."

"I'm amazed that he would call."

"Honey, sometimes you're a little slow about social things."

"Oh? How's that?"

"Obviously, Whiskey really likes you. He's going out of his way to do nice things for you . . . for us. I think you need to pay closer attention. Try to find something you can do to be appreciative."

"For instance?"

"Well, for one thing, he wants you to run for state senator."

The light came on.

I leaned back in my chair, away from her. "And what do *you* want me to do?"

"You know," she said. "You don't have to ask."

She was right about that. Without question my wife wanted me to become a candidate.

"And Art wants you to run," she continued. "He and Linda think you'd be a shoo-in."

I stopped to think about my circumstances. My wife, my partner, the state's political leader—all joining forces to twist my arm. At first I had thought it would be easy to decline a role in state politics. Now it didn't appear so simple.

"Linda's organizing the Midland County Republican women," Suzie continued. "They have a slogan for you."

"Oh, no."

"Super Sam, he's our man!"

I cringed.

Then she stood, and it got worse. She sang it like a girl in a TV commercial, using a jumpy little tune, repeating the words over and over, snapping her fingers and adding hand motions. When she finished, she flashed a big, toothy grin and said. "Of course, we'd do it with a polka band—with lots of accordions."

12

The Crockett Hotel Ballroom, Austin

I hate dances. Especially big mob scenes like the Governor's Ball. Why people want to get all dressed up in uncomfortable clothing, gather in a dark, crowded room, subject themselves to music so loud they can't converse, and spend an evening getting drunk . . . defies reasonable understanding. Did I mention that I hate dances?

Linda, Art, Suzie, and I sat at a small table in the corner and sipped our drinks while the band, a country western group called Texas Tornado, hammered out the loudest arrangement of *Tennessee Waltz* I'd ever heard. Suzie and I had just finished dancing the Texas Two-Step to an upbeat version of *San Antonio Rose*. I welcomed the chance to sit this one out.

Art leaned over and yelled in my ear, "You looked good out there on that last number."

It was an effort to respond, but I tried. "Not as good as you and Linda."

Art nodded and smiled. Obviously he didn't understand what I'd said. Together we sipped our drinks and looked out over the dance floor. I guessed there must be a hundred couples attempting to dance in three-quarter time. Some could do it—most were just walking around. I leaned over until my lips were only six inches from his ear. "How much longer you want to stay?"

Art looked at his watch. "It's only eleven fifteen."

The music stopped—a guy on the mike announced a fifteen-minute break. The dance floor slowly cleared as couples made their way back to tables and more alcohol. I found it a relief to converse in a normal tone of voice.

Art leaned over and in a hushed voice said, "Don't look back, but the governor and the first lady are two tables behind you and headed this way."

In spite of Art's instructions not to, I turned and looked. The governor's eyes locked with mine, and he smiled. I nodded. He and his wife stepped to our table.

Art and I stood.

The governor shook Art's hand, and his wife took Linda's. "Good to see the Midland contingent so well represented," he said.

The first lady moved on to Suzie. I couldn't hear their conversation, but Suzie's facial expression said it all. She glowed.

The governor extended his right hand to me. "I understand you're our candidate for the Senate's Thirty-first District."

I could have said, "No." But I didn't. Instead I concentrated on maneuvering so that my left hand grasped his right with as little awkwardness as possible. And without thinking—trying my best to sound agreeable—the word that came out my mouth was, "Yes."

"Good," the governor said. "Whiskey tells me you're certain to win."

Art jumped into the conversation. "Midland County Republicans are hoping you'll have time to make a few stump speeches for him next fall."

"Of course," the governor replied. "Count on it."

The first lady smiled, a benevolent gesture to indicate her approval, and then moved on toward the next table.

The governor put his hand on my shoulder, "Let me know what I can do to help." He, too, moved on.

Art and I sat down.

"That was a biggie," he said.

Suzie squeezed my hand. "I'm so glad you decided to run."

Linda held up her glass in a toast. "To our candidate," she said.

Art, Linda, and Suzie clinked their glasses.

I wanted to say wait a minute. But the band chose that moment to break out in a loud rendition of "Deep in the Heart of Texas." Everyone started singing. I made one feeble effort at a disclaimer, but with a thousand people clapping the three quick notes, there was no way.

I had become a Republican candidate for the Texas State Senate.

13

Austin, the next morning

After a short night, the four of us—Art, Linda, Suzie, and I—hailed a cab to Bergstrom International Airport. Whiskey's secretary had told us not to eat anything. Breakfast would be served en route to Midland.

So we boarded the little Lear Jet to find, in addition to the two pilots, a uniformed flight attendant. One of the pilots introduced her as Caitlin, a sociology major at UT who worked part-time for an Austin catering service. Caitlin was a knockout—slender, blonde, early twenties, and a smile that would probably win the Miss America contest.

As soon as the plane was airborne, Caitlin went to work. She served us a great breakfast of cheese omelet, orange juice, croissant, fruit compote, and steaming hot coffee. Racing across the stratosphere at close to the speed of sound, I savored the gourmet food, served amid conversation with friends, and wished that all aspects of my life could have such elegance. I had barely finished my food when Caitlin came to pick up the service items and announce that we'd be landing in five minutes.

Suzie took Linda with her in our car. I rode with Art in his. The girls headed for home—the guys to work.

A few seconds after I had settled into my McComas and Davis office, on the twenty-seventh floor of the Bank of America Building, Art came into the room and closed the door. "The Midland Republican Committee wants to meet with you," he said as he plopped down in one of the chairs in front of my desk. "How about four o'clock?"

"Today?" I asked.

"Hey, it's important to get started. You're already behind."

"Art, I just decided to run. I need a few days to let it sink in."

"There's something else."

I looked out the window to the north and surveyed the flatness of the West Texas, desert-like landscape. And I thought about how politics was taking over my life. I turned back to my partner, shook my head, and said, "Art, why is it that there's always 'something else'?"

"Hey, this is good news." He leaned forward in his chair, his face animated like he'd just found key evidence to win a murder trial. "Whiskey's sending his Austin political team to help us."

"Political team?"

"His top three guys—a fundraiser, an advertising expert, and a pollster."

"Suppose I don't want the help of an Austin political team?"

Art relaxed back into his chair and let loose with a big, old-fashioned, Texas hee-haw. It came at me as a sound of derision, like I was the chump on *World's Funniest Videos*.

I waited.

He wiped his eyes.

54

"I didn't think it was that funny."

He shook his head, his laughter subsiding. "How can a savvy, intelligent lawyer like yourself be so naive?"

"Maybe I'm inexperienced, but I also have a small measure of personal integrity. If I'm going to run for office, I want people to vote for me because of my qualifications. Not because some Madison Avenue hacks have marketed me like a ham sandwich."

He started laughing again, this time not as loudly. After a moment of mirth, he said, "Let me ask you a question. Do you object to a defendant seeking the help of a lawyer in a lawsuit?"

"No. Of course not."

"Suppose it's a big, important case, with complicated litigious factors. Would you think it wrong for the defendant—or plaintiff— to assemble a team of legal specialists to help them win?"

"That's different."

"No, it's not. And even if you're trying to sell a ham sandwich, you'd do well to assemble a team of experts to do it well."

"Goddammit, Art, all I'm asking is for you, Whiskey, and the Midland County Republicans to back off. For Christ's sake, I don't even have an opponent yet."

He pulled out a newspaper, unfolded it, and laid it out flat in front of me. I looked at the masthead and read *Amarillo Globe-News*. Someone had circled the headline in red:

FORMER MAYOR FILES FOR
STATE SENATE RACE

"Clarence Anderson is a seasoned politician," Art said. "He's going to be a formidable opponent."

14

The office, later that afternoon

Seated at my desk, I studied the résumés of Whiskey's "political team" and wished I had more than fifteen minutes before our four o'clock meeting.

I picked up the phone and dialed my secretary. "Mrs. Harris, I have a request."

"Yes, sir," came the crisp reply.

"When people start arriving for the meeting, would you show them into the conference room, please?"

"Of course, that's what I was planning to do."

"And if anyone requests to speak with me, just tell them I'll be there in a few minutes."

"Yes, sir."

"I need a little time by myself to prepare for the meeting."

"Yes, sir. I understand."

In spite of my continuing frustration with Mrs. Harris, at times like this I was grateful to have her forceful personality guarding my door. I leaned forward in my chair, resolved to shut out distractions, and summoned all of my concentration to focus on the biographical information of the three experts from Austin.

Thomas Long, fundraiser, had a three-page résumé. With an MBA from Harvard Business School and a PhD from Texas A&M, he had both a national and Texas perspective for raising money. His info listed over a quarter-century of fundraising campaigns and the amounts of money raised. I scanned it quickly and on the last page found an impressive total—over $100-million in funds raised.

Richard Klemkowski, advertising expert, showed an MBA from Yale. While his six-page résumé seemed longer than needed, or than I would have liked, it gave dozens of national and Texas political campaigns where he had successfully elected candidates. As I read through his summary, the material that intrigued me the most was his listing of several clients who were not elected. He gave specifics—why the candidates failed and his opinion of what should have been done to reverse the outcome. This guy's résumé gave the most impressive details on how to market political candidates that I'd ever seen.

Harriet Wong's résumé listed a mixed background in both music and political polling. Her degree was in piano from the New England Conservatory. But she was originally from Dallas and had worked at the national level for both Roper and Gallup. She came across as a highly intelligent Asian woman, a Texan who had learned her skills in political polling through actual experience. She gave three examples of Texas campaigns where her research had guided candidates to victory.

I looked back through the stack to memorize names. Often I use some ditty or word association to help, and I found one. These three came close to "Tom, Dick, and Harry"—not exactly profound, but a crutch that worked for me. The phone rang, and I picked it up to hear the voice of my obsessive-compulsive secretary.

"Two minutes," Mrs. Harris said.

"Thank you," I said and hung up. I grabbed a legal pad and hurried down the hall to the conference room. I found it full of people.

Art stood by me, put his arm on my shoulder, and in a commanding voice said, "Ladies and gentlemen, our candidate." Everyone clapped. Then he held up his hand, a gesture asking for quiet. "Please take a seat."

We did. And Art went around the table giving names and a single-sentence descriptor for each. I appreciated the fact that he had finessed the usual procedure of shaking hands.

I counted. We had five members of the Midland County Republican Committee, the three Austin experts, Art, and myself—a total of ten. Art sat at the head of the table—I at the other end. The room crackled with energy.

I thought back to the day I had taken the appointment to finish out Abner Stone's term. It seemed like each day that passed brought an increase in the way politics dominated my life.

15

The Conference Room

I love our conference room. I think it must be the best place in all of Midland to hold a meeting. Lined on three sides with shelves filled with law books, the other wall, by contrast, consisted entirely of glass. Not just a window, but a huge glass wall that went from floor to ceiling and offered a magnificent view to the east. That afternoon I could see heavy truck traffic on I-20 heading toward Fort Worth, a subtle reminder that those of us gathered around the table were now above and beyond the hectic world of commerce.

The enormous, mahogany table filled the center of the room. Normally we have eight high-backed swivel chairs around it. But for today's meeting, someone had brought in a couple of extra chairs from Art's office.

The smell of rich leather and the visual impact of so many law books have always brought an ambiance of seriousness to meetings held in our conference room. Today I sensed something even more somber—a special, thoughtful expression on the faces, an unusual feeling of tension, or an unspoken word of caution. I worried that these people were plotting to take control of my life.

Art started the meeting by calling on our polling expert, Harriet Wong. "How soon can you give us an estimate of where we stand?"

"A week from today," she answered. "I've hired Roper and Associates to do a telephone survey this weekend." She passed out copies of a single sheet of paper. "Here are five questions we plan to ask."

I read the questions:

    a.   Where do you reside? Give city and/or county.

    b.   Did you vote in the state senatorial election four years ago? Yes or no.

    c.   Do you plan to vote in the primary election on May 5th? Yes, not sure, no.

    d.   Who are you most likely to vote for? Sam Davis, Clarence Anderson, other.

    e.   Rate the following political issues on a five-point scale with "one" being of little interest and "five" being of great interest to you.

        • Education

        • Health care

        • Immigration

        • Oil and gas regulations

        • The Texas economy

"Does anyone have an additional question you'd like added to the survey? Harriet asked.

No one did.

Art turned to Thomas Long, the fundraiser. "Tom, let's talk about money," Art said, "How do you want to start raising funds for the campaign?"

"Basically, I see us building our war chest from two distinct sources—local and state."

"What do you want us to do?" Art asked.

"Help me build a list of potential donors at the local level." He passed out copies of a form. "First, I assume everyone in the room will want to make a personal contribution. This could be a pledge, but if you have your checkbook handy, it would help me to receive your gift now. A thousand each would give us a good start."

Half the people pulled out their checkbooks and started writing. I didn't have mine, so I turned my attention to his form. In the space for donors, I wrote "Sam and Suzanne Davis," and in the column for pledges, I listed "$1,000."

Tom continued. "Art has agreed to serve as our campaign treasurer. Pass your checks to him—your list of prospects to me."

This took a few minutes.

"Whiskey Williams offered to help me contact the State Republican Committee," Tom said. "I think you can leave fundraising at the state level to me."

Art nodded and turned to Dick. "Tell us your thoughts about publicity."

"To start with, we'll do yard signs," Dick said. He held up a small cardboard sign, about eighteen by thirty-six inches.

Several of the locals chuckled and made supporting comments.

"Red, white, and blue," one said.

"I like the fact that there are only five words," another said.

"You get the message with one quick glance," a third added.

"We need volunteers," Dick said. He passed out a form titled *Names*.

"Especially, we need people to serve as County Chairmen. And if you know of people in the Amarillo area who would work for Sam—instead of his competitor—those are names we'll want to call tonight."

Everyone started writing names on their forms. I knew a few Amarillo names: a fellow who worked at the American Quarter Horse Association, Suzie's cousin and his family, a couple of lawyers with whom I had worked. Then I went on to add a client who lived in Tulia and a bunch of names in Odessa.

"And we need speaking engagements," Dick continued. "If you have any contacts with civic clubs, churches, or special events, write 'em down."

No one asked me. I could see that if the Kiwanis Club in Podunk, Texas, invited me to come as guest speaker, I was expected to go.

Politics had taken over my life.

16

Breakfast, at home, ten days later

Suzie handed me the morning paper. Seated in my usual chair at the kitchen table, I opened the *Midland Reporter Telegram* and glanced briefly at what appeared to be a routine headline:

SENATE RACE HEATS UP

I scanned the lead article. It stated that the deadline for filing had passed, that there were now four candidates who had filed, and that yard signs were popping up all over senate district twenty-one, especially in Midland and Amarillo.

"Your ad's on page five," she said.

I turned the page and found three ads placed by my political opponents. Clarence Anderson—Amarillo's former mayor, whom Harriet Wong's telephone poll named as my most serious competitor and likely challenger in a runoff election—had a professional-looking

63

advertisement, which I estimated to be eight by ten inches. The other two ads were half as large. After studying all three carefully—reading each announcement word for word—I flipped over to page five and nearly dropped the newspaper. I was expecting a small ad, something similar in size to my rivals, or at the most, maybe an advertisement twice as large. Instead I found a full-page display.

"Wow," I said.

Suzie filled my cup with coffee. "Sorta' knocks you over, doesn't it?"

Tim and Emily came to the table and took their chairs.

"What knocks you over?" Tim asked.

I showed the page to the kids.

"Daddy, are you famous?" Emily asked.

"Nah, he's just a politician," Tim said.

I folded the paper and laid it on the floor by my chair. "Let's talk about something else. What about the barrel races next Saturday?"

"What about them?" Tim asked.

"Do you and your sister need to practice?"

"I don't. But she does."

"He needs the practice more than me," Emily shouted.

"Shush," their mother said, "no need to yell. And you should say 'more than I'."

"He started it," Emily rejoined, her voice softer, but her face filled with resentment.

"I didn't start anything," Tim said. "I merely stated a fact."

"Mama, should we take them out to the practice arena after school today?" I asked.

Suzie winked. "Only those with good manners. Those who support their brother or sister."

We finished our breakfast in silence.

PUPPET POLITICS

I left the table to brush my teeth, came back, picked up the newspaper, kissed my wife, and turned to the door. "Call me if you get things settled."

Suzie walked me out to the garage. "They both want to go," she whispered. "It's only a matter of how to save face."

I kissed her again. "Call me."

I drove east to an old, rundown shopping center, a strip of tattered businesses at the corner of Marionfeld and Ohio. We had rented a vacant building, what had once been a grocery store, for our campaign headquarters. Huge signs booming our "Vote for Sam Davis" message—with the red, white, and blue caricature of Uncle Sam holding a tiny American flag—filled the front of the old building. I went inside to find a dozen or more desks, all with phones and computers. Next came rows of tables, many heaped with yard signs, others piled high with mass= mailing flyers. Immediately, Arthur McComas rose from one of the desks and came forward to greet me.

In a commanding voice, one that filled the old grocery building, he shouted, "Ladies and gentlemen, our candidate."

I guessed that there must be thirty or forty people now working in our campaign headquarters. They all stopped what they were doing and clapped. I raised my good hand and waved, doing my best to mimic the traditional gesture of political candidates. "Thank you, thank you," I repeated over and over with a smile and a wave. Gradually the applause subsided. Then Art and I drifted over to his desk.

On the way I greeted Thomas Long, Richard Klemkowski, and Harriet Wong, who occupied the first three desks. When we came to Art's place, he and I grabbed a couple of chairs.

"Art, where did all these people come from?" I asked.

"Well, you know Tom, Dick, and Harriet. Three more are from Austin, pros that Whiskey hired. The others are all volunteers—members of the

Midland Republicans." He handed me a flyer.

I studied the leaflet. Eight-and-a-half-by-eleven, full-color, tri-fold, printed on heavy glossy paper—it reeked of Madison Avenue professionalism. On the front page, a headline, "Vote for Sam Davis," gave the standard political commercial followed by a collage of pictures of my family and me. The surprise was on the reverse side.

Flipping the little pamphlet over, I found a huge photo of me and our two horses, one that completely filled the page. Imbedded into the lower half of the photograph, a brief message in white letters proclaimed the news of my recent appointment to the Committee for Equine Standards and Activities. While the communication was factual, the image it conveyed came across as wildly exaggerated. As I read the note, it made me think this person, me, was out to save the horses of the world.

I shook my head and looked at Art, "I haven't yet attended a meeting of this committee."

He smiled. "Guess you'd better get busy and call one." Then he changed the subject. "What'd you think of the ad in this morning's paper?"

"I was bowled over."

"We have a video team coming from Los Angles this weekend to shoot footage for your TV ads. And Sunday, the audio guys from Austin have asked for three hours to meet with you for radio commercials."

"We need to talk," I said. "Could we step outside?"

"Sure." He led the way out to the parking lot, and we stopped by my old dilapidated pickup.

"How much did that ad in this morning's paper cost?" I asked. "And these flyers, the yard signs, six professionals from Austin, radio and TV ads—where's all the money coming from?"

17

Campaign Headquarters, the parking lot

Art "artfully" dodged my question. "We need to get you some signs for this old rust bucket," he said. "Then we can feature it in the video ads."

"Can we talk about campaign finance?" I asked.

"Sure. What'd you want to discuss?

"How can we afford all this?"

He looked away across the nearly empty parking lot. After a few seconds he turned, and our eyes met. His expression and tone of voice reminded me of a kindergarten teacher addressing a wayward student.

"Well to start with," he said, "we received seven thousand at the planning meeting last week. Since then, the Midland Republicans have been sending checks."

"What's the total?"

"I don't have it memorized, but I'd guess we've doubled the original amount."

Mentally I calculated an estimate of the cost of flyers, signs, and advertising in the print and electronic media. I guessed that this morning's full-page in the *Midland Reporter Telegram* would be over a thousand dollars. "What happens if we spend more than we have in contributions?"

Art smiled. It was a patronizing look, a facial gesture that implied ignorance on my part. "We also received a check from Whiskey. Don't worry, Sam, money's no problem."

"How much was Whiskey's check?"

"You don't need to know," he said. "Probably better if you don't."

"Art, damn it. How much?"

"One hundred thousand."

His words took my breath away. I didn't know what to say. So I turned and walked around my truck. In thirty seconds I ended up back at the spot where Art stood.

"See, I told you," he chastised me. "It's better if you leave the finances to others."

"Where'd the hundred grand come from?"

"Honestly, I don't know," he said. "Furthermore, I don't want to know."

"This has to be reported," I argued. "We've both read the laws about campaign finance. Eventually it all has to come out."

"Sam, there are ways around it."

"Such as?"

"Well, for instance, Tom, Dick, and Harriet—and these other professional consultants—can be listed as volunteers."

"That's breaking the law."

"No, it's just categorizing their status differently. And no one will ever know."

"I'll know."

"How are you going to find out?"

"I'll ask you and Whiskey."

"And here's what I'm telling you. Tom, Dick, Harriet, and the others are volunteers. Whiskey will tell you the same."

"I don't like it."

"You don't have to." His manner stiffened, and he pointed a finger at me. "I've got work to do. For Christ's sake, Sam, get out of the way and let us get you elected. And it wouldn't hurt for you to show a tiny bit of appreciation to those of us who are doing all of this on your behalf."

He stomped off back to the old grocery store, leaving me alone in the parking lot, feeling nonplused about my status, bewildered about my friends, and completely flummoxed about what to do.

With a heavy heart, I drove to the office where Mrs. Hughes greeted me with scorn. "It's almost ten o'clock," she said as she handed me a handful of pink slips—telephone calls she had taken because I was late to work.

I settled into my desk chair and looked at the top message. It was from my wife.

"The kids and I will meet you at the horse barn at five o'clock. I'm counting on you to supervise the barrel racing. Don't be late."

Mrs. Hughes had written the last three words in capital letters.

18

The Midland County Fairgrounds Arena

I made it to the arena fifteen minutes late. But one of the things I had learned over the years was to keep a set of riding clothes at the office. So I arrived, properly dressed, boots and all, ready to do my part in helping Tim and Emily practice for the Midland County 4-H Horse Show.

The featured event for our kids was barrel racing, and the first order of business was to saddle the horses and get them ready for strenuous, vigorous riding. Fortunately, the horses and the kids knew the drill. When I arrived, I found Tim on Champ and Emily on Midnight—both were out in the arena warming up, riding in circles at a fast trot in preparation for the routine to come. Suzie had things organized beautifully.

I called our two riders over to the side, to a point near the starting line.

"Tim, how about going first?"

He smiled and immediately maneuvered Champ back about thirty feet from the starting line. Once in position, I stood on the line of white flour, held the stopwatch high with my finger on the button, and called out. "You ready?"

"Yes, sir," he said.

"Let'r rip," I yelled.

Barrel races are conducted with a running start. Tim urged Champ forward, and they took off at full speed headed for the first barrel. Tim leaned forward, low in the saddle, his knees pressed against the horse in perfect form, rider and mount fused together at a breathtaking pace. As they sprinted past me, I clicked the stopwatch.

The 4-H Races are ridden in a cloverleaf pattern around three barrels. Three standard fifty-five gallon steel oil drums are placed in a triangle formation, ninety feet apart. Barrels one and two are sixty feet from the start/finish line, with the third barrel farthest away at the tip of the triangle.

Rules require that riders cross the line, run to barrel number one, pass to the left of it making a right turn of approximately 450 degrees, then go to barrel number two, pass to the right of it making a left turn of approximately 450 degrees, then go to barrel number three, again passing to the right and making a left turn, followed by the final sprint to the start/finish line.

Champ had the route drilled into his memory. I watched as horse and rider neared the first barrel. Tim shifted his weight to the inside in perfect form. Dirt flew, and they took the first barrel at maximum speed.

Suzie laced her arm through mine. I could feel her heart pounding as we watched Tim and Champ race toward the second barrel and lean in the opposite direction for the first of two left-hand turns. Again they took the circle at breakneck speed, passing very close to the barrel. Too close, I thought.

I held the stopwatch up so both Suzie and I could see it. "Nine seconds," I said as Tim raced toward the third barrel.

"That's too fast," Suzie replied. She squeezed my arm even tighter.

Obviously, neither horse nor rider could hear her remark. And as though in defiance of her admonition, I sensed that Tim urged Champ on to greater speed.

Champ tried.

And as a result they tipped the barrel.

Without breaking stride, horse and rider sprinted for the finish line. I clicked the stopwatch as they thundered past. Thirteen seconds—a new record for our family.

The rules say a five-second penalty must be added for knocking over a barrel. So a total of eighteen seconds. A very good time, enough to win some contests. Suzie and I walked over to congratulate our son and his horse.

Tim slid down.

Suzie and I gave him a hug. Even Emily threw her arms around her brother in a rare moment of congratulations.

"We're mighty proud of you," Suzie said.

"And the next time," I added, "if you can do it without knocking over the barrel, you'll win the championship."

Tim patted Champ on the nose, took a small plastic bag of sliced apples out of his pocket, and fed them to his horse. "Good job, fellow," he said.

"Take him for a cool-down walk," I said. We'll get Emily and Midnight ready."

Tim started leading his horse away, stopped, turned and asked, "Emily, will you wait until I get back? I want to be there to see your race."

Emily looked at me.

"Sure, we'll wait," I said.

Tim led Champ away.

"This would be a good time to walk Midnight around the barrels," I said.

Emily led her horse around the path while Suzie and I watched.

"How about riding through it at a slow pace?" I asked.

"Okay," Emily said.

With Emily in the saddle, I took the reins and led them through the barrels. I ran. Midnight easily kept up with just a light trot.

After we'd crossed the white line and had stopped, I looked up at my daughter and asked, "Want to do it one more time?"

"Sure."

"This time you go without me. Take it easy, a light lope, a bit faster than what we just did."

"Daddy, we can do it. Don't worry."

They looked good.

Tim returned and watched. "Good control," he said. "She's learning."

I thought it interesting that he wanted to be present for the run, a gesture of support for his sister, and that when she wasn't present to hear, he voiced complimentary remarks.

Emily maneuvered her horse to a spot about thirty feet behind the start/finish line.

"Ready?" I asked.

"Not too close to the barrels," Tim yelled.

Emily waved.

"Go!" I shouted.

Our seven-year-old took off at a speed I thought dangerously fast. I clicked the stopwatch as she dashed over the white line and raced toward the first barrel.

Midnight knew the way. All Emily had to do was hold on. She looked awfully small as her beautiful black horse tore around the circle, dirt flying, hooves pounding.

"She needs to rein Midnight in," Suzie said. "That's too fast."

Horse and rider headed to the second barrel, the pace increasing.

"Go, Emily," Tim yelled.

Switching to a left turn, they made the second barrel like seasoned competitors.

"Easy, now," Tim shouted. "Watch the barrel."

Again, horse and rider leaned in against the turn, making a perfect circle. Then on the final dash, Emily took the end of the reins and whipped Midnight, urging her on. As they darted past the white line, I clicked the stopwatch and held it up for Suzie and Tim to see.

Seventeen seconds.

"Oh, no," Tim said. "I'll never hear the end of this."

19

Friday, April 18, fifteen days before the election

Art had called the meeting, made coffee, and brought doughnuts. At his request, five of us, what we called our *executive committee,* met in the conference room at eight o'clock. The early morning sun beamed into the room with blinding intensity. While the others squinted to pour coffee and get doughnuts, I adjusted the blinds.

With the brightness blocked, I took my seat at the big, mahogany table and scanned Art's outline for the meeting.

AGENDA
1. Overview – Arthur McComas
2. Poll numbers – Harriet Wong
3. Advertising – Richard Klemkowski
4. Finances – Thomas Long
5. Speaking appearances – Sam Davis

"Things are looking good," Art said. "But I'm anxious to hear your reports. Harriet, what've you got for us?"

"Like you say, the news is good. Roper e-mailed me these numbers last night." She passed out a sheet.

ROPER POLL: SENATE RACE #31
- Sam Davis – 42 percent
- Clarence Anderson – 37 percent
- All others – 11 percent
- Undecided – 10 percent
- Margin of error – plus or minus 3.5 percent

"No surprise, it's a two-man race," Harriet said. "And it seems certain we'll have a run-off."

"If there's a run-off, when will it be?" I asked.

"Election laws state that it's always four weeks after the primary," Art said.

I shook my head. "Bad news. That means we'll need more money."

Art smiled. "Maybe that's good news." He turned to Thomas Long. "Tom, how's the war chest?"

Tom passed out his financial report:

CAMPAIGN FINANCES: SENATE RACE #31
- Expenses to date: $253,550
- Expenses anticipated to May 5: $225,000
- Total expenses for primary: $478,550
- Campaign donations to date: $500,000
- Anticipated balance: $21,450

"Looks like we're cutting it pretty close," Art said.

"We'll be fine," Tom replied.

A quiet settled over the room. I expected Tom to continue. Instead, he relaxed back into his chair, sipping coffee.

Finally, after a pause of at least twenty seconds, I raised the obvious question. "What're we going to do about finances if we have a run-off?" I asked.

Again, an awkward silence. I looked around the room. Tom continued to sip his coffee. Harriet Wong and Richard Klemkowski stared down at the table, waiting. Art sat in his chair, immobile, his face reflecting an image of indecision.

I clenched my teeth and resolved not to be the first one to break the silence.

Tom leaned forward, set his cup on the table, and turned to Arthur McComas. "Art, you're the chairman. I think you need to explain our financial circumstances to the candidate."

Art shook his head, obviously reluctant to speak. I had the image of a delinquent taxpayer being grilled by the IRS.

"Sam, how many times do I have to tell you? Money is no problem."

"You think $21,450 is enough to finance a hotly contested run-off election?" I asked.

He chuckled and turned to Richard Klemkowski, "Dick, how much do you estimate we'll need for the run-off?"

"I've budgeted a half-mil," Dick said. "Could be more."

"A half million? Another $500,000?" I asked.

"At least," Dick said. "It depends on the issues, on how hard the Anderson campaign fights us."

"Where's the money coming from?" I asked.

"You don't want to know," Art replied.

"Wait a minute," I shouted. "This is my campaign. I *demand* to know."

Art looked around the room. No one moved. It was so quiet I could hear dust settle.

"From Whiskey," Art said.

I didn't like his answer. "From Whiskey, personally?"

"From his friends."

"What friends?"

"His oil and gas friends."

20

The Conference Room, McComas and Davis Law Firm

The meeting over, Tom, Dick, and Harriet picked up their stuff and left. I asked Art to stay for a minute. He looked at his watch. "I have a nine o'clock appointment," he said. "Could we do this later? How about this afternoon?"

"Only take a minute," I answered as I closed the door. "I'm going to confront Whiskey and tell him no more contributions from the oil and gas lobby."

Over the past ten years that Art and I had been law partners, we'd had our ups and downs. But I had to give Art credit for one thing; he'd never lied about his position on issues. I might not like his opinion on a certain subject, but when he told me where he stood, it was always the truth. His body language at that moment indicated we were about to have another moment of truth—a big one. I braced myself.

"Goddamnit, Sam," he said, his voice rising, his face an ugly scowl of frustration. "You can't have it both ways."

"I understand."

"No, you don't," he snorted. "You've got to get it through your thick head that campaign financing is tough. Money's scarce and hard to come by."

"Yes, I know."

"You've got a bird nest on the ground," he said, shaking his head to emphasize his passion against my intentions. "You have the oil and gas lobby behind you, money in the bank, and a comfortable lead going into this election."

"And I appreciate all that you, Whiskey, and the others are doing for me," I said.

"You sure as hell have a funny way of showing it."

I didn't know how to answer him. For the next few moments I tried to think how I could show my appreciation.

Meanwhile, he appeared to back off. Lowering his voice, he said, "Don't mess this up. A confrontation with Whiskey will not help you win the election."

I gestured to the table and the two nearest chairs. "Let's sit for a moment."

He checked his watch again, walked over to the phone on the credenza, picked up the handset, and dialed a number. "Mrs. Hughes, tell them I'll be there in five minutes." He acknowledged her response. Then he came over and sat next to me.

"I really appreciate all the time—" I started.

Art held up a hand. "Stop. I don't want to hear it."

"But . . . " I tried again.

"Just listen," he said.

Our eyes locked, and I nodded. "Okay."

"No one has done anything illegal," he said. "Not you, not me, not

Whiskey, not anyone connected with the oil and gas lobby."

I waited.

"It's a common practice for various constituencies to support political candidates who favor issues that concern them. Doctors and healthcare professionals contribute to nominees who go on record for medical issues. Teachers and their associations rally behind those who endorse education. Farmers give money in the hope that their representatives will vote for agriculture support."

I nodded.

"There's nothing wrong with the Texas oil and gas lobby giving money to your election campaign fund," he said.

"As long as it's open and above board," I replied.

"And it is."

"I'm not so sure," I said. "I get the feeling that there's money under the table."

"Where?" he asked. "Show me."

Art had me. I didn't have any specific examples. I changed the subject.

"I'm worried about what these people who are supporting me with huge campaign contributions are expecting in return," I said.

Again, Art looked at his watch. "We don't have time to go into all of your presumptions. But you know, and all of us know, that once you're elected, you have only to vote your conscience." He stood and picked up his legal pad.

"God, I hope you're right," I said.

He didn't answer. Instead he turned away and hurried out of the room, leaving the door open.

Alone, I stared at the doorway and wondered what I should do about calling Whiskey.

Mrs. Hughes came into the room and started cleaning up the coffee cups and leftover doughnuts. "You okay?" she asked.

I nodded, thought about my desk, and pictured neat little stacks of paper. After Mrs. Hughes, I probably wouldn't be able to find Whiskey's contact numbers nor any of the questions I'd written down about his campaign contributions.

21

My office, a week later

The phone buzzed. I picked up to hear Mrs. Hughes say, "Lieutenant Fuller is here to see you."

"Who?" I asked.

"Lieutenant Charles Fuller, of the *Texas Rangers*."

I knew from her exaggerated pronunciation that Mrs. Hughes was really pissed at me for forgetting his name. For a moment I thought about various ways I could play it. I could say, *Tell him we're not buying any protection today*, or *We've already given to their baseball fund*. Instead, I said "Please, ask him to come in."

Seconds later the door opened, and she ushered him in.

"Morning, Charlie," I offered him my left hand.

"Morning, Sam," he replied. He remembered my situation and clasped my left with his right. He did it with unusual smoothness and grace—accompanied with a warm smile.

I gestured to one of the chairs in front of my desk as I sat.

HARRY HAINES

Mrs. Hughes hovered. "May I get you a cup of coffee?"

She didn't ask me.

"No thank you, Ma'am," he said.

"We're honored to have a lieutenant from the *Rangers*," she continued.

"Thank you, Ma'am. It's an honor for me to be here, to call on one of our senators."

I didn't say anything. Neither did Fuller.

Mrs. Hughes remained silent. After a moment of awkwardness, she stepped back toward the door.

"Thank you, Mrs. Hughes," I said.

With obvious reluctance, she went out and closed the door.

"What brings you back to Midland?" I asked.

Just like before, he pulled out his small tape recorder. "Mind if I record this?"

I smiled, shuffled through the papers on my credenza, found mine, plopped it down on the desk next to his, and said, "Here we go again."

He chuckled. "You're the only person I know who has a tape deck just like mine."

We each clicked on our recorders.

"The Midland County Sheriff found evidence that the oil well fire was arson."

"Really?" I shuddered at his announcement.

"Yep. And this creates a whole new set of circumstances around Abner Stone's death."

"You think it was murder?"

"For sure it wasn't an accident."

I thought back to the morning we first read about Abner's death in *The Midland Telegraph Reporter*. "That's what my wife thought."

"So did a lot of other folks," Charlie said.

"Any suspects?" I asked.

"All the people who are supporting the oil and gas lobby."

A cold shiver ran down my spine. And for the first time I realized why a Texas Ranger from the Austin Crime Lab was here, making a tape recording, and asking me questions about the demise of our state senator.

"What does this have to do with oil and gas people?" I asked.

"We've discovered a 'behind the scenes movement' to re-write the laws that govern fracking, oil well spacing, and the oil depletion allowance, the ODA."

"And?"

"And old Abner was the leader of the opposition."

"Wow."

"Just a theory. But we have to investigate."

I shook my head. "So I'm now a suspect?"

"Your campaign finances are a matter of public record," he said. "So far this year, you've reported more money from the oil and gas lobby than any other politician in Texas."

"Double wow," I said. "I didn't know that."

"What commitments have you made?" he asked.

"Commitments? I don't understand."

He smiled, shook his head. "Come on, Sam. We all know that when political candidates accept campaign donations, especially big ones like you're getting, promises are exchanged to support certain issues."

"None that I know of."

His smile faded. Instead, a look of anger filled his face. "I don't like it when people lie to me."

I reached up to the shelf above my computer and took down an old tattered Bible I've kept in my office since law school. I occasionally use it to quote scripture when I'm making summations before a jury. I reached over to Fuller and asked that he hold it.

Then I placed my hand on the Bible and said, "I do swear that I have not made any commitments, any promises, nor any agreements to any person or group, in return for their support of my political campaign."

Fuller sat there, speechless for a moment. Then he reached over and turned off his tape recorder. "I'd like you to turn yours off, too."

I did.

"Look, Sam, I don't think you killed Abner Stone, but I need to know who you talk to. Off the record, who's your contact from the oil and gas lobby? Who gives you the money?"

"I honestly don't know," I said. "Let me ask my campaign treasurer, Thomas Long."

Obviously, Lieutenant Charles Fuller didn't believe me. Without saying a word, he packed up his tape recorder and stomped out the door.

22

The office

I called Tom Long. He picked up after the first ring. "Sam Davis campaign headquarters," he said.

"Tom, we need to talk," I said. "Could we go for coffee?"

"Now?"

"Yes, I can be there in ten minutes."

He said okay. Minutes later I arrived at the old grocery store to find him standing outside, waiting. We drove three blocks to Starbucks, picked up our coffee, and seated ourselves at a table by the window.

"What's up?" he asked.

"I had a visit this morning from the Texas Rangers."

"So?"

"So, they now think Abner's death was murder, and they're investigating possible suspects."

"They're investigating you?" Tom asked.

"Apparently they believe the motive for Abner's murder is linked to his opposition to oil and gas legislation."

Tom poured cream into his coffee and stirred—his face a studious expression, as though trying to connect the dots.

"The Rangers want to know about campaign contributions I've received from oil and gas lobbyists," I said.

"Why would they ask?" Tom frowned and shook his head. "It's all a matter of public record."

"Lieutenant Charles Fuller asked me for a list of names of the specific individuals who give us the money."

Tom sipped his coffee. I could almost see the wheels turning inside his brain. "He doesn't want *Chevron*, *Shell*, or *Conoco-Phillips*. He wants names?"

"Exactly."

"What'd you say?"

"I told him I didn't know. And that I'd ask you."

"Ouch," Tom said. "Wish you hadn't said that."

For the first time I had an inkling of trouble. Tom had always appeared so nonchalant about our finances. Throughout the campaign, time and time again, when we discussed money matters, he spoke with confidence. "Money's no problem," he said, repeatedly. I had never thought to question him about specific names.

Now I wished I had.

"Tom, I told Lieutenant Fuller I would get names. Is that a problem?"

"Sorta. I don't have all the names."

My heart sank. "Okay, give me the ones you have."

"Sam, you're making a mistake," he said. "We need to stick with corporate names. I've served as treasurer for dozens of campaigns, and that is how we've *always* done it. You should tell the Texas Rangers we're in compliance."

Tom's intransigence baffled me. I studied him for a moment and tried to think of what to say.

"I've studied the election rules and regulations," he continued. "There is nothing that requires us to list specific names of people."

"Except that I gave my word. I told him I would give him the *names* of our contacts."

Tom gave me a hard look. Then he shook his head as he said, "You'll have to go back to him and say you're sorry. We don't give out names. That we don't have to."

Our eyes locked, and it was flint against flint, igniting an open flame into our confrontation. In a slow, soft voice, I said, "Tom, it's my campaign, it's my neck on the line. I need to know the names of those who have given money to finance my election expenses."

He looked away. Beads of perspiration formed on his forehead. It was obvious that he felt intense pressure to do something he didn't want to do. I questioned how disclosing a list of names from oil companies could cause such anxiety. One thought led to another, and I wondered if the size of the list or the magnitude of the money was the problem. Perhaps he hadn't kept good records, and he was worried about revealing erroneous amounts or a list of inaccurate names. My thoughts roiled.

Finally, I asked, "How many names are there?"

He turned back and our eyes met. "One," he said.

I couldn't believe his answer. But before I could say anything else, he told me.

"Whiskey Williams."

23

My office

I put off calling Whiskey. A day went by, then another. But I realized that, before I gave his name to the Texas Rangers, I had to call him. So, three days later, I mustarded up my courage and dialed his direct line—his secret, personal number to the phone on his desk in the Texas State Capitol. He answered on the first ring.

"Good morning, Senator Davis," he said. "How goes the campaign?"

I knew he read my name on his caller ID. Still, it jarred me when he answered my call with my name and an immediate question. "Fine," I said.

"Good," he continued. "Harriet called me a couple of days ago with the Roper Poll numbers. Looks like a run-off with the guy in Amarillo."

"Yes."

"No problem. Tom, Dick, and Harriet all tell me you'll win in a breeze if not a landslide."

"They're more optimistic than I."

"You question Harriet's numbers?" he asked.

"Actually, I think she has a good grasp on our present position," I said.

"But?"

"But I had a visit from the Texas Rangers—Lieutenant Charles Fuller."

"Big Charlie, the bloodhound?"

"You know him?"

Whiskey chuckled. "Yeah, you might say that. Charlie and I go way back."

I sensed danger. Whiskey knew something I didn't, and for a nanosecond I debated with myself about whether or not to pursue it.

He decided for me.

"Thirteen years ago, in my first year as lieutenant governor, I failed to support a big budget request for the Texas Rangers. They wanted a fleet of helicopters—a request for several hundred million—and I quashed it. Charlie has never let me forget."

"*Thirteen* years ago?"

Whiskey laughed. "Hard to believe, ain't it."

I didn't know what to say. But with Whiskey I'd learned that sometimes I didn't have to say anything—he'd carry the conversation.

"Charlie's pressing you about campaign finances?" he asked.

"Yes," I answered. "How'd you know?"

"Sam, this ain't about you. It's about an old bruised ego—it's about those damned helicopters." Whiskey paused, obviously thinking back.

Thirteen years ago? I, too, let my mind scroll back to a time when I was just getting started with my law practice in Midland. Suzie and I were thinking about getting married. But I couldn't remember anything about state politics, a multi-million-dollar helicopter deal, or a budget fight in the Texas legislature. It seemed best to return our conversation to the present.

"Fuller wants me to give him names," I said. "I thought I could get them from Thomas Long, but Tom says he doesn't have any—names of individuals who represent our corporate donors."

"Tom's right," Whiskey replied. "He depends on my contacts with the oil and gas lobby."

There it was—the bare facts of Texas political reality.

Shell, BP, Chevron, Conoco/Phillips, and all the other players in the oil patch, including the little independents like our local companies in Midland, had found the most effective way to legislative influence. I took a big breath and thought about the pockets of our beloved lieutenant governor.

His fourteen-million-dollar jet.

And that even my ten-year-old son could read about Texas's crony relationships, about Brown and Root, Halliburton, and the billions that were at stake in foreign oil.

The millions Whiskey was pouring into my campaign seemed insignificant.

"Sam, you still there?" Whiskey asked.

"Yeah, I was just thinking," I replied.

"Okay, Sammy, what're you thinking?"

"I'm thinking, I don't know what to say to Charlie Fuller."

Whiskey let out a raucous sound, what I've heard called the good ole boy laugh. "When all else fails, tell him the truth."

"But that's like pointing a finger at you."

"Which is the truth."

"God, Whiskey, this is about more than campaign finances. Charlie's investigating the death of Abner Stone."

"You think I killed Abner?" he asked in a somber voice.

"That's the furthest thought from my mind."

Then in another roar of laughter, Whiskey said, "Why don't you say that to Charlie Fuller?"

24

Friday evening, television station KMID, 6:15 p.m.

I arrived fifteen minutes early. Actually, forty-five minutes before the scheduled interview. KMID's public affairs head, a youthful-looking blonde named Kaye Kelly, had asked me to meet her at the station thirty minutes early. This being my first ever interview on live television, I added another fifteen minutes. Normally, people liked it when I came early. The KMID receptionist didn't.

"I'm a little early," I said.

The receptionist, a redhead who looked like a high school senior but was probably a twenty-something employee, apologized for the fact that Ms. Kelly was not yet at the studio. "May I get you a cup of coffee?" she asked.

"No, I'm fine."

"Kaye is always here early," the receptionist said. She impugned the weather, the traffic, and the Lord Almighty as reasons why Ms. Kelly was not available—her third apology since I'd arrived.

PUPPET POLITICS

Just as I was about to shush the apologetic receptionist, in walked Kaye Kelly. "Sorry to keep you waiting," she said.

"You haven't kept anyone waiting," I said as I looked at my watch. "We're not scheduled to meet for another five minutes."

She smiled. "Thanks. I appreciate your patience. But you're right, we have plenty of time." She walked over to a door marked *Authorized Personnel Only* and held it open for me. "Come on back."

I followed Kaye Kelly into unfamiliar surroundings—down a narrow hallway to Studio A, a large room with high ceiling, lights, and cameras. "This is where we'll do the interview." She introduced me to the director, two camera operators, and a sound engineer. "We'll do a five-minute run-through, then we'll take ten minutes for makeup."

One of the technicians fitted me with an earpiece and a lapel mike. The lights came up. Kaye asked me some rhetorical questions, and I improvised responses. Then the director's voice came into my ear. "We're all set. Kaye and Mr. Davis, take a few minutes. Be back in place no later than 6:55."

"Time for them to make us beautiful," Kaye said.

I followed her back into the hallway and on farther down to the dressing rooms where she introduced me to a makeup technician—an older woman who reminded me of our Mrs. Hughes. Much like going to a barber shop, I sat in a high, swivel-chair facing a huge mirror while this authoritarian individual draped a protective cover over me and proceeded to apply makeup with her own ideas and standards. She didn't ask my opinion about anything. I could have been a fence post. It wouldn't have mattered.

At five minutes until seven, Kaye and I took our seats in front of the cameras. The lights came up, and before I knew it we were on the air.

Kaye Kelly lobbed a few easy questions about me, my family, and my

---

background.

I relaxed and tried to make brief, cogent answers. Kaye smiled a lot. Things seemed to be going well.

Then her facial expression changed, and her voice took a stern, crisp manner. "Mr. Davis, are you aware that the Midland County Sheriff's Office is conducting an inquiry into the death of Abner Stone?"

"Yes," I replied. "I've spoken with sheriff deputies who are working the case."

"And that a CSI unit from the Texas Rangers has been called to assist?"

I nodded and wondered where this was going. "I've met Lieutenant Fuller and tried to help with his investigation."

"Both the *Midland Reporter Telegram* and the *Odessa American* have recently printed editorials about Stone. Both newspapers are calling it *murder*."

With her introduction of the word *murder,* I could feel perspiration on my forehead. My mouth turned dry. I hesitated, tried to swallow, and then nodded. "Yes, I've read those."

"And there seems to be considerable evidence that, if Stone was assassinated, it was somehow linked to his vociferous opposition to big oil."

"That's pure speculation," I said.

"However, it is true that he was leading the charge against the oil and gas lobby, is it not?"

"In Texas, yes. Abner made his views known that he was against any changes in the ODA."

"The ODA?"

"The oil depletion allowance."

"Is it true that you were out near the oil well fire on the night of

Senator Stone's death?"

"Yes, I was feeding my horses."

She shuffled her papers, selected a computer printout, and leaned forward in her chair. "I have here a summary of campaign expenses as reported by the state election board." She held up the computer paper, a gesture of *here's the evidence*. This, combined with her body language—moving forward toward the camera—and the scowl on her face, gave an unmistakable inference.

Kaye Kelly was accusing me of the murder of Abner Stone.

25

Friday night and Saturday morning

Friday night I tossed and turned. While Kaye Kelly had not, in so many words, accused me of murder, she certainly left no doubt about her thoughts. Anyone who watched the TV interview would instantly grasp the idea. I felt powerless. This young reporter had set a trap, and I'd walked right into it. Accused and convicted in the court of public opinion, there didn't seem to be anything I could do.

At two a.m., I slipped out of bed, fixed myself a double scotch, and watched a 1930s film on Turner Classic Movies. Gradually, as Greta Garbo flirted with Clark Gable, I fell asleep sitting on the sofa in the den.

Suzie woke me as the sun was coming up. "It's 6:30," she said. "Remember, we're taking the kids to the barrel races this morning."

When life's problems threaten one's public persona, it's a relief to have family responsibilities. Grateful for my two kids and their 4-H activities, I showered, shaved, and struggled into a pair of tight jeans, western shirt, and boots. The four of us piled into our old dilapidated pickup and headed for Art's barn on the south side of town. The taste of Suzie's still warm blueberry muffins gave a festive air to our morning travel.

I backed our pickup into the barn. Tim stood by the horse trailer, ready to secure the hitch. Suzie guided me with hand signals. Emily watched.

At the appropriate moment, Suzie signaled me to stop. Seconds later I heard the familiar "clank" as Tim secured the coupling and began to lock down the trailer hitch. I killed the motor, climbed out of the pickup, and ambled over to the horses. Both Midnight and Champ stuck their heads out over the half-doors. Animals can read the signs of human behavior—the pickup backing into the barn, the sounds of the horse trailer, the presence of all four members of the Davis family—and recognize when a trip is eminent. Trips almost always include apples and other tasty treats. Both of our horses crowded their doors, ears forward, obviously anxious and ready to go.

Tim went to Champ, Emily to Midnight.

Suzie and I watched.

This was the payoff for our kids and their horses.

I thought back to the day of the fire, to the uncertainty of life. And I remembered how Tim calmed his horse, then led him to the trailer and eventual safety. Those frantic moments had no doubt added to the trust we now saw between a young rider and his mount. Tim loved his horse. It appeared that Champ felt the same for Tim.

Tim opened the door to the stall, snapped a lead rope on Champ's halter, and led him into the trailer. I stood there with my wife and marveled at how easily our ten-year-old son handled this thousand-pound animal.

Suzie started to go with Emily, to help her load her horse.

"Wait," I whispered.

Suzie stopped.

Emily stretched up to the tack board for a lead rope. Barely tall enough to reach it, she grabbed one, lifted it off the holder, and carried it over to Midnight. She opened the stall door. For a moment tension filled the barn, and I sensed that Suzie held her breath. I took a half step toward the stall, ready to leap if Emily needed my help.

For a moment nothing happened.

Then Emily reached up and patted her horse on the nose, whispering words that I couldn't hear. Watching closely, I suddenly realized Emily could not reach Midnight's halter—either Suzie or I would have to help. But before I could react, the horse lowered her head and Emily snapped on the lead rope. Amazed, I stepped back and held my wife's hand.

"How about that?" I whispered.

"She's doing fine," Suzie replied.

We watched as our seven-year-old led her horse into the trailer and secured the lead rope.

I closed and locked the trailer.

The Davis family crowded into our old pickup and headed down the road toward the Midland County Fairgrounds. It felt good to be surrounded by family support, love, and laughter.

My cell phone rang.

I handed it to Suzie.

"Good morning, Whiskey," she said.

She paused, listening, and looked at me.

"We'll be at the Midland County Arena," she said. "Our kids are competing in the 4-H Barrel Races this morning."

Again, she listened for a few moments.

"Sure, we'd love to have you join us. Art knows how to find us." She punched off.

She looked at me and shook her head. "That was Whiskey calling from his plane. He and Art are worried about last night's TV interview."

"And they're both coming to the barrel races?" I asked.

Suzie nodded.

The feeling of family, so pervasive only moments ago now dissipated to a fleeting memory. Thoughts of the election came rolling over me like a ten-ton truck.

26

The Midland County Fairgrounds

We unloaded and saddled the horses. Tim and Emily joined about fifty other youthful riders who were warming up in the field next to the arena. Over to the side, not far from the arena building, the event organizers had placed a set of barrels for practice. I motioned for Tim and Emily to ride over and get into the queue.

First Tim and then Emily made a practice run. Both had good times. And more importantly, both looked good, really good. I felt proud of our children, and for a moment the outside world—elections and murder accusations—left my conscious thinking.

Tim and Emily led Champ and Midnight toward the arena. That's when I saw Art McComas and Whiskey Williams. I almost failed to recognize Whiskey. In the half-dozen times I'd met the lieutenant governor, he'd always greeted me with his "politician's smile," a face that glowed with a cheerful, upbeat countenance. Sincerity might be questionable, but his beaming expression was so consistent that I'd come to accept it as endemic, an essential part of his persona.

That morning his expression was grim. Eyebrows together and his eyes glaring, he scowled at me with a hard look that left no doubt about his exasperation. "Davis, we need to talk," he snarled.

I pointed toward the arena's open door. "Join us," I said. "Our kids are about to make their run."

Whiskey and Art had no choice. They had to walk with us or be left. Inside the arena we gathered at the staging area with other contestants waiting their turns. A contest official came with clipboard in hand, "Only one adult with each contestant," he yelled. "All others must either take seats in the bleachers or go back outside."

Art took my arm. "Whiskey's about to lose his cool. He's gone to a lot of trouble to fly up here this morning to speak with you."

"And I'll be with him just as soon as this is over," I replied.

"Why don't you let Suzie look after the kids? I'll bring you back as soon as you're finished with Whiskey?"

I turned to Art. Using my good hand, I gently removed his grasp from my right arm. "Art, my first priority is this barrel race. Tell Whiskey I'll be with him as soon as it's over." I walked away.

The announcer called, "Emily Davis."

I boosted my daughter up into the saddle. "Not too fast," I said.

She smiled down at me and said, "Don't worry Daddy. Midnight and I can do it." She rode back, about thirty feet from the starting line.

As the official with his stopwatch stood on the white line ready to give the signal, I glanced up in the bleachers to see Whiskey and Art take seats in the back row. The lieutenant governor's face looked hard, his features projecting a mixture of impatience and furry.

Words boomed over the PA, "Okay, Emily," the announcer said.

Emily slapped Midnight on the rump and urged her forward.

My daughter looked small and fragile as she leaned forward on her horse. I watched as they dashed across the white line, unbelievably fast for a seven-year-old girl. She took the first barrel in stride, a fast pace but with good control. The second barrel went even better, with dirt flying as Midnight's hooves dug into the turf. I worried that Emily was pushing too much for such a tiny rider.

Then it happened. On the third barrel, the big black mare slipped. One leg went down in a turn taken too fast. My heart stopped as I watched horse and rider try to recover. A gasp went up from the crowd, and it looked certain that a thousand pound horse would tumble, sure to fall on my daughter.

And then, somehow, a miracle happened. Midnight made the turn on three legs and pulled up straight. Horse and rider paused for a moment and then loped across the white line—to a safe finish.

The crowd clapped long and loud, the biggest ovation of the morning. Moments later the PA boomed, "Twenty-one seconds for Emily Davis," he said, "and a great recovery for a seven-year-old rider."

With heart pounding, I went over to congratulate my daughter and caught her as she slipped down from the saddle. We hugged.

Suzie put her arms around Emily. "I'm so proud of you," she said.

Tim hugged his little sister. "Way to go," he said.

"Ruined my time," Emily whimpered.

I knelt. Put my arms around her a second time. "Hey, that was a great ride. Not many riders could pull out of a slip like that."

"Is Midnight okay?" Emily asked.

I stood, pleased that she would think about her horse, and together we led Midnight around in a circle. The big, black mare seemed fine.

Whiskey and Art returned from the bleachers. Whiskey approached with a solemn, somber face. "Where can we go to talk? he asked.

Before I could answer, an announcement boomed over the PA, "Tim Davis, are you ready?"

"I'll be with you as soon as I can," I said. "Tim's run is next. And if he does well, we'll have the trophy presentation. It may be an hour."

I turned to help my son up into the saddle. "Watch the barrels," I said. "Not too fast. Control is more important than speed."

"Don't worry, Dad, we're not coming close to any barrels," Tim said. He rode back to the usual spot behind the white line.

The official starter stood on the line. I glanced around to see Whiskey and Art just outside, the lieutenant governor's face beet red.

I turned back as my son thundered across the white line, the fastest I'd ever seen him ride. My breathing stopped.

Tim leaned precariously to the inside of the left-hand turn as Champ's hooves churned the dirt in a tight circle. The second barrel followed immediately, and Tim urged Champ to an even faster speed. Coming out of the turn, heading toward the third barrel, Tim leaned so low I worried he might fall out of his saddle.

But he didn't. Instead he circled the last barrel perfectly and headed past the white line like a bullet. I relaxed. My breathing restarted.

"Thirteen point eight seconds for Tim Davis," the announcer said. "The fastest time so far today."

A wave of exultation fell over me like a warm, fuzzy, blanket—a mixture of joy, of pride, of a release from tension. I went over to congratulate my son. We hugged.

Then his mother and his sister grabbed him.

And I realized, neither Whiskey nor Art were anywhere to be seen.

27

Sunday morning at the breakfast table

Front-page articles in the Sunday edition of the *Midland Reporter Telegram* hit me with conflicting emotions. On the left side, a photograph showed my son with Champ—accepting his trophy with a big smile. The caption read, *Davis Wins County 4-H*. The article described Saturday's events at the Midland County Arena and devoted an entire paragraph to Tim's winning performance in the barrel races.

The opposite side of the same page featured a photo of Texas Ranger Charles Fuller and the Midland County Sheriff, both in uniform, both with somber expressions. The caption read: *Local and State Law Enforcement Consider Indictment*. My hands shook. Working to hold the newspaper steady, I slowly and carefully read about the possibility of criminal action against me.

Oblivious to the indictment story, or to my reaction, Emily, Tim, and Suzie laughed and chattered about Tim's trophy. I watched and wanted desperately to share in their euphoria.

But the implications of an investigation of Abner Stone's murder, and the likelihood that charges might be filed, caused me to withdraw. I looked at the trophy sitting on the kitchen cabinet with a heavy heart and tried to muster a smile at the breakfast table.

"Something wrong with your waffle?" Suzie asked.

I folded the newspaper, dropped it on the floor, and said, "Pass the blueberry syrup, please."

Emily handed the bottle to me. "The only reason he won that trophy was because Midnight slipped."

Tim chuckled. "That's not true." He shook his head. "You weren't even close."

"Was too."

"Was not."

"Hey," my wife said, her voice loud, projecting a ring of command. "I have something I want to talk about."

Both kids stopped. When we heard that tone of voice, everyone in the family knew to proceed with caution. Even me.

The room became so quiet, no one dared breathe.

"Let's talk about how to be a gracious loser."

Tim snickered. A tiny little sound. So soft I almost missed it.

The voice of steel returned with stinging rebuke.

"*And* . . . how to be a gracious winner."

The room became even more quiet. If I could have stopped my heartbeat, I would have.

I stole a glance at Emily.

She rolled her eyes.

Then came the lecture. Short and sweet. But to the point, as a mother told her offspring about two important lessons in life. Seconds later our meal resumed.

I wished my parents had taught me how to accept a criminal indictment for murder.

But they hadn't. So I tried to restart breakfast conversation. "Emily, a lot of people have told me how impressed they were with your recovery after Midnight's slip."

"Thanks, Dad," she replied.

No one said anything for a moment.

I looked at Tim.

He returned my gaze. And for a nanosecond I felt the electricity. It was a moment of brief emotion. An unspoken communication between father and son I will always remember.

"That could have been disaster," Tim said.

I heard a deep sigh, a soft release of breath. It came from the direction where my wife was seated.

"If Midnight had fallen on your leg, you'd be in the hospital," Tim continued.

"Thanks." Emily said the word softly. So soft I could easily have missed it. But in the passion of the moment, it was all that was needed.

Breakfast ended on a happy note.

The kids excused themselves.

The trophy remained on the kitchen cabinet.

Suzie and I admired it without speaking.

She broke the silence. "What's going to happen about the indictment?"

"Impossible to predict," I replied. "That's up to the district attorney."

"What does this do for the election?"

"That's what Whiskey and Art wanted to talk about yesterday."

"And they're gone?"

"Obviously."

"So now it's up to you?"

"Yeah," I said.

And as she always does when we have moments of intense emotional interaction, she reached over and put her hand on my deformed right thumb and forefinger—her closest, most intimate gesture of support.

"And I've got to find a way to fight back," I said.

28

Breakfast at home

Nothing happened Sunday. No phone calls, no e-mail, no visits. Nothing. Monday broke as a bright, sunshiny West Texas spring morning, temperature in the mid-sixties, a light breeze from the southwest. Breakfast with the family was normal for the last week in April. The kids scampered off to school with energy and enthusiasm.

And I was left to face massive uncertainty.

I dreaded going to the office, but once there I felt a sense of relief. Something was going to happen. Either they would indict me or they wouldn't. And whichever way it fell, I'd have direction.

The uniqueness of the day started with Mrs. Hughes's reaction. Instead of her usual clipped, impersonal greeting, she appeared subdued. "Is there anything I can do?" she asked.

I gave her my best smile. "Thank you," I said, and I meant it. "Right now, I can't think of anything."

She handed me a cup of coffee, a first in our ten-year relationship. "I'd like to help."

I thought about giving her a hug. But the coffee cup made it awkward. And I thought the gesture might cause her to fall into apoplexy. Instead I said, "Thanks," gave her another smile, carried the coffee into my office, and closed the door.

Ten seconds later, before I could even sit at my desk, Art burst into the room. "Morning, Sam," he said. He, too, carried a cup of coffee. "Let's talk." He plopped down in one of the two chairs in front of my desk.

Instead of taking my usual seat behind my desk, I turned the other guest chair around so it faced Art and sat next to him. The gesture brought us close, an action I hoped was not lost on him.

"You really ripped it with Whiskey," he said.

"Hey, if I have to choose between him and my kids, guess who wins? Hands down, every time." I raised my voice. "No one comes between me and my family. I don't allow it."

"The point is you didn't have to choose," Art continued. "You could have found some way to handle the situation with diplomacy."

"That's your interpretation. I didn't see it that way. Still don't."

"If Whiskey could have dumped you on the spot, he would have," Art continued. "I've never seen anyone so steamed."

"He doesn't have to dump me," I said. "I quit."

Art shook his head.

"Want me to call him now?" I leaned forward, ready to reach for the phone.

"Goddamnit, Sam, it's eleven days until the primary. Everybody knows it's too late to change horses. We're stuck with you."

"Whiskey knows it?" I asked.

"*Especially* Whiskey. We've already spent two million on you, and he's authorized us to spend another three this week."

"Three million?" The thought took my breath away.

"We've got to," Art continued. "Clarence Anderson smells blood in the water. He thinks he has the election won."

"With this talk about indicting me for Stone's murder, he's probably right."

"We spent all day yesterday, brainstorming. We have a plan."

"Who's we?"

"Your executive committee."

"You were meeting without me?"

"Whiskey insisted."

"Whiskey was here in Midland?"

Art nodded. "All day Sunday."

Emotion surged through me like super adrenaline. Partly anger, some amazement, maybe even bewilderment. For a moment I felt like I would explode, I couldn't control it.

I got up, went to the door, and asked Mrs. Hughes for more coffee. She brought the carafe into my office and filled both our cups. Her presence created a sense of closeness among the three of us—her, Art, and myself. It felt like we'd formed a new team—a team that was circling the wagons. It was a good feeling, one that calmed me. I thought I saw her smiling as she left the room and closed the door.

"I am amazed," I said. "That's the last thing I would've thought Whiskey would do."

Art snorted, shook his head, and said. "Sam, I think you must be the dumbest dumb-ass on the planet."

I chuckled.

"Don't hold back. Tell me what you really think."

"Whiskey, wants to win this election," Art said. "He thinks you still can."

I caved. "Tell me what you want me to do."

Art looked at his watch, and then he lectured me. "Tom, Dick, and Harriet are coming at nine o'clock. I've scheduled a three-hour meeting in the conference room."

"Okay."

"And I want you to clear your schedule . . . for the next eleven days."

29

The Conference Room, McComas and Davis Law Offices

We started with reports. Tom had bad news as did Dick. But Harriet's statistical report was the worst—more devastating than anyone had expected. According to Sunday night's Roper Poll, my campaign dropped thirty points.

"In the thirteen years I've been in the polling business, that's the record—the largest weekend drop in a political campaign. Ever," she said.

"Give us the details," Art said.

"Before the Friday night interview, all three major polls gave us about 60 percent of the vote," Harriet said. "Roper predicted 59 percent for us, 33 percent for Anderson, and the remaining 8 percent either undecided or split among the other two candidates."

Art sighed, an audible sound of exasperation. "And now?"

Harriet continued. "As I said, Sam dropped 30 points and is now at 29 percent. Smithson got most of it, and Roper gives him 52 percent. The remaining 19 percent is split three ways among the other two and undecided."

"So, to force a run-off election, Sam has to win back 3 percentage points?" Art asked.

"This is a highly volatile election. With so many voters shifting, the margin of error is extremely unpredictable. Roper, Gallup, and USA Today all say it's at least 5 percentage points—maybe even 10."

"What's the bottom line?" Art asked. "How many points do we have to gain to force a runoff?"

"To be safe," Harriet answered, "I'd say thirteen points."

"Sounds impossible," I said.

"In a normal election," Art said, "I would agree. But when you lose thirty points in one weekend, gaining thirteen in the next ten days sounds doable."

"How?" I asked.

"We have a plan," Art said. "We call it 'Fireside chats with Sam Davis and his family.'."

Art went on to describe the plan the team had devised. It would consist of a series of fifteen-minute television programs that would be done nightly just after the ten o'clock news for the next nine evenings. Originating from KMID-TV, and carried by a network of eight stations throughout District 31, a series of guests would be interviewed along with me, Suzie, Tim, Emily, and our Dachshund, Gretel. I was amazed to learn that the hostess for the series would be Kaye Kelly, the reporter who had started my downfall with her murderous interview on Friday night.

As Art droned on with details of the plan, I thought about a little ditty my mother had made me memorize: Mine is not to reason why, but to smile and willingly comply.

If there had been any question about politics taking over my life, the next ten days would remove all doubt and, like a metaphorical ball and chain, would script my every word, thought, and deed.

The *chats* started that evening. Our first guest was Reverend Gene Garrison, our minister at the Midland Presbyterian Church. Reverend Garrison wanted to help us, and he did. Kaye led him through a series of endorsements that extolled my family's involvement in the church and its programs. While nothing overt came out, the inference was that someone, like Sam Davis, who was so heavily committed to the church could not possibly have murdered Abner Stone.

Tuesday night the guest was our PTA president at Cactus Elementary School, Mary Jane Eckor. Mary Jane and her husband were our good friends and members of our dinner bridge club. We played cards and had dinner with the Eckors once a month. Their kids and our kids were the same ages, in the same grades at school, and often shared rides during bad weather. Mary Jane came across great with her responses to Kaye Kelly's questions. The interview conveyed an image that no person so heavily involved in PTA could have had anything to do with the murder of Abner Stone.

Wednesday night, Tim's scoutmaster, Roger Johnson, laid it on thick with home movies of the scout troop's recent canoe trip—paddling down the Rio Grande through Big Bend National Park—with me as one of the dads and co-sponsor. The highlight of the film came when my canoe tipped over, and I pulled Tim and another boy out of the water. In the voiceover, no mention was made of the fact I caused the accident, and that the water was only three feet deep. Roger gave testimony that *any* dad who sponsored boy scouts and saved lives could not possibly be considered a suspect in the murder of Abner Stone.

One of the little-known social clubs in Midland was the DAR, the Daughters of the American Revolution. Organized back during World War I as a flag-waving women's group to encourage patriotism, it had grown over the next century into a somewhat elitist assemblage of wealthy dilettantes who sponsored Memorial Day activities at the Midland Cemetery and raised money for a municipal fireworks display on the Fourth of July. Whatever, these women played bridge at the Midland Country Club, were among Suzie's best friends, and wanted to be a part of the parade of people endorsing me. On Thursday evening, six of them brought a dozen American flags and filled Studio A at the TV station. Kaye Kelly led the "Pledge of Allegiance," made sure we had a piano, and led the singing of the *Star Spangled Banner*. I had to bite my tongue to keep from laughing as Kaye went through testimonials about how such a patriotic American as myself could not possibly be connected, in *any* way, with the murder of Abner Stone.

On Friday evening we were joined by the girls on Emily's soccer team. If "cute" could win elections, I had this one won in a landslide. A dozen seven-year-old girls, all in uniform, gave a cheer.

"Two, four, six, eight, who do we appreciate? Mr. Davis!"

Three attractive moms, again, all in matching uniforms, gave individual testimonials.

The girls closed the program with another cheer.

The coach, Suzie's friend Elizabeth Johnson, said, "Anyone who thinks that Emily's dad could have anything to do with the death of Senator Stone simply doesn't know Sam Davis."

The circus went on for seven more nights. I thought the prize for most ridiculous went to our veterinarian, Zackary Brown. Don't get me wrong. Zack is a great vet, and he takes excellent care of our dachshund, Gretel. But his endorsement of me, based on his praise of my care of the family pooch, was more than ridiculous, I thought it preposterous.

Gretel stole the show.

And I don't think anyone cared anymore about Abner Stone.

By Election Day—by the time we'd spent almost three million dollars on television specials—I was sick of political life.

Suzie planned a "victory" party in our backyard and invited a hundred or so people, what she referred to as our friends of the election. She hired a caterer who set up tables loaded with finger food and an unlimited supply of cheap champagne. Nobody expected me to win the election. If we could just squeak out enough votes to force a runoff election—that would be our victory.

People started coming shortly after the polls closed, a little after seven o'clock. By nine, the place was crowded, the champagne flowed, and the streets filled with cars for several blocks in every direction.

By eleven o'clock, Clarence Anderson had built a small lead, but not enough to command a clear majority. With the major question, the runoff, still in doubt, people started leaving. Most came by to shake my hand, or pat me on the back, and wish me well.

By midnight the caterers had carried barrels of trash to the dumpster, folded the tables, and pretty much restored our backyard to a modicum of normalcy.

When the clock struck 1:00 a.m., I counted noses. Less than a dozen diehards gathered around the TV in our living room.

The last two things I remember from an evening filled with anxiety were Art working at his laptop at the kitchen table, trying to predict how many votes remained uncounted, versus the number needed to settle the question of runoff, and the clock chiming 2:00 a.m.

I fell asleep in the lounge chair in front of the television.

30

At home, 3648 Everglade

The next morning Suzie woke me with a kiss. "Congratulations," she said. "They're calling you the comeback kid." I blinked, rubbed my eyes, and tried to understand what she was saying.

"Anderson won." She kissed me again. "But you forced a runoff."

"Really?"

"The kids and I are having breakfast," she said. "Why don't you join us?"

"What time is it?" I asked.

"Five minutes until nine." She kissed me lightly on the forehead. "Channel Five has scheduled an election special at nine o'clock."

Minutes later I joined my family at the breakfast table.

I scanned the TV screen. Someone muted the sound, but a narrow line at the bottom scrolled election numbers. First I tried to read the raw numbers but found it too difficult to keep up. Then, the scroll disappeared and we got a full-screen announcement about the nine o'clock election special.

Seconds later I punched the mute button and we got a live, "Good morning," announced by a female news anchor. "Welcome to KMID's Sunday morning election special, the only comprehensive summary available in West Texas. We'll have all the details right after these important messages."

Ten seconds into the news and we get a commercial. I thought about a few choice words, but remembered, just in time, that the kids were at the table. I punched the mute button.

"Daddy, now that the election's over, can we take the horses out for a ride?" Emily asked.

Tim snickered. "It's not over," he said. "There's a big runoff next month and the general election in November."

"How many elections do you have to win to be a senator?" she asked.

Suzie laughed. "Too many."

I reached over and patted Emily's arm. "Usually, just one in a heavy republican area like West Texas. This is an unusual situation. And, yes, we can go riding this morning if you want."

The TV announcer returned. I hit the mute again.

"Yesterday's hot contest for State Senate District 31 produced a record turnout," she said. "And the big news is Midland candidate Sam Davis's remarkable comeback. Less than two weeks ago the polls reported him trailing badly and his leading opponent, Amarillo Mayor Clarence Anderson, predicted an easy victory. Here are the surprising numbers."

The screen changed to show that the republican primary in Senate District 31 ended with me in second place. Barely. The final tally, with 98 percent of votes tallied, was as follows:

Anderson – 220,125 or 44 percent
Davis – 215,515 or 43 percent
Gonzalez – 50,116 or 11 percent
Yerbanski – 10,013 or 2 percent

A runoff election was scheduled in four weeks.

The phone rang.

"Congratulations," Art said. "You've just pulled off one of the biggest miracles in the history of West Texas elections."

"Thanks, Art. You and I both know this wouldn't have been possible without you and the team."

"Before we get round-shouldered from patting ourselves on the back, let me remind you that the toughest is yet to come."

"June 7? The runoff election?"

"That's why I'm calling. Whiskey wants to fly up for lunch with you and then an afternoon meeting with the team."

"Fine with me."

Art rang off. Fifteen minutes later he called back to confirm details.

So, on a Sunday morning after the election, I drove to the Midland/ Odessa Airport and waited for Whiskey's familiar jet. Art had told me 11:00 a.m. The little white plane touched down on time. I watched as the lieutenant governor scurried off the plane and over to the terminal. A minute later he came through security and greeted me with his usual politician's smile.

"Senator Davis, the newly famous comeback candidate," he said.

I held out my left hand, a gesture he'd come to expect.

He shook it with his right, a response I'd come to expect.

"Congratulations," he said. "I saved this for you." He handed me the morning edition of the *Austin American-Statesman*. A front-page article carried the headline, RUNOFF SET FOR SENATE DISTRICT 31. Someone had circled the second paragraph with a red pen.

I scanned it quickly—enough to see that they referred to me as Comeback Sam.

"You're being compared to Landslide Lyndon," he said.

We both laughed at the newspaper's reference to LBJ's narrow victory over fifty years ago. But a comparison with one of Texas's legendary politicians wouldn't hurt, and might even help. I re-opened the paper and read the article again, more carefully.

Whiskey lit a cigar and waited for me. "In a couple of years you'll be running for the U.S. Senate." He chuckled and blew a cloud of smoke. "And one of these days, old *Comeback Sam* runs for President."

I folded the newspaper and used it to give him a playful whap on the shoulder. "Hey, we haven't won this election yet."

He laughed.

I laughed.

And as we walked to my old pickup, I marveled at how different our relationship seemed. The acrimony and distrust of two weeks ago now gone, Whiskey reveled in our success of the moment. He was a political animal.

And he loved to win.

31

The Conference Room, McComas and Davis Law Office.

All the world loves a winner. And while I hadn't actually *won* the primary, the fact that my candidacy had risen from twenty-nine to forty-three points, a gain of fourteen, was enough to shake the Texas political world and cause everyone to think of me as a winner.

My executive committee—now gathered around the conference table—bubbled with the enthusiasm of a winning team. Art, Tom, Dick, Harriet, and, most of all, Whiskey, exuded a spirit akin to having won World War II. The lieutenant governor led our discussion with such a pervasive upbeat attitude that it seemed the runoff election was in the bag. As he talked, I thought about our circumstances.

It was impossible not to like Whiskey when he came at you with his "politician's smile." His affability glowed with a power that smothered all doubts or hesitations about our topic of the day. Such was the case as we discussed the future.

"This will be easy," Whiskey said. "We'll win with the Latino vote."

PUPPET POLITICS

He passed out a single sheet of paper that gave a breakdown of the primary election figures. It was a summary I'd seen on television so much that I practically had the numbers memorized.

Anderson – 220,125 or 44 percent
Davis – 215,515 or 43 percent
Gonzalez – 50,116 or 11 percent
Yerbanski – 10,013 or 2 percent

"Whoever takes the largest share of Gonzalez's 50,000 votes will nail the runoff," Whiskey predicted.

I studied the data. His premise sounded reasonable. The question was how to do it. I hadn't the foggiest.

But Whiskey did. In fact, he was so full of ideas, it made my head swim. For the next two hours we listened, made notes, and learned about ethnic politics from a master politician.

Harriet asked if we could take a break. She left the room.

The others stood and meandered around.

I studied my notes, which now ran to five handwritten pages. While the others filled coffee cups, listened to Whiskey's jokes, and exchanged election stories, I organized my list of Hispanic political strategy.

1. Secure endorsements from state and national Latino celebrities.
2. Publicize these endorsements.
3. Research Latino issues, especially immigration.
4. Formulate favorable statements on these issues and repeat them at every opportunity.
5. Attend Catholic services every Sunday.
6. Hold meetings at Mexican restaurants.

7. Attend as many Latino social events as possible.
8. Find opportunities to be photographed with children who have Hispanic names.
9. Identify local Latino leaders and cultivate their support.
10. Make it subtle. Don't ever let it sound or look gratuitous.

Gradually the break ended, and everyone returned to their seats.

"What do you think Anderson's strategy will be?" Art asked.

"I know what I'd do," Dick said. "I'd blast away at the possibility of indictments for Abner Stone's murder."

"Yeah," Tom added. "I'll bet he develops a mudslinging campaign."

"I expect him to come after Sam with both guns blazing," Harriet said.

Whiskey laughed. "Let's hope he does."

"Aren't you worried?" Art asked.

"Hey, what's Anderson been doing for the past two weeks?"

"Hitting me as hard as he could," I replied.

"And while he was screaming indictment, spending millions, and yelling about law enforcement, you gained an unbelievable fourteen points." Whiskey chuckled. "The most ever seen in Texas politics."

A quiet settled over the room.

I looked around. Whiskey smirked—a half-smile radiating supreme confidence. The others looked subdued, as though thoughtfully doubting his cockiness.

"Sam's the Teflon candidate," Whiskey said. "And our strategy should be to let his persona speak for itself."

Harriet nodded. "Avoid the old Shakespearian syndrome, *Me thinks milady protesteth too much.*"

"Or to quote another time-worn cliché, the more he tries to *ride a dead horse*, the better we'll like it."

I wasn't so sure the horse was dead, but I didn't protest.

"What's our budget for the next four weeks?" Tom asked.

"Let me worry about that," Whiskey replied. "You folks concentrate on how best to spend campaign money."

"Tamales, enchiladas, and tacos—anyone?" I asked.

"Okay, Sam," Harriet said, "Translate."

I didn't have to.

Whiskey did it for me. "Friends, you have a blank check to go after the Latino votes."

32

Monday morning at home, 3648 Everglade

I had just finished shaving when Suzie came into the bathroom, stood in front of the mirror beside me, and pulled open her robe exposing her bare breasts.

"Honey, I'd like you to feel my right breast," she said.

"Aw, do I have to?" I joked as I washed my face with a washcloth.

"This is serious," she said. "I think there's a lump, and I need your opinion."

There are some things one doesn't kid about. Also, there are times when one doesn't show fear. My instincts told me this was a time for both.

As nonchalantly as I could, I hung the damp cloth on my towel rack, dried my hands, and turned to feel her soft right breast. As expected her nipple hardened. That was good, and I was tempted to crack a joke—but I didn't. Then, still using my good hand, I moved over to massage her left breast.

"No," she said, her voice cold, dispassionate, bordering on anger. "The lump is in my right one."

My fleeting thoughts of light humor—and playful lust—returned to complete seriousness. As I concentrated on the physical sensation of gently massaging her right breast, I felt the lump. As much as I hated to acknowledge it, the feeling of a rather large mass of hard tissue was definitely there.

"Dear, I think you should have that looked at."

"Oh, God." A tear rolled down her cheek. "I was afraid you'd say that."

"It's probably nothing. But the smart thing is to have a mammogram."

She broke out in tears. "I did," she said. "And they called and said I should consult with my doctor."

"And you didn't tell me?" I took her in my arms and held her. "They sent the X-rays to Dr. McAfee?"

She nodded. "I'm so scared."

"I know. I know." I caressed her back and pulled her closer. "But you need to go see the doctor about a biopsy."

"I don't want to," she said, the words coming with sobs.

"I'll go with you." I relaxed my grip and handed her a Kleenex. "Sooner the better."

She wiped the tears.

"Want me to call Dr. McAfee?"

She shook her head, wiped her eyes, and then blew her nose. "No, I can do it."

"I'm going with you," I said.

"You're busy. The election—"

"To hell with the election. You're more important than a thousand elections."

She smiled. "I'd like you to make the appointment."

"And then I'll call you?"

"Okay. I'll meet you at the doctor's office."

"No, I'll pick you up and drive you."

"Sam, you don't have to do that."

"Look at your hands. They're shaking."

She hid her hands behind her back. "I'll get over it. Give me a minute."

I hugged her—tightly. And while I held her, I rubbed her back some more. "I love you," I said. "And you need to think of this as just something to have checked."

She stepped back and tried to smile, an effort that failed.

"Better if we don't upset the kids."

She wiped her eyes and tried again. This time the smile looked almost normal. "How's this?"

"Academy Award," I said.

She kissed me, our lips touching for only a second, and then left.

I dressed and joined the usual bickering at the breakfast table.

"It's her fault. She started it," Tim said.

"Started what?" I asked.

"He called me a complainer," Emily said. "He complains more than me."

"More than I," Suzie corrected.

Tim laughed.

"And he makes fun of me," Emily said.

Suzie gave me a pleading look. She seemed close to tears.

"Stop it," I said. And I said it loudly. Too loud. So loud that an edge of raw anger came out, unmistakable in my voice.

Both Tim and Emily flinched. I remembered reading somewhere

about the need for consistency with your children. Immediately I regretted yelling. These were two good kids, and my reaction was over the top.

"Mama, I want the kids to clean up this morning. Is that okay?"

She nodded. I was afraid she was about to break down in front of the kids. But she didn't. Instead she left and silently hurried back to our bedroom.

"Mama's not feeling well this morning," I said. "But there's something you can do, if you want to help."

"Sure," Tim said.

"Tell us," Emily added.

"First, you can clean up," I said. "Do a really good job—make the kitchen look spic and span."

"We can do it," Tim said.

Emily stood and carried her plate to the dishwasher.

"And second, if you could, do it without quibbling or bickering."

"I'll do my part," Emily said.

"Me, too," Tim replied.

"Come here a minute," I said.

They both came close.

I picked up Emily and put her on my knee with my arm around her. Then I put my arm around Tim's shoulder and pulled him close. "Your mother's not feeling well, and I'm taking her to the doctor. The three of us need to do what we can to be supportive. You can help most by being good kids. By not arguing. By not causing her worry. How about it?"

"You can count on me, Dad," Tim said.

"Sure," Emily said. "Me, too."

"I'm sorry I yelled at you," I said.

Tim smiled. "I knew something was wrong."

HARRY HAINES

Emily kissed me on the forehead. "I love you, Daddy, even when you yell at us."

"And I love you both." I patted them each on the back. Immediately they started clearing the table and loading the dishwasher.

33

At the office

First thing, I called Dr. McAfee's office. The receptionist said he was booked solid. I argued. I pleaded—softly but urgently. Finally, she relented and said if we'd come at four-thirty, she'd *try* to work us in at the end of the day.

I called Suzie and arranged to pick her up at four o'clock.

The day whizzed by. But I kept my eye on the time. At four o'clock, I closed my office and headed for 3648 Everglade.

The kids were already home from school. Linda McComas greeted me when I drove up. Suzie had called her about the lump, and Linda offered to come and stay with the kids.

"Thanks for coming," I said.

"Hey, what're friends for?" she replied.

Suzie and Linda hugged. Suzie got in our old pickup, and I quickly backed down the drive, trying my best to avoid a teary scene.

Everybody waved, but nobody cried—overtly.

HARRY HAINES

When we got to the doctor's office, we waited. As the first hour dragged by and the second crept slowly along, I began to understand the reluctance of Dr. McAfee's appointments secretary. She knew this was going to be a long day and that we'd make it longer. My wife and I struggled to make conversation.

Suzie asked me about the election.

I told her everything I knew.

I asked her about the kids and their horses.

She told me everything she knew.

We talked about a summer vacation, after the June runoff election. She suggested a week at the YMCA of the Rockies, a family vacation facility west of Estes Park, Colorado. I argued against it because I thought it was probably too late to get reservations. But she'd been searching for rentals nearby and had found one across the road in Windcliff Estates. We talked about it for a long time, about how nice it looked on the Internet, about how close it was to the YMCA's program for the kids, and about how she and I could go hiking in the mountains.

The word cancer never entered our conversation.

All the while, the waiting room gradually emptied until, finally, we were the only two. At a little after six o'clock, the nurse called, "Suzanne Davis."

It sounded like the call of doom.

Suzie grabbed my hand, and we followed the nurse to an examination room.

A few minutes later, the nurse came back with a gown and asked Suzie to take off her blouse and her bra and to put on the gown.

Lawrence McAfee, M.D., came into the room with his nurse. He did his best to sound reassuring.

"You want me to leave?" I asked.

"Let's ask Suzanne," the doctor replied.

"I'd like him to stay," she said.

Dr. McAfee put the X-rays on the fluoroscope and turned on the light. Suzie stood next to him. I stood behind and looked over their shoulders. Using his pencil, McAfee pointed to the outline of her right breast on the mammogram. He focused on an area which he called "the lump."

Then he pulled down the gown and gently massaged her breast. "Right here," he said, "you can feel it."

Suzie followed his example. "Yes," she said.

"We need a biopsy immediately," he said. "I'll make an appointment for you at Midland Memorial Hospital."

34

The next morning

I took Suzie to Midland Memorial Hospital for the biopsy. Any thoughts about the election fell off the radar. The procedure went quickly. They said they'd get the results to Dr. McAfee and that he, in turn, would contact us.

I dropped Suzie off at home and went to the office. In the elevator, I checked my watch—almost ten o'clock.

First thing, Art and Mrs. Hughes came in, and closed the door.

"I'm expecting a call from the doctor," I said. "Suzie and I will go to his office to hear about the biopsy."

"I'll put it through immediately," Mrs. Hughes said.

"I'll take care of the office," Art said. "Just let me know what needs to be done."

They left, and I tried to get my thinking turned back to the election. Not an easy task.

Political details that had seemed important now appeared mundane.

PUPPET POLITICS

I looked out the window and studied the horizon. Some people take a measure of inspiration from viewing mountains, others the sea. While I've never heard poetry that describes the flatness and the sagebrush of West Texas, I've repeatedly found solace for the soul in the view from my office. My thoughts roiled and eventually returned to Whiskey's list of Latino projects. It all felt so petty. But if I had to work on the election, immigration seemed a good place to start.

Harriet had prepared two documents on current issues. The first was a big, thick, three-ring notebook filled with clippings from newspapers and magazines. I leafed through it to find the articles arranged chronologically, a comprehensive sampling from national newspapers like the *New York Times, Washington Post, Wall Street Journal,* and *USA Today*—followed by magazines such as *Time* and *Newsweek.* State newspapers ranged from big ones like *Dallas Morning News* and *Houston Chronicle* down to small ones from border towns such as Brownsville, Del Rio, and El Paso. Thirty minutes of scanning page after page was enough to show me that a daunting task lay ahead. I could spend days on this material and not cover all of the complex, conflicting details.

I closed the notebook and went to the second of Harriet's two documents, *Immigration: An Executive Summary.* It was ten pages, letter size, in a manila folder, and written by an analyst from the lieutenant governor's office.

I started reading and had waded through about half of the material when the phone rang. "Your wife on line one," Mrs. Hughes said.

I looked at my watch, 11:00 o'clock, and punched the button, "How're you doing?" I asked.

"Dr. McAfee's nurse called," Suzie said. "They have the results and want us to come now."

"I'll pick you up."

Fifteen minutes later we reported to the check-in counter in the doctor's waiting room. Remembering our long wait of the previous visit, I wondered if we'd have to sit through the noon hour. But Dr. McAfee's nurse was watching for us. We had barely taken our seats when she called Suzie's name and immediately led us to one of the examination rooms where the doctor stood at the door, waiting.

Normally, immediate medical attention would be welcomed as a good omen.

Not this time.

I felt urgency in the room as both Dr. McAfee and his nurse faced us with their news. Suzie took my left hand and held it tightly.

"You have a mass in your breast," McAfee said.

"Yes, I know," Suzie replied.

"It is malignant."

Suzie's hand gripped mine like a vise. Her body tensed, and I worried she might faint.

"I've discussed your case with Dr. Robert Gross, Midland's leading oncology surgeon. He and I think you should have the malignant tissue surgically removed tomorrow morning."

"Tomorrow?" I asked.

"Time is critical," the doctor replied. "Any delay only makes the situation worse."

"We have to decide now?" Suzie asked.

"Wait," I said. "Maybe we should get a second opinion?"

"In most cases," McAfee continued, "I would suggest it. However, in this situation, I think it necessary that we act immediately. It might mean the difference between a lumpectomy and a mastectomy."

"Wha . . . what . . . what do you recommend?" Suzie whispered, her voice so soft I could barely understand her words.

"A lumpectomy," McAfee said. "We'll do everything possible to save the breast."

"There's no question about doing this tomorrow morning?" I asked.

"None."

The next four or five seconds seemed like an eternity. No one spoke. No one moved.

Finally, the doctor broke the silence. "We'll wait outside," he said. Then he and the nurse left the room and closed the door.

I took my wife into my arms. We held each other for a long time, and I experienced a flood of emotion, a time of intense, silent communication. It was as though we faced the world together in an unspoken pledge of mutual support. Of love that cannot be described with words.

Finally, I felt her grasp ease. "You have a Kleenex?" she asked.

I released her and handed her a tissue.

She wiped her eyes. "Damned mascara," she said.

I handed her another tissue. "You okay?" I asked.

"As okay as a person can be when they might be about to lop off part of your body." She smiled a little smile, not a full-blown happy grin, but a slight firming of the lips with the corners turning up, what I've heard called a sardonic smile, a disdainful gesture of irony. "I never wanted to be sexy, anyway."

"Hey, you're sexy enough for me." I pulled her close and kissed her.

The kiss lasted several minutes.

She broke the embrace and pulled back. "We'd better open the door or the doctor and his nurse will wonder what's going on in here."

"Let 'em wonder." I pulled her to me and kissed her again.

She pulled away, gently. "I'd like this better tonight in our bedroom."

"Promises, promises."

35

The next morning, Midland County Hospital

Art sat with me in the waiting room and did his best to manufacture conversation. It wouldn't have mattered how hard he tried—it takes two to have a discussion. He rattled on about problems with the election, problems with our law practice, problems with the weather. For almost an hour, his comments sailed past me without a word of response.

"We haven't had rain in almost ninety days," he said.

Finally he gave up his monologue, and we sat silently.

As one silent minute followed another, I felt the need to respond. "Ninety days?" I asked.

Immediately he responded. "February sixteen," he said. "Driest spring since 1935, the height of the Dust Bowl."

"And what else is new?" I asked.

"You listen to the weather?"

"No, I've had a few distractions." I tried a smile that failed. "Things like being accused of murder. Losing thirty points in an election. And now cancer."

Art acted like he hadn't heard me, "And if it doesn't rain in the next three days, we'll have a new record."

I pondered the inane direction of our conversation—was weather better than talking about cancer? "What're the chances?"

He turned and stared at me. "Chances for what?"

"Chances we'll break the record."

"They don't report that."

"Okay, what are the chances for rain in the next three days?"

"The weather girl on KMID-TV says 50 percent today, 75 percent tomorrow."

"And day after tomorrow?"

"She doesn't give percentages for long-range forecasts."

"Day after tomorrow is long range?"

The doctor came into the waiting room. "Suzanne's doing well." He took a seat. "No complications. She can go home in a few hours."

"The cancer?" I asked. "You got it all?"

"We won't know for a while."

I nodded.

"I need to prepare you for what to expect." The doctor looked at Art. "Would you excuse us for a moment? I'd like to visit with Mr. Davis in the conference room."

"Of course." Art stood as if to leave.

"You stay here," the doctor said. "This will only take a minute." He led the way to a small room down the hall.

I followed.

He closed the door. "The breast will look much different. She's lost quite a bit of tissue. And there will always be a scar on the lower side. In a month to six weeks, I suggest you consult with a plastic surgeon about reconstructive surgery."

"A breast implant?" I asked.

"That would be one possibility."

"Whatever she wants," I said.

"Often we find that post-operative depression is the most serious part of breast surgery, the patient's psychological reaction."

I nodded. "What can I do to help?"

"Be supportive. The worst thing that can happen to a woman who has gone through this procedure is sexual rejection from her spouse."

"I understand."

"I'm not sure that you do. It's the *degree* to which our culture emphasizes the appearance of our bodies. Television is full of advertisements for body building, for perfect abs, and for all the associative qualities of an attractive body."

I held up my right hand.

He looked at. It took him by surprise. He didn't know what to say.

I helped him out. "Birth defect."

"So, you do understand what I'm trying to say?"

"There's a difference in a disfigured breast and a deformed hand. But the psychology of dealing with people's reactions has a common quality."

"Suzanne's lucky."

His comment took me by surprise, and I tried to think of something to say in response. I couldn't.

It was the first time in my adult years I'd heard something good about having a deformed hand.

36

Breakfast felt almost normal. The kids were on their best behavior. No bickering. No arguments. It was their way of showing how much they appreciated having their mother back.

I lingered at the breakfast table and read the morning paper a third time, waiting until Tim and Emily left for school.

"You're going to be late for work," Suzie said.

"They can get along without me," I said.

"And the election?"

"Screw the election. I want to be with my wife." I stood, took her in my arms, and kissed her—long, slow, lingering kisses.

"We have to wait," she said. "I'm recovering from surgery."

"Waiting makes the heart grow fonder." I kissed her neck.

"What's gotten into you? You haven't been this randy since our honeymoon."

I stepped back. "I'll leave if this bothers you."

She pulled me to her. "No, I love it." She kissed me. "But—"

I kissed her back and mumbled a response. "But what?"

"But I'd like to continue this tonight."

I held her, tight. With my lips to her ear, I whispered, "I love you."

We parted.

"Guess I have to go win an election," I said.

She whacked me on the butt. "I'll be glad when this damned election is over."

In the car I listened to the radio and caught an interview about the election. Consuelo Hernandez, an investigative reporter for the *Austin American-Statesman*, was interviewing Texas Ranger Charles Fuller in Austin. They shifted from the election to the investigation of the death of Abner Stone.

"Where's the investigation now stand?" Hernandez asked. "You have any indictments?"

"We have suspects," Fuller replied. "No indictments. The case is pretty much at a standstill."

"You've given up?" Hernandez's voice rose in pitch and in volume.

"Of course not," Fuller said. "We still have a CSI detail working with the Midland County Sheriff's Office."

"How many people are working on this case?"

"About a dozen."

"You have a dozen law enforcement officers on this case, and you call it a standstill?"

"We're following up leads. Looking for a break in the case."

"What about Sam Davis? A month ago he was thought to be your prime suspect?"

"He's one of the leads we're following."

"Who are the others?"

"I'd love to give you all the names we have under investigation."

"Well, why don't you?" she asked. "If we knew who your suspects were, maybe we could help you."

"If we tip our hand, it just makes it harder to break the case."

I parked in the parking garage and turned the key, stopping both the engine and the radio. I'd have to find out later what Ranger Charlie Fuller and reporter Consuelo Hernandez thought about the murder investigation.

"How's Mrs. Davis?" my secretary asked.

"Fine," I replied. "She fixed a big breakfast this morning. Things are almost back to normal."

"*She* prepared breakfast?" Mrs. Hughes didn't say it, but I could read the accusatory implications.

Art came out of his office. "How's Suzie?"

"Fine," I repeated. "Art, would you come in for a minute?"

He followed me into my office. I closed the door.

"They got all the cancer?"

"Presumably. They won't know for a while."

"Anything Linda or I can do?"

"Give us a few days."

"Let us know when you're up to it. We'll have you over for steaks in the backyard and celebrate your victory over cancer."

"Thanks. We'll look forward to it. But—"

"But?"

"On the radio just now I listened to an interview with the Texas Rangers. They say they're still investigating me."

"Of course. What did you expect they'd say?"

"I was hoping Charlie Fuller would say that they had cleared me, that I was no longer under investigation."

"He can't say that until they have someone else charged with the murder."

"How long is that going to be?"

"Sam, they may never find out who killed Abner."

37

The Law Offices of McComas and Davis, two weeks later

Suzie's recovery progressed. The election tightened. I worked harder. Whiskey flew to Midland and held a meeting of our executive committee in the conference room.

"How's the wife?" he asked.

"Good," I said. "She passed the first test."

"Tell me."

"Biopsies are scheduled at strategic intervals."

"And?"

"And the first one was the day before yesterday—Suzie's cancer free."

"Congratulations."

One of Whiskey's greatest assets was his ability to give an *atta-boy*—a word of celebration. When he smiled, patted you on the back, and gave you his stentorian phrase of acknowledgement, you felt like a million bucks. And even though I knew it was mostly his political bullshit coming at me, I reveled in it.

"Thanks," I said.

"Give my best regards to Suzie," he said. "Tell her we're all pulling for her."

"I will. And thanks for the flowers."

Whiskey dismissed my comment with a wave of his hand. Then he immediately started talking politics. "How about events with Latino children?" he asked.

"Two next week," Harriet said.

"Details?"

"Sam's the commencement speaker at Lee High School's graduation. The valedictorian is Carlos Reyes, who's receiving a full scholarship at Midland College. Sam will do the presentation. We'll have newspaper photographs and probably TV interviews."

"Good. And the second?"

"Alamo Middle School," she continued. "Sam's giving citizenship awards to the top 10 percent. Most are students with Hispanic names. Again, lots of coverage. Newspapers eat it up, and we'll try for television."

I expected the usual big smile from Whiskey. Instead, he frowned. "Only two?"

"School's out at the end of next week," Harriet said. "It's getting harder to find kids."

Harriet's excuse produced a wall of silence.

Most of the time Whiskey's personal demeanor was bright, upbeat, and cheerful. His smile, especially, was legendary. But it turned when something ticked him off. He became vicious. I watched as he snarled at Harriet. "Two events ain't enough. In fact, two a day, every day until the election will not be enough. Harriet, if you can't cut it, we'll have to get someone who can."

Harriet turned pale and shrank back in her chair.

Whiskey vented his wrath on the rest of us. "Listen up. We have an election to win. We're spending a ton of money and expect to see results." He looked around the room until his eyes locked with mine, and I felt the conflict. Like electricity at 100,000 volts, it surged through me, attacking my will to resist. My heart sank. What had I gotten myself into?

Somehow I found the strength to stare back, clench my teeth and not look away.

Finally, when he saw that I wasn't going to yield, he turned to Art. Then I watched as his gaze moved around the room, giving each person in turn "the treatment."

Just as the conflict in the room felt like it was ready to explode, Whiskey stood. "Get busy," he yelled, his voice loud, angry, and backed with a menacing scowl. He stomped out, slamming the door behind him.

"Whew," Tom said. "That's not the same lieutenant governor I've known."

"Did you see the way he looked at me?" Dick added. "I thought he was going to fire me on the spot."

"Settle down," Art said. He handed a box of Kleenex to Harriet. "He's right about one thing—we have an election to win."

"But we don't have to take that kind of shit," I said. "This is a good team. We have a good plan. We're all trying."

"Sam, a good plan isn't worth squat if we don't make it work," Art said. "And Whiskey's right. Two events in two weeks don't convey enough Hispanic association to win the Latino vote in this election."

"Okay, maybe he's right about Hispanic events," I said. "But that doesn't give him the right to come down on Harriet the way he did. Besides, we have a ten-point plan, and that's just one of the objectives we're all supposed to be working on."

Art changed the timbre of his voice. In a softer, well-modulated tone, he said, "Let's take our goals one by one and each of us report on how we're doing."

For the next three hours, that's what we did.

We had good endorsements, and Harriet had arranged excellent publicity for them. I'd attended Catholic services every Sunday and planned to continue. Art, Tom, Dick, and Harriet had lined me up with daily meals and meetings at Mexican restaurants. Harriet's research on immigration gave us more information than we could use.

But because I needed to schedule more events with children, everyone pledged to pitch in and work on it. Also, we needed more Latino social events. Again, everyone took notes and promised to do more.

By the end of the day, we had our plans made.

Harriet looked better. Before leaving the room I gave her a hug.

She smiled and said, "Gracias, amigo."

38

W hen I came into the office and Mrs. Hughes greeted me with, "Buenos diaz, Señor Davis," I knew that Operation Latino was in full swing.

"Buenos diaz," I replied. "Como esta usted?"

She smiled, shook her head, and said, "I know that means 'How are you?' But I don't know how to answer."

"Bien, gracias," I suggested.

"Good, thank you," she translated. "I'll remember that."

"I don't know much Spanish. But it helps to use a few words occasionally."

"You know more than I."

A compliment from Mrs. Hughes? What was the world coming to? I thanked her, went into my office and closed the door.

If only I could find some way to keep her from rearranging the papers on my desk.

HARRY HAINES

Immediately I reconciled myself to stop worrying about things that can't be changed. So I fired up the little coffee pot on my credenza. Then, as the gurgling sounds and aroma of fresh brew filled the room, I started through the stacks looking for my schedule. Luckily I found it halfway down in the second stack, about the time the gurgling stopped.

I poured myself a cup. It smelled wonderful.

Then I studied the schedule and tried to plan my day.

At ten o'clock a reporter and a photographer from the *Midland Telegraph Reporter* were scheduled to meet Midland Fire Chief Roberto Guzman and me at the Central Fire Station to do a story about summer safety for children.

At eleven a television crew from KMID-TV would meet Midland City Park Supervisor Manuel Mata and me at the swimming pool to film a story about the pool's opening next weekend.

At noon I could look forward to lunch with city councilman Ricardo Rodriquez at Rosa's Taco Café.

The afternoon remained unscheduled. Maybe I could get some work done.

The phone rang. "Lieutenant Governor Williams on line two," Mrs. Hughes said.

I pushed the button. "Buenos diaz," I said.

Whiskey laughed. "That's what your secretary said when she answered the phone."

"Yeah, we're all practicing the two or three words of Spanish that we have in our vocabularies."

He changed the subject abruptly. "I'm calling to give you a heads up about Consuelo Hernandez. She's coming to Midland this afternoon."

"I've heard that name."

"Works for the *Austin American-Statesman*. Late twenties, good looking, trying to make a name for herself as an investigative reporter."

"What does this have to do with me?"

"You're her ticket to fame and fortune. If she can prove that you're the perp who murdered Abner Stone, she'll become the most famous journalist in Texas."

"But what if I'm innocent?"

"Hell, she don't care. You're just a means to an end."

"Yeah, but this renewed interest has to be coming from somewhere," I said. "She wouldn't be traveling to Midland if she didn't have something."

"Usually that's the case," he said. "However, we're in the middle of the most competitive election in the state. That alone would be reason enough for her to do a story on you."

"What can I do?"

"Smother her with kindness and attention. Invite her to lunch. Or better yet, have her over to your house for hamburgers in the backyard. Have her meet your wife and kids. Be sure she knows all about Suzie's cancer."

"Hey, I draw the line at my wife's illness. That's private."

"Sorry, Sam. No way."

I felt my blood pressure rising and a nasty scene looming. More than any person I'd ever met, Whiskey Williams could really aggravate me. Especially when he tried to push me on family issues.

"When you signed the form agreeing to become a candidate for state senator," he said, "you effectively gave up your rights to family privacy."

"We're not gonna talk about Suzie's breast."

"Too late," he said. "Everyone in Texas already knows about it."

"Fine. Then I don't have to say anything."

He kept pushing. "You can't hide it."

My resentment kept rising.

"My point is," he continued, "if you don't answer questions, this reporter will assume you have something to hide."

"Goddamnit, what's there to hide about my wife's breast?"

"It's the principle that's at stake. If you're not forthcoming about this, what's to keep you from hiding something about Abner Stone?"

I could see that this discussion wasn't getting us anywhere. Whiskey, at his worst, was like a bulldog that wouldn't give up. I changed to a topic I knew I could win. "I'll resign as a candidate."

"We've been through this," Whiskey said. "You can't resign, not after we've spent almost ten million on your campaign."

"Who's we?"

"Me for one," he said. "And hundreds, even thousands of your friends."

"My friends, all of 'em, haven't given a tenth of the money you're talking about."

He stopped talking.

I held the telephone receiver but said nothing.

Finally he resumed speaking. His words came slowly, in a soft voice, in a tone that let me know this was to be the end of our conversation. "Sam, you'll have to handle Consuelo Hernandez as best you can. I can't help you." Then I heard a click and a dial tone.

Mrs. Hughes knocked and then stuck her head in the door.

"You're going to be late for your appointment with the fire chief."

39

The Midland Central Fire Station

Chief Guzman shook my hand, the usual awkward—his right, my left—exchange. A reporter and photographer from the *Reporter Telegraph* greeted both of us.

Guzman and I posed for pictures in front of their biggest fire truck, a huge hook-and-ladder.

The reporter interviewed us and took notes about summertime safety for children. As the chief rattled on about more bicycles in the street and the need for motorists to drive cautiously around city parks, I shook my head in disbelief. This was news?

When it was over, a five-minute meeting that lasted forty-five minutes, I drove to the swimming pool where I found a television truck and a dozen or so people gathered at the edge of the water.

Manuel Mata, Midland's park superintendent, had assembled a handful of pre-school kids, all in bathing suits. The kids, of course, had come with their mamas. The TV station sent two cameramen and a

155

director. With Manuel, me, and the pool's maintenance crew, we had a crowd large enough for a Hollywood media event.

The kids gathered around me. We talked about summertime and swimming while the cameras rolled. And then the kids all jumped into the water.

So goes a slow news day in Midland, Texas.

But everyone smiled.

The moms loved having their children on television. The news crew had filled another three-minute segment for their noon news program. Manuel and the city park department came off looking good.

And I had what I wanted—television with Latino children.

I drove to Rosa's Taco Restaurant, hoping that lunch with City Councilman Ricardo Rodriquez would be more meaningful. He was waiting for me in the lobby.

"Morning, Sam," he said. He knew me, smiled, and extended his left hand.

"Ricky, good to see you."

Rosa herself led us to a table by the water fountain. The aroma emanating from the kitchen smelled wonderful.

The menu listed endless varieties of tacos—tacos with hard shells, with soft shells, with ground beef, with shredded beef, with peppered beef, with fajita beef, with chicken, with shrimp, with crab, with lobster, with six different kinds of salsa, with an uncountable variety of cheeses.

I requested two soft tacos with ground beef, guacamole, and pepper jack cheese.

Ricky ordered two with lobster, red salsa, and mozzarella.

"How's the campaign going?" he asked.

"I'm working on the Hispanic vote," I replied. "What can I do to win you and your family?"

He laughed. "You've got 'em. You had them even when Gonzalez was in the race."

"Any suggestions for how I can win those fifty thousand who did vote for him in the primary?"

"You're asking me? Hell, everyone knows you already have the guru of Texas politics as your advisor."

"Who's that?"

"Whiskey Williams, of course."

"What makes you think he's advising me?"

"Well, for one thing, his Lear Jet flies into Midland-Odessa Airport on a regular basis."

"How in God's name would you know that?"

He chuckled and shook his head. "I'm on the city council, remember? City councilmen talk with city police. City police patrol the airport. There's hardly any gossip making the rounds in Midland that I don't come into contact with."

The waitress brought our food—big plates loaded with huge tacos, beautifully arranged on beds of bright lettuce and tomatoes. It looked delicious.

Ricky picked up a taco and chomped down.

"What does the gossip mill have to say about me?" I asked. Then I took a big bite.

He chewed for a few seconds. "None of the locals think you had anything to do with Abner Stone's death. But for some reason, the Texas Rangers have you in their crosshairs."

"You got that right."

"And the *Austin American-Statesman*."

"You noticed."

"More than noticed. How can anyone miss all the front-page news?"

He took another big bite of taco.

"Maybe this is coming from my political opponent in Amarillo?"

"Maybe it started there. But do you want my opinion?"

"Please."

"I think there's too much smoke for this to be just Clarence Anderson. If it were only an Amarillo mayor trying to win a state senate seat, the story would have died long ago, probably even before the primary election."

"Who else could it be?"

Instead of answering, he took a huge bite of taco.

I waited while he chewed.

Then he took a big swallow of iced tea.

And I waited.

He smiled and said. "I've heard it's the greenies—the Greenpeace in Austin. They're the folks against the oil and gas lobby."

40

Law Offices of McComas and Davis

Back at my desk I resolved to change my thinking, to refocus my thoughts away from discord. Easier said than done. Ricky's comment about the "greenies" wouldn't go away.

My life used to have far less conflict.

So, because I couldn't force my brain out of clash mode, I decided to change my strategy and attack it head on. I took a yellow pad and started making a list of those with whom I was doing battle.

"Clarence Anderson" headed the roll. Next I wrote the word "temporary," then "eleven days until election." Immediately I felt better. Just writing those three things on the pad made my struggles seem less personal and more manageable. I knew the Anderson/Davis contest would soon be history. I sighed with relief.

Troubles with law enforcement worried me far more, so I scribbled down all the related words that came to mind: Abner's death, Texas Rangers, Charlie Fuller, Midland County Sheriff, Austin, no indictment, why?

Media came next on the list. The *Austin American-Statesman*, Consuelo Hernandez, Ricky's statement "should have ended." Why was Hernandez coming to Midland?

Tensions with oil and gas people bothered me: big bucks from Austin. Why did they continue to give me money? Why did they support my election in the first place?

Next I wrote Greenpeace. People in Austin, opposite side of every issue with the oil and gas lobby. How could I be at war with both a greenie and an oily?

Conflict with Whiskey? Definitely. He was pushing me; I did not want to be pushed.

What about Art? I wrote "ten years."

I put down the pencil, poured myself a cup of coffee, and studied the yellow pad.

The bottom line on the list troubled me most. Art and I had had ten years working together, almost entirely without conflict. Now we found ourselves on opposite sides of every issue. The more I thought about it, the more unhappy it made me. If I didn't do something, and do it soon, it could destroy our friendship. I shuddered at the consequences—the possible end of our law firm.

A sense of despair filled the room as I scanned the list again. Like a paralysis of the brain, it gripped me and barred my rational thinking. For a third time, I read the words I'd written on yellow paper. One stood out.

Austin.

Duh.

Most of the conflict in my life came from the state capitol.

I sipped my coffee and suddenly felt energized.

In our thirteen years of marriage, Suzie frequently commented on my ability as an analyst. "It's your best quality," she often said. "And the main reason I'd want you as my lawyer is because you are really good at researching all the details—finding and selecting the best resolution to a problem."

I tossed the Styrofoam cup and dialed Art's extension. "Got a minute?" I asked.

"Sure," he replied.

I picked up the yellow pad and joined him in his office.

"There's too much conflict in my life," I said. "I'd like your help in reducing it."

He laughed. "Maybe you should write Abigail Van Buren."

I showed him my legal pad.

His smile faded when he came to the line with his name.

"Me too," he said. "I've worried about the conflict between us. We should talk over our differences before they get out of hand."

"I'm here and ready to listen," I said.

"First," he said, "what can I do to help?"

"You're already doing it."

He chuckled. "I remember ten years ago, we hardly ever had an argument."

"So what're we at odds about now?"

"Money, the election, Whiskey. His role in the campaign."

"That'll all come to a screeching halt next week," I said. "What else?"

He paused, rereading my list, looking for an answer.

"Notice," I said, "that almost all of the disagreements come from Austin?"

He nodded as he studied the yellow pad. "And related to the election."

"Why is the oil and gas lobby spending so much money on my campaign?"

"That's easy," he said. "They want you to support legislation that's favorable to them. Hell, I'm an investor in oil and gas. And, as a member of the O&G lobby, I'm expecting you to support my best interests."

"And if I don't?"

He smiled. Not a big smile but a friendly, benevolent expression that one business partner gives another. He relaxed back into his chair, scooted the yellow pad across his desk toward me, and said, "Two things. First, if you don't, there's nothing that I can do about it. And second, I'm not really worried about that possibility because you and I think alike."

"Most of the time," I said.

Then he laughed, and it disarmed the tension between us. "Sam, are you looking for a fight?"

"No," I said. "But I'm wondering what's going to happen. What if I get elected, if there's a bill to liberalize the ODA, and if I vote against it?"

Again he laughed, this time more restrained. A nervous little sound that revealed for the first time that we were getting close to a nerve. "That's a lot of ifs."

"And how would we handle it?"

"Like I said. There's not a damned thing I could do about it. Neither could Whiskey, nor any of our friends who're investing in stripper wells."

"And you think that we could agree to disagree?"

"You and I could." He paused, looked out the window for a moment, then turned, and with a frown said, "I'm not sure the big investors could."

"Name some big investors."

"Whiskey. He's the biggest."

"How big?"

"Millions," Art said.

41

Driving home from the office

I felt discombobulated. The face-to-face with Art was a good thing. It made me feel better. But on that evening, with cancer worries at home, an election yet to win, and Whiskey's millions looming on the horizon as major conflict, I found it impossible to relax.

Somewhere in the dark, hazy recesses of my mind, I remembered a song—I think Judy Garland sang it—about how "Troubles Melt Like Lemon Drops." But that's the problem with a dysfunctional memory, the harder one tries to remember, especially a melody, the less likely one is to get it.

I gave up when I turned into the drive.

Gretel, our dachshund, came to greet me. She danced a little jig and barked short, happy sounds. I bent down to pet her, and she licked my hand. For an effusive show of affection, it's hard to beat a dachshund.

I dropped my coat on the sofa, pulled off my tie, and followed the aroma of roast beef into the kitchen. "Yum," I said.

"Linda McComas brought us a pot roast." She lifted the lid, and the whiff of a home-cooked meal flooded the kitchen.

"How's our number-one patient?" I asked.

Suzie put down a potholder, put one arm around my neck and kissed me. "Each day's a little better," she said.

"What'd the doctor say?" It had now been five days since the lumpectomy, and I knew she had an appointment scheduled.

"Everything's progressing perfectly. They removed the bandages, and I got fitted for a padded bra."

"Stitches?"

"They take them out next Friday."

"And you'll be good as new?"

"Not exactly." She kissed me. "They made an appointment for me to see a plastic surgeon about a breast implant."

"When?"

"I have the date written down. About a month. I have to go to Dallas."

"We could make a trip out of it. Stay at the Anatole, dinner at Turtle Creek."

She smiled. "Food and sex?"

"Hey, this calls for some kind of celebration."

Tim barged into the room. His entrance killed our conversation. "When's supper?" he asked.

"Right now," Suzie answered. "Call your sister."

He left.

"What can I do?" I asked.

"Pour milk for the kids."

I did.

The four of us gathered around the table. Linda had provided a magnificent pot roast with potatoes, carrots, onions, and gravy—a happy time for the Davis family.

We heard about school, about how many days were left, and about plans for summer activities.

Not a word was said about cancer, nor the election.

Tim and Emily excused themselves to do homework.

I cleared the table.

Suzie asked how the election was going.

I told her about meetings with the fire chief, the park supervisor, and the city councilman. While recounting my meeting with Art, the phone rang.

It was Consuelo Hernandez, the investigative reporter for the *Austin American-Statesman.*

"I'm here in Midland for the next couple of days," she said. "I'd like to do a feature article on you and the run-off election."

"You want to do it now, on the phone?" I asked.

"I could have done that in Austin," she said. "I've traveled to Midland in the hope we could do a face-to-face interview."

"Sure," I said. "When and where?"

"How about ten o'clock tomorrow morning in your office?"

"Okay. Uh . . . I caught part of your NPR interview with Charles Fuller."

"Good for you."

"And I was a bit surprised at the depth of your questions about my possible role in the death of Abner Stone."

"Yeah, well, you know that's the major part of the assignment when you do a story involving the Texas Rangers. It's the reason we interview them. In this case, people want to know who killed Senator Stone, and they want to know what law enforcement is doing to catch the killer."

"Ms. Hernandez, from my perspective, I thought it was more than that."

"Oh? How so?"

"Your questions about me were very suggestive. You all but accused me."

"Now who's accusing whom?"

"I had my secretary get the NPR transcript of the interview. I'd like to discuss it with you at our meeting."

All of a sudden the conversation died.

After a few seconds, I asked, "Ms. Hernandez, you still there?"

"Yes, I'm here."

"See you tomorrow morning."

"Uh, I have a request," she said. "If I came a few minutes early, would you let me have a photocopy of that transcript? If we're going to discuss it, I'll need to look it over first."

I chuckled. "Sure, I'll have my secretary run a copy for you. Nine-thirty okay?"

"Thank you, Senator Davis."

42

The next morning, 7:30 at the office

I got to the office early for one reason—to study the transcript of the previous week's NPR interview of Consuelo Hernandez with Charlie Fuller.

I couldn't find it.

So I made a pot of coffee and waited for Mrs. Hughes.

As usual, she arrived exactly at eight o'clock. I could set my watch on the promptness of her coming and going.

I complain a lot about Mrs. Hughes. But I have to admit she's good at organizing and filing things. It took her ten seconds to find the radio transcript. I took it into my office, closed the door, poured a cup of coffee, and sat at my desk to study the document.

The first two pages contained nothing but history. Ms. Hernandez's questions about details of the case reminded me of Sergeant Joe Friday on the classic TV show *Dragnet*. "Nothing but the facts, ma'am." But on page three, Hernandez shifted from facts to opinions.

Consuelo Hernandez: So you now think Senator Stone's death was murder?

Lieutenant Charles Fuller: We're reasonably certain the fire was arson.

Hernandez: Arson that led to murder?

Fuller: When authorities thought the fire was an accident, the Midland County Sheriff called Stone's death an accident.

Hernandez: But now that they believe it's arson, you and he call the death murder?

Fuller: We're leaning in that direction.

Hernandez: Let's assume your investigation verifies Stone's death was murder, then your leading suspect is Senator Sam Davis?

Fuller: We can't comment on a case that's under investigation.

Hernandez: This is not a totalitarian society; people have a right to know. In America it's called freedom of the press.

Fuller: Yes, but a free society also has rules that protect citizens against false arrest and intimidation.

Hernandez: You've not arrested anyone, have you?

Fuller: No.

Hernandez: So if the press asks about suspects, about how law enforcement is investigating a crime, that would come under 'freedom of the press,' it seems to me.

Fuller: That's your interpretation.

Hernandez: What other interpretation is there?

Fuller: Some might call it yellow journalism. That you're printing names just to inflame the story and sell more newspapers.

Hernandez: Not if it's the truth.

Fuller: The truth is, we don't know who killed Abner Stone. Or even that his death was murder rather than an accident.

Hernandez: How about facts. Will you answer questions about facts?

Fuller: Usually.

Hernandez: Usually? My God, what are you hiding?

Fuller: Ms. Hernandez, we're just trying to do our job. And our job includes being careful not to falsely accuse people of murder. You asked about facts?

Hernandez: Is it a fact that Sam Davis was out at the oil well the night Abner Stone was killed?

Fuller: Yes, in the area . . . the night Stone died. But so were the crewmembers who were working on the rig.

Hernandez: And these men are also suspects?

Fuller: I think the term suspects *is too strong. They are persons of interest, and we're checking them out because they were there.*

The transcript went on for many more pages. I went back to reread these two.

I poured myself another cup of coffee and thought about the transcript. The material didn't seem as damning as when I heard it over the radio. Was I overreacting? Possibly.

I checked the time—8:55 a.m. Consuelo Hernandez would arrive soon. I asked Mrs. Hughes to Xerox a copy of the transcript.

At 9:30 Mrs. Hughes announced Ms. Hernadez. I led our guest into the conference room, to a chair at the big mahogany table, gave her a copy of the transcript, a cup of coffee, and left her to read. I returned to my desk.

At ten o'clock Mrs. Hughes buzzed me. "Ms. Hernandez is here for her appointment."

I invited her in, and we went through our routine with the two tape recorders.

For the first fifteen minutes of the interview, Hernandez lobbed easy questions. Mostly she asked about facts. What was my name, my address, my job, etc?

Then she switched to opinions.

"Do you think Abner Stone was murdered?" she asked.

"I have no way of knowing," I replied.

"Prior to Stone's death, had you spoken to the governor about your interest in the senate position?"

"No, of course not."

"How about to Lieutenant Governor Williams?"

"No, and I resent the implication of your questions."

"Surely you realize that you're the major beneficiary. You gained more than anyone from Stone's death. I have to ask, or I wouldn't be doing my job as a reporter."

"I'd like to ask you a question," I said. "May I?"

She chuckled. "Role reversal?" Then she added, "Go ahead."

43

Tuesday, ten days before the election, my office

The interview dragged on for almost an hour. Like two wolves scrapping over a chunk of raw meat, we parried each other's questions and answers, attempting to block or deflect any damage to our respective side of the issue, to evade the blow by cleverly saying something that avoided the answer.

Our exchanges soon became repetitious. Then tiresome.

"Is this enough?" I asked. "It's almost eleven o'clock."

She looked at her watch. "I'd hoped for more."

"Okay, one more question."

She frowned and shuffled through her notes. "We haven't discussed the possibility of a debate," she said.

"I'm all for it," I said.

"Why haven't we had one?"

"Ask my opponent."

"I will. But right now I'm asking you."

"You may remember we tried to set up a televised debate the week before the primary."

"Yes," she said. "But there were four candidates, and we could never get all of you to agree on rules and procedures."

"Anderson was the roadblock," I said. "He kept changing the location, the date, the moderator, the questions—everything. Each time he insisted on a change, it took three days to contact the others. Eventually, we ran out of time."

"He says it was you."

"What do you think?"

She threw her pencil down and held up her hands. "Hell, I don't know. All I can say is that petty bickering caused multiple postponements and eventually the date for the election arrived."

"It's now been two weeks and three days since the primary."

"Yes, I can count."

"And we have only ten days until the runoff."

She pulled out a small pocket blackberry. "I count eleven."

"We can argue about how many days, but I don't think anyone wants to have the debate on Election Day." I chuckled at my own joke. "Meanwhile, I have a suggestion."

"Okay."

"Why don't you write a news article about the disagreement over debate procedures. Get a copy of my rules, Anderson's rules, and then ask the League of Women Voters—or some neutral party—for their rules, and publish all three."

She looked doubtful. "I don't know—"

"I have a list of my proposed rules and procedures for a debate." I pulled out a single sheet of paper. "Would you like a copy?"

Her demeanor changed, and she smiled. "You bet."

"When you ask Anderson and the League, you might limit their response to 250 words or less."

She looked at my sheet and started counting.

I saved her the trouble. "My computer counted the words. The number is in the lower right-hand corner. It's 186."

She nodded. "Good point. We couldn't publish the article if any one of you submitted long, rambling rules."

I relaxed back into my chair. "We done?"

"Yep." She gathered up her stuff, put everything in her briefcase, and stood to leave. "Good luck in the election."

I walked her to the door. "When's your meeting with Anderson?"

"How'd you know I have a meeting with him?"

"Just assumed," I said. "You don't have to tell me."

"No secret," she replied. " It's tomorrow morning. I'm driving to Amarillo this afternoon."

"You going to give him a 'heads up' about publishing the three different versions?"

"You trying to do my job for me?"

"Hey, I know how a candidate thinks." I gave her my best campaign grin. "I *are* one."

"So how does a candidate think?"

"Well, if a newspaper reporter asked me for something that I didn't want to commit to, and he asked for it in writing, then I'd say, 'Gosh, golly, gee-whiz, I wish I'd known you wanted this'."

"That answer has a familiar ring."

I didn't say anything, but I thought about how many times I'd used those exact, same words.

44

A week later, three days before the election, the conference room

An uneasiness about Harriet's report flashed in my subconcious like a neon warning sign. I looked around the room and tried to read the reaction of the others.

Tom Butler looked smug. We had plenty of money, and he was pleased with himself. Tom evaluated the election in terms of finances, and right now he felt things couldn't be better.

Dick Klemkowski radiated self-confidence. He'd orchestrated a magnificent advertising campaign—one that would likely be quoted in textbooks for years to come. Dick had media he could brag about . . . especially if we won the election.

Harriet Wong's face didn't give me a clue. Her Asian features projected an inscrutable lack of emotion.

Art, like me, viewed the election with bottom-line mentality. He looked worried and didn't try to hide it. "So here we are, less than seventy-two hours until the polls open, and you say we're still behind?"

"Less than two percentage points," Harriet replied. "But the margin of error is probably three points, so we're not sure."

"Behind is behind," Art said. "I believe we're in trouble."

"I think it comes down to the TV debate tomorrow night," Harriet said. "Both Roper and Gallup tell us its impact could easily swing three or four points."

"Damn. What happened to the lead we were supposed to get from our ads?" He turned to Dick. "Tom says we've spent three million on advertising. That's twice what Anderson has done, and yet Harriet says—"

"She says it won't matter," Dick cut in. "That the election's going to be decided by the debate." He turned to Harriet. "Right?"

"Probably." She opened her laptop and rapidly punched the keyboard. "Here's Roper's exact statement." She read aloud: "Because there were no debates during the primary, experts predict that Thursday night's televised debate will have an impact unprecedented in Texas political history. This 'one-and-only opportunity' for citizens to compare the candidates side by side will influence voting more than any other factor."

"Where does it say four points?" Art asked.

Harriet continued to scroll. "I guess that was in yesterday's press release. Give me a minute, and I'll find it."

"Doesn't matter," Dick added. "We can't do anything about it."

"We can help Sam prepare for the debate," Art replied. Then he turned to me. "Tell us about your preparation. What can we do to help you?"

"Nothing," I said.

"Tell us what you're doing. Maybe there's something we know that you don't."

"Harriet has prepared study books on state politics. These are clippings from Texas newspapers that report the pros and cons of the issues. I have three, big, thick notebooks."

"You getting any coaching?"

"More than I can handle," I said. "The debate coach at Midland College has been meeting with me two hours a day. He has a Wednesday night class and tonight he's devoting the entire session to a mock debate. One of his friends, a political science professor, is going to act the role of Clarence Anderson."

"Sounds good," Art said. "Want me to come?"

"Sure," I replied. "And a history professor at WTAMU, who's been tracking my opponent's position on issues, is flying to Midland tomorrow to spend three hours briefing me on what he thinks are the vulnerable spots in Anderson's platform."

"What can any of us do to help?" Tom asked.

"Nothing I can think of," I said.

Harriet perked up. "I have something."

"Let's have it," Art said.

"As the stakes grow, I'm wondering if the debate is rigged," she said. "Especially I'm worried about Consuelo."

"Worried?" Art asked. "What are you worried about?"

"How often does *The Austin American-Statesman* send one of their reporters 350 miles to cover a debate for a state senate election? Frankly, I've never heard of *The Dallas Morning News,* or *The Houston Chronicle,* or any Texas newspaper spending money for that kind of coverage."

"So you think there's something going on?" Art asked.

Harriet shrugged her shoulders, extended her arms, palms out—a gesture of *the situation speaks for itself.*

"Something fishy?"

"You asked if there's anything any of us could do. Well, I think some of us could look into it."

Art turned and looked at me. "What'ya think?"

I shrugged. "You're out of my league. I haven't the foggiest."

45

Midland College night school, The Business Building

Professor Cody Myers called the class to order and handed out an information sheet about the evening's lesson. While he circulated his handout, I looked around the room and sized up his students. Not many were youthful, eighteen-year-olds, the typical college-age freshmen one expects to find enrolled at a community college.

Most were what Midland College called "returning students"—working adults, ages twenty to fifty, attending night school to improve their competence in the business world. They appeared serious as they listened to Myers and looked over his outline. I followed along.

> *MIDLAND COLLEGE*
> *BUSINESS 2013:*
> *PRINCIPLES OF MARKETING*
>   *Tonight we will have a "mock" debate, a run-through of*
> *an actual political event, which will be broadcast tomorrow*

evening on KMID-TV. Tomorrow's live debate will be between the two Republican candidates for State Senator—Sam Davis of Midland and Clarence Anderson of Amarillo. For tonight's class we have Midland College Professor James Calvi, playing the role of candidate Anderson, and Senator Davis playing himself. I will portray the role of Veronica Young, President of the Texas League of Women Voters (TLWV), who will moderate tomorrow night's television program. Please, no comments about the gender—I was unable to secure a suitable female actress with knowledge of TLWV rules and procedures. You'll just have to stretch your imagination a bit and refer to me as Ms. Young.

There will be ten questions. Davis will go first on questions 1, 4, 5, 8, and 9. Anderson will go first on questions 2, 3, 6, 7, and 10. Candidates will have two minutes to respond to each question. Following the ten questions, each candidate will have three minutes to summarize his candidacy.

The room had three speakers' stands at the front. Myers took the one in the middle. Calvi, playing the role of Anderson, walked over to the one on the right, and I stood at the one on the left.

Professor Myers read the first question: "What are the major issues facing the state of Texas in the next four years, and what strategies do you advocate for meeting these challenges? Mr. Davis, you have two minutes."

"Two minutes to answer a question like that is comparable to asking us to write a summary of World War II in two minutes," I replied.

The class laughed.

"But I'll give you three. Immigration. Gun control. And taxes, or what I like to think of as 'financing state government'."

I started with immigration and did my best to explain a complex, virtually irresolvable issue for almost two minutes. Next I gave two sentences to gun control. And had barely started on taxes when Myers called "time."

While I was giving my poorly organized, three-part answer, I had seen my opponent scribbling notes. And I learned a valuable lesson. Calvi, the political science professor, gave a list of six issues—twice as many as I had presented—with hardly any detail.

Like me, he started with immigration, but he didn't waste time trying to give the specifics of his resolution strategy. He was a scholar who had studied Texas political issues. He knew the magnitude of the immigration problem and anticipated the hopeless task of finding a solution.

While I had ranted about immigration's conflictive details for two minutes, he summarized its main points for only thirty seconds and went on to his next topic.

His response to the first question came across as clear, organized, and easily understood. Mine was frantic, disorganized, and a jumbled mess of ideas that must have sounded confusing to the listener.

Next, Myers questioned us about our priorities for state government. Calvi had a list. I half-listened to his responses and thought his ideas sounded reasonable. When it came my turn, I had all of his topics plus a couple more: the committee on equine standards, of which I was chairman, and the need to address legislation for oil and gas production.

Our responses to question number two, while similar, gave me a slight edge. Horse lovers would like my concern for equine protection— who could be against the care and safety of horses—and the general nature of my platform for the oil and gas industry probably wouldn't hurt.

The debate rushed on, questions attacking us like a machine gun. In fact, I had the distinct feeling that I was dodging bullets. Much of the material sounded familiar—topics I had studied and for which I could pull out prepared responses. The only question that contained entirely new material had to do with state prisons. Fortunately, my opponent went first, and that gave me a chance to gather my thoughts.

The closings, by comparison, offered a sense of relief. I had mine down pat. So I delivered it word-for-word as prepared, a straightforward declaration of how I planned to fight for right, to support the people, and provide leadership for the great state of Texas.

The students of Midland College clapped for us.

Cody Myers gave me a video recording.

And I headed home, exhausted.

46

Eleven o'clock that evening, at home

"How'd it go?" Suzie asked.

"I have the DVD," I replied. "Want to see it?"

"Yes, my love. How about a glass of wine to go with the movie?"

"I'd love one, darling."

I set up the playback. She poured the drinks. We plopped down together in front of the television to critique my performance.

"Honey, you lost the first question," Suzie said, after we had watched the opening responses.

Suzie had never been one to hesitate when it comes to criticizing me. And as much as I have resisted her critical remarks over the years, tonight it was exactly what I needed.

"I agree," I said, reluctantly, and then took a heavy draw of wine. "But I thought my opening remarks were okay."

"Maybe."

I took another slug of wine.

After the second round she said, "Much better, but after the first question, I still have the feeling you're behind."

"The old cliché about *first impressions* and *lasting impressions*?"

She nodded. "It takes more spin to 'turn around' an impression than it does to 'create one.' I think that's in the Dale Carnegie book."

I made notes.

We progressed on through the recording. I won some and lost some. We stopped the DVD and discussed the losses. I made notes of ways to improve.

Finally we came to the closing statements.

I felt good about my "Onward, Upward" speech.

Suzie didn't.

"I worked hard on that summary. It has patriotism, selflessness, and idealism all wrapped up in short, concise verbiage. What could be better?"

"A summary of your opponent's misspeaking," she said.

Her answer floored me. I had always thought of the closing statement in terms of myself—a prepared précis of my political ideals.

"It's your best opportunity," she continued, "while it's fresh in the minds of your audience, to make points about why you're the better candidate."

"By pointing out his shortcomings?"

"Exactly."

I thought about the ramifications. "You mean I'd have to come up with it *on the spot,* to summarize Anderson's debate performance while the cameras are rolling." I shook my head slowly. It didn't sound feasible.

"Yes."

Hell, I wasn't sure anybody could do it under that kind of pressure.

Suzie could read my mind.

"I can tell by your reaction that you don't like the idea," she said.

I nodded.

"You're probably thinking how much easier it would be to read a prepared statement. And how difficult it would be to come up with a closing speech if you have to do it right there, on stage, under lights, and with super severe time restraints."

"I think of it as the o-u-s effect." I chuckled at my own joke, thinking she probably didn't get it. "Ex-tem-po-rane-OUS is dan-ger-OUS."

"It's not entirely thinking on your feet."

She got it, she just didn't agree.

"You have a few minutes to reflect and organize your points."

I raised my voice. "Damn few. It's more like seconds than minutes."

"Well—" She hesitated, and then said, "Yes."

"I don't know if I can do it." I smiled. "I'm damn sure I can't do it well."

She smiled back, a coy little grin indicating she still didn't agree.

I pressed. "And if I do it poorly, that's infinitely worse than doing a canned speech well."

She shook her head. "Two things," she said. "First, I'm confident you'd do it well. You're a quick thinker. It's one of your best qualities. And second, you've told me yourself . . . quick thinking is what makes you a successful lawyer."

"I've never said that."

"Shall I go wake the kids and get them to confirm it?"

I laughed. "No."

"See? You admit it."

"You're exaggerating."

"Exaggerating or not, I feel sure you'd do it well. It's your best chance to win. After all, it is a debate." She looked at her watch. "And it's almost two o'clock in the morning. It's been a long day. Tomorrow's the debate. I'll—"

I raised a hand, my indication for her to stop. "Together?" I gestured for her to say it. So we said it, in unison, her infamous four-word phrase.

"I'LL THINK IT OVER."

We laughed.

Then we kissed.

47

The next morning

When I awoke, I felt like I'd been run over by a Mack truck—an eighteen-wheeler. I opened one eye. The other side of the bed was empty.

I showered, shaved, dressed, and found Suzie in the kitchen reading the morning paper. She showed me the headline:

TV DEBATE TONIGHT

I scanned the article and learned some startling news. The president of the Texas League of Women Voters was ill. The television station, KMID-TV, had selected Consuelo Hernandez to fill in. The newspaper writer gave several paragraphs of justification for the decision.

A spokeswoman for the Anderson campaign approved of the Hernandez selection. She pointed out that Hernandez was from a neutral city—Austin—that she was well informed about the campaign issues, and had recently interviewed both candidates. The *Austin American-Statesman* article, which I thought heavily favored Anderson, was praised as the most definitive and scholarly coverage of the runoff election.

My campaign spokesman, Arthur McComas, was also quoted. He criticized the choice of Hernandez to serve as moderator of the debate. Art made a good effort. He excoriated her views, listed numerous examples of partisan comments in her writing, and, I thought, gave sufficient grounds to disqualify her. Art suggested Midland College professor Cody Myers for the moderator.

All to no avail.

KMID-TV stated that time for the debate was imminent, qualified people who had a grasp of the campaign issues were in short supply, and that the one other name, Cody Myers, had to be disqualified because his Midland College ties showed bias.

The only alternative for the Davis campaign was to withdraw, thereby conceding the debate and probably the election. Art said the Sam Davis campaign staff would consider the decision and have an answer by noon.

The phone rang.

"Good morning, Sunshine," Art said.

I looked at my watch, 10:00 a.m. "It was a late night," I said.

"Suzie told me," he said. "She refused to wake you when I called this morning at seven."

"Good for her."

"Not so good. Have you seen the morning paper and that the completely *impartial* reporter from Austin is going to moderate?"

"Just saw it."

"When can we talk?"

"I'm on my way to the office now."

"I'll assemble the executive committee and get Whiskey on the speaker phone. Can you be ready in thirty minutes?"

"Sure."

On the drive to the office I thought about the choices. No question that Hernandez favored my opponent. She had destroyed any semblance of impartiality during the interview in my office the previous Monday. But what could she do to hurt me tonight? If she blatantly slanted the debate to favor Anderson, that might actually help me. Blatant was the key word. How about subtle? I thought about how much damage could be done subtly. Then I parked and took the elevator to my office.

Art had things set up in the conference room with a closed circuit, two-way video hook-up instead of a speakerphone. We took our places in a semi-circle before the camera. Moments later Whiskey's face appeared on the TV monitor.

"What a god-dammed, rotten turn of events," Whiskey yelled.

48

Friday morning, the day before the election, the conference room

Y ou think we should cancel?" I asked. I directed the question at the television monitor, but then I let my gaze roam, making eye contact with Tom, Dick, Harriet, and Art—a gesture that invited each to respond.

"Hell no," Whiskey replied, his voice booming from the video hookup. "In a close race like this, we'd be conceding the election."

"What else can we do?" Art asked.

"Fight like hell," came Whiskey's reply from the TV. "And try to anticipate what this bitch will do to sabotage our chances."

"Questions," Harriet said. "She'll do everything she can to ask questions that look impartial but subtly favor Anderson."

"Any ideas?" I asked.

"Campaign spending," Art said. "She'll ask questions about how much each side has spent in order to prompt Anderson's accusations that we're trying to buy the election."

"Experience," Dick said. "Let Anderson brag about all those years he's held elective office."

"Abner Stone," Tom said. "That's the issue that put us behind. Hernandez is sure to use it again to cast aspersions."

The discussion continued for over an hour. Everyone had ideas of how the moderator would use her bias to direct the debate in Anderson's favor. I made notes of each topic.

Then while the committee haggled over how best to deflect the prejudicial slant of the moderator, I racked my brain to find countermeasures for each subject. On campaign spending, I noted Anderson's personal wealth, and then I contrasted my circumstances—that I drove a dilapidated old pickup, that I had young children, that we were saving for our kids' college fund. Anderson had money to spend. I didn't—I had to raise my campaign funds. And the fact that I raised more money than he did showed initiative, that I was working harder to win the election.

For experience I focused on the political advantages of change. Voters knew about the old guard, and a role call at the Texas State Capitol showed that fresh new faces were in short supply. Yes, Anderson had held various political offices for over a quarter century, almost as many years as I was old. But one of the things Texas government needed most was dynamic new ideas in Austin. A vote for Sam Davis was a vote for change.

I looked over the list of topics. Some would be easier to refute than others. I could see a danger of repetition and realized that it wouldn't be smart to "make excuses" over and over. Better to pick the most powerful of Hernandez's questions—I started to say accusations—and then work to defeat them. If I could challenge Anderson's strongest, most damaging topics, then by comparison the lesser subjects would seem ineffective.

PUPPET POLITICS

The biggie on the list was Abner Stone.

Just as I started to build my theory about Abner's death, Whiskey addressed me on the video box. "Sam, there's no magic bullet. You're just going to have to stand toe-to-toe against Anderson and find some way to lick him, even when the deck is stacked against you."

"Hey," I answered, "I plan to give it my best shot."

Whiskey signed off.

The TV went black.

Tom, Dick, and Harriet left the room.

"What can I do to help?" Art asked.

"You going with me to the TV station tonight?"

"Of course. Linda and I will pick up you and Suzie at six. It's all arranged."

I worked at my desk for a while and got to thinking about Veronica Young, the president of the TLWV. She had dropped out at the last minute. I wondered why.

I called Sean O'Brien, my old UT Law School buddy, who now worked in Austin, an assistant in the Office of the State Attorney General.

"Sean, old friend, I've called to ask a favor."

He laughed. "That's what friends are for."

"This is a big favor. It has to be done this afternoon."

"Let me guess," he said. "You need to borrow a million dollars."

"It's almost that bad. Are you sitting down?"

When he said yes, I told him about Veronica Young. I asked him if he could find out why she cancelled at the last minute. He said he'd give it his best and call me before six o'clock. I gave him my cell phone number and thanked him, saying that my political future was on the line. Which, it was.

HARRY HAINES

No sooner had I hung up than Mrs. Hughes buzzed me to say that the history professor from WTAMU was here for my briefing.

After quick introductions, we adjourned to the conference room. We ordered pizza and started on Clarence Anderson. I soon learned that a quick comprehensive briefing on a sixty-year-old political opponent was an impossibility. I don't know how I thought it could be done in a couple of hours. It reminded me of trying to get a drink out of a fire hose.

But we persevered. And in between pizza and coffee, I learned a lot about the Amarillo mayor, some of which I could probably use in the debate.

At 4:40, we called it quits. I thanked him for his help and gave him a ride to the airport. Then I headed home to shower and change clothes.

Art, as promised, picked us up and drove us to the TV station.

49

I knew the drill. We hurriedly went through the studio check, the lighting check, and the mike checks. Then came the make-up. And promptly at seven o'clock, we were on the air.

Consuelo Hernandez gave introductions and read her first question to me.

"Senator Davis," she said, "I've gone over the campaign expenditures that both candidates have reported to the state election commission. You've spent over twice the amount reported by Mr. Anderson. Some columnists are accusing you of trying to buy this election. What do you have to say?"

I gave a short response about raising money, that it was a sign of public support, and that, unlike Mr. Anderson who had personal funds, I was dependent on fund raising.

Hernandez frowned, and said, "You've used less than half of your two minutes."

"I think I've answered your question," I said.

She shook her head—a gesture of incredulity—and turned to Anderson. "Go ahead, sir."

Anderson gave a long repetitive answer about having to sacrifice a significant sum of his own money and that, despite being outspent almost two-to-one, he was still ahead in the polls. Hernandez had to cut him off.

The moderator addressed the next question toAnderson. "How has your background in public service qualified you to serve in the Texas State Senate?"

"I'm glad you asked that question,"Clarence Anderson replied. "I'm proud of my record in Texas politics. Just to remind our voters, I'd like to take a minute to go over my thirty years of public service and highlight the offices I've held." He then proceeded to list every office and the dates he held it. Unfortunately, the long record sounded both repetitive and boring. Again, Hernandez had to call time.

"Senator Davis," she said. "Here's your opportunity to tell us about your public service."

"I have none," I said. "Which may be a good thing. Some political columnists have commended me as being a new face with fresh ideas for state government."

I paused. The camera went back to Hernandez. She looked flustered. "You have more time. Senator, is there anything you wish to add?"

"No."

She shuffled her papers. One dropped to the floor, and she stooped to retrieve it. The more she struggled to find the next question, the more discomfited she appeared. Drops of perspiration appeared on her forehead.

"Education is a major expenditure of state government. Mr.

Anderson, what should Texas do to improve educational opportunities for our children?"

Again, Anderson gave a long answer and had to be cutoff.

Mine was short.

But this time Hernandez was ready. She didn't ask if I wanted more time. Instead she went directly to the next question.

"What do you think about the enormous budget for Texas State Prisons? What can we do to fight crime with less money?"

I gave a concise answer.

Anderson's was long and detailed.

Hernandez continued to fire questions.

Anderson persisted with lengthy responses.

I stuck with short answers.

"This is our final question," Hernandez said. "Mr. Anderson, we've all read about the murder of former Senator Abner Stone and the fact that the Texas Rangers and the Midland County Sheriff have identified your opponent as the leading suspect in their investigation. I'd like you to comment, please."

Anderson acted like he'd just been given a free ticket to win the debate. He pounced.

"I'm the candidate of law and order. The Texas Rangers are widely recognized as one of America's leading law enforcement agencies. I'm glad to see, after almost a year of little or no action, that the Midland County Sheriff's Office is now working with the Rangers to find and bring to justice the perpetrator of this horrible death Voters should know that, unlike my opponent, I am not, nor have I ever been, a suspect in this or any other homicide. And I hope every citizen in Senate District 31 will join me in support of our law enforcement agencies, in furthering the cause of justice and in seeing that no crime in our area goes unpunished.

We must be aggressive in finding and indicting suspects in all murder cases, and it is only with—"

"Mr. Anderson, sorry, but your two minutes are up."

"Support of law enforcement is essential," he added. "Thank you."

"Senator Davis, you have two minutes," she said.

"I agree completely with Mr. Anderson, so I don't believe there is anything to add."

Consuelo Hernandez dropped her jaw. "Surely you have some response to these accusations?"

"I just gave my response. Find those who are guilty and prosecute."

"But, you're a suspect."

"Says who?"

"Newspapers. It's reported all over the state."

"Name a newspaper? Singular."

"Well, uh—"

"Ms. Hernandez, you work for the *Austin American-Statesman*, correct?"

"Yes, I'm an investigative reporter."

"Has the *American-Statesman* named me as a suspect?"

She started to answer. I could see the "yes" being formed on her lips. But she didn't say it. I could almost read her thoughts—lawsuit—we could be sued for liable. Then her expression changed, and her face formed an ugly scowl.

"It's just a matter of time until charges are filed."

"Your opinion? Or would you like to announce here on this public affairs program the name or names of law enforcement officers you can quote?"

I've seen hate. And I've seen anger. However, I don't recall any occasion when I've seen both emotions so pronounced in the facial features of one person and filmed on television.

After a moment, Clarence Anderson came to her rescue. "Perhaps we should go to closing statements. I believe I'm first. Would you like me to begin?"

Hernandez took a big breath and exhaled slowly. "Thank you, Mr. Anderson. Yes, please begin. You have three minutes."

50

Clarence Anderson read his summary, a prepared statement and obviously written by a professional speechwriter. For the first time in our debate, he finished on time. I guessed he'd carefully timed his closer to be sure that he would not be stopped.

It was the sort of presentation I originally planned to give.

Thanks to my wife, I now had a different plan—an outline, written frantically while my opponent spoke.

"Senator Davis, you have three minutes."

Sweat beaded on my forehead and dripped on my notes, but I knew the plan. What I didn't know was if I could pull it off. Just behind the lights and to the right, I spotted Suzie. She held up both hands with her fingers crossed.

"Thank you, Ms. Hernandez," I said.

She stared at me, eyes blazing with antagonism. Her facial expression communicated anything but thanks., but she said, "You're welcome."

PUPPET POLITICS

I returned her gaze without the antipathy, and in a voice as calm as I could make it, I said, "I hope the viewers of this program have taken note of your bias in the questions presented tonight. I have a few thoughts which I'd like to share with our audience."

Like a lighted match tossed into a can of gasoline, the television studio erupted into an emotional explosion. I could feel it. But almost immediately a hush fell over the room and it became eerily quiet. Camera operators froze. No one moved or even breathed.

In a slow, measured voice, I proceeded to read my scribbled notes. I started with campaign spending, then her question about experience in political office, and on to the next nine queries, each time adding a short comment about how each question was designed to favor Clarence Anderson.

I took a deep breath and shifted from the actual debate to my research about it.

"I was puzzled about the last-minute change in moderators for tonight's program. As all of us know, the President of the Texas League of Women Voters, Veronica Young, was to have presided. Because of the hurried and secretive manner in which the change occurred, I contacted an assistant in the Texas State Attorney General's Office and asked that they investigate."

I heard slight movement and a gasp for breath. For a nanosecond, I looked away from the camera to see that Consuelo Hernandez had changed.

Earlier, she had shown hate, anger, even revulsion—all of it directed at me.

Now the color drained from her face, and she fidgeted with her watch, refusing to look me in the eye.

I faced the camera and continued.

"Assistant State Attorney Sean O'Brien visited Ms. Young at her home in Austin this afternoon. He found that she had been a victim of apparent food poisoning under suspicious circumstances. And he returned my call—just as this program was about to go on the air—to ask that I forward a detailed list of the questions used tonight. He told me he plans to submit them to Ms. Young to see if they are identical to the ones she gave KMID-TV for the debate."

At this point I realized I could be in hot water. Anderson and his lawyers would come after me, and if I were wrong, they'd sue for libel and probably take me for everything I had.

Probably?

A small voice in the back of my brain warned me. *Quit while you're ahead, while your statements are about facts.*

I hesitated. Then I looked at Hernandez. Her hostility was no act. I wasn't wrong . . . .

So I threw caution to the winds and said the words that would guarantee a lawsuit.

"The questions were changed."

When I delivered those four words, all the chips were now on the table. If this were Texas Hold 'Em, I was *all in*.

With nothing to lose, I plowed ahead and pushed to win the election.

"Voters, especially viewers of this program, may want to pay particular attention to question number ten, the closing question. You will recall that it focused on the investigation of Abner Stone's death. Notice that I switched words. I said 'death' not 'murder.' That's because both the Texas Rangers and the Midland County Sheriff are using the former rather than the latter in all official communications about the case. Again, another example of pejorative action on the part of the moderator."

"So, for my closing thought, I ask that voters consider the fairness of tonight's debate. And if you think that one side has not participated fairly, I ask that you take such behavior into consideration when you enter the voting booth tomorrow."

If looks could kill, I'd now be a dead man.

Instead of appearing on camera to give the moderator's closing, Consuelo Hernandez turned and stomped off the set.

The television cameras tracked her exit.

It was a dramatic moment. One I'll never forget. I felt a burden lift from my shoulders and a breeze of fresh air float over me.

I turned to Anderson and offered my left hand. He didn't know what to do, so I reached for his right hand. It was awkward, but I managed to make it look like a handshake. The cameras caught it as the final scene of our debate.

The lights went down.

People gathered around.

"Wow," Art said. "Where'd that come from?"

"Tell you later," I said.

Suzie grabbed me, took me into her arms, and gave me a big, passion-filled kiss.

People around us clapped.

51

The next morning, Election Day

In my heart of hearts, I didn't care if I won or lost the damned election. But the elation of clearing my name—of appearing on television with the largest audience in West Texas history, which included my friends and neighbors of a lifetime—was worth it.

I felt sure that we had caught Hernandez and her cohorts with their hands in the cookie jar. She had taken a foolish risk, thinking that she could subtly shift the tenor of the debate and get away with it.

In my mind, she wasn't very subtle. She deserved to be castigated—the more public, the better.

And I had been lucky. Lucky that I didn't try to debate the questions. Lucky that Anderson overplayed his answers and gave me the setup. Lucky that Suzie's idea, about my response, had worked so perfectly.

At breakfast I felt like I was on top of the world. But as the day wore on, the feeling ebbed. The reality of the numbers dominated everyone's thinking. Anderson was ahead. And no one had any idea how many voters would be affected by Friday night's TV broadcast.

Our local NBC affiliate tried to compile an exit poll.

I watched the six o'clock news with jaded expectations. Exit polls, I've heard Whiskey say, are the worst—the most inaccurate of all political predictions. NBC reported the election as "neck and neck."

"Thanks, NBC," I said aloud, talking to myself. Then silently I pondered the TV reporter's implications. He didn't say it in so many words, but his message came through loud and clear. He thought the impact of the debate was little to none.

I felt worse than before.

Art and Linda had planned a victory party in their backyard. They scheduled it to begin at nine o'clock. Suzie and I arrived at 10:30. The news of the evening was the tightness of the election. KMID-TV showed that, with 50 percent of the precincts reporting, Anderson was ahead by 1 percent.

Shortly after midnight, with 75 percent of the vote in, the TV commentators announced that I had pulled ahead. The vote, Anderson 249,103 to Davis 250,311, gave me a half-percent lead. People cheered. I smiled and took another glass of Champagne.

At 1:00 a.m., people started leaving. I still had a razor-thin lead, but those who were going home shook my hand like it was a landslide victory.

At two o'clock, I decided to call it a night. I expressed my gratitude to Art and the few remaining die-hards and asked them to call me in the morning. Suzie drove, and I fell asleep on the way home. Somehow, I staggered into bed and fell into a deep slumber the second my head hit the pillow.

Tim and Emily woke me.

"Daddy, you won," Emily chirped, her voice almost a squeal.

"It's on TV," Tim said. "With 100 percent of precincts reporting, they're saying that you won by fifty-seven votes."

I looked across the room to see Suzie standing in the doorway, a big, happy smile filling her face.

"What time is it?" I asked.

"Almost eleven," she said. "The KMID-TV truck is here, and Kaye Kelly's waiting on the front steps for you to make a statement."

"My second-most-favorite reporter," I said. "Did she bring Consuelo Hernandez with her?"

"No, but if you don't get dressed and give her an interview, I think Kelly will go looking for Hernandez."

I threw back the covers and sat on the side of the bed. Tim and Emily plopped down by me, one on each side. I put my arms around them. "What'ya think, kids, should I go on TV like this or should I shower, shave, and get dressed?"

"And brush your teeth," Emily said.

"When you want the plain, unvarnished truth, ask a seven-year-old," I said.

Suzie laughed. "I'll go tell the paparazzi you'll be there in ten minutes."

They left.

I went through my morning ablutions.

Then I gathered my family and, together, the four of us went out on the front steps to face the cameras.

Kaye Kelly wasted no time.

"Senator Davis, what are your thoughts about the recount?"

52

An hour later, at home

The TV truck and all the news people left. Art came. We gathered for coffee at the kitchen table. "What'd you think?" I asked.

"I think it's just a matter of time," Art replied. "You're in the catbird's seat."

"Only fifty-seven votes," I said. "A recount could go either way."

"And if it goes their way, we'll ask for another recount."

"How many recounts are there?"

"Theoretically, the number is unlimited," Art replied. "As a practical matter, money will decide."

I shook my head. "How can that be?"

"For an election this size, each recount will cost about a quarter-million. The person who requests the recount has to pay the tab. We have more money than Anderson."

I took another sip of coffee and thought about what Art was saying. Art continued. "After several recounts, a contested election usually ends up in court with the loser suing the winner."

"Sounds expensive," I said.

"All depends. But the rule of thumb is that a lawsuit will cost twice as much as a recount."

"Ouch."

"But good news for us," Art said. "Have you read the morning paper?"

"No."

"Your friend, the Assistant Attorney General, spilled the beans." Art handed me a copy of the morning paper. It was the headline story.

DEBATE MODERATOR SHIFTS QUESTIONS

Apparently Consuelo Hernandez, moderator for the Davis/Anderson televised debate, substituted a different set of questions than those scripted by the Texas League of Women Voters. This accusation was made by Sean O'Brien, Assistant Attorney General who investigated the matter, and who interviewed Veronica Young, the designated TLWV moderator. Hernandez, now widely acknowledged as an Anderson partisan, selected questions designed to favor the Amarillo Mayor. It is not known if Anderson was personally involved.

The article went on to say that, in spite of the rigged questions, political commentators were virtually unanimous in their opinion that I won the debate. And that the debate, which had been widely heralded as an "election decider" in a hotly contested race, turned out to have little or no effect.

"So if this election winds up in court, how does all this affect our case?"

PUPPET POLITICS

"We win," Art said. He leaned back in his chair—a pensive look on his face. "I think."

"What kind of an answer is that?" I asked.

"Everything about this election has turned 180 degrees from what we expected. You had a big lead, then lost an unbelievable 30 points. Anderson was heavily favored to win the runoff, but the race tightened. Next, Hernandez's treachery, when exposed, should have given you a victory. Instead, it now appears that the debate had virtually no effect."

"Art, skip the political spin and cut to the chase. Where do we stand?"

"I think Hernandez will hand you the election," he said.

"Think?"

"You've seen all the ups and downs," Art said. "This is a political race for the history books."

"When will I know for sure?"

"Probably not until *after* the November general election."

"Good God, why does it take seven months?"

"Because the Republican candidate, whether it's you or Anderson, has to run against old what's-his-name—the Democrat that no one knows or even cares about. After that it becomes virtually impossible to take the case to court and question the legality of the primary elections."

"Time becomes the final arbiter?" I asked.

"I like the word history," he replied.

"Heck of a way to run the country."

"Democracy," he continued. "Who was it that said, 'It's the worst form of government, except for all the others'."

"I think it was the cartoon character who lived in a Florida swamp."

"Pogo?"

I smiled. "My all-time *fave-oh-rite* philosopher."

53

A rt was right. The general election, when it finally happened, came as an anticlimax. However, I worried right up to election day that some unexpected turn of events would empower the democrats, and that old whatzisname—the obscure candidate from Bushland—would stage a come-from-behind miracle and defeat me. It didn't happen. So, when I won in a landslide vote, everyone yawned and left the "victory party" right after the ten o'clock news.

When you're supposed to win and you do, there's no drama.

The next morning our executive committee—Art, Tom, Dick, and Harriet—gathered at eight o'clock for a video conference with Whiskey to wrap up the campaign and close our operations. The lieutenant governor radiated cheerfulness over the video screen that dominated the meeting.

"Congratulations, *Senator* Davis," he said. "Preliminary results give you 80 percent of the vote, and, if that holds, you'll have established a new record."

Everyone clapped.

Art laughed. "Yesterday, our candidate was worried about an upset." He reached over and slapped me on the back.

"Hey, I remember the primary and the runoff," I said, "when *everyone* was worried."

"Enjoy the moment," Whiskey replied. "I've gotta go. See you in Austin in January."

The screen went black.

"What do we have to do to close down the campaign operations?" I asked.

Art went through his list. Tom would close out our finances and prepare the election reports required by Texas law. Dick would pay the bills, shut down the campaign headquarters, release the employees, and organize our volunteers to take down signs. Harriet would help me with the mountain of thank you notes.

The meeting ended on a high note.

Tom, Dick, and Harriet left the room wearing big smiles.

Art and I paused at the door. It was a moment to be savored, one of those emotional milestones when words fail and communication comes by innuendo. Art stared at the floor, avoiding my gaze. With my bad hand, I formed a fist and jabbed him playfully on the shoulder.

"You're one helluva campaign manager," I said.

"Ah shucks, Senator," he replied.

"I don't know how to tell you how much I appreciate all you've done to get me elected."

"You already have." He gave me a wry smile, returned the punch to the shoulder, and walked away, heading down the hallway toward his office.

HARRY HAINES

I went to my office and had barely settled into my desk chair when someone knocked on the door.

"Come in," I said.

Mrs. Hughes walked in with a cup of coffee. It was the first time in our ten-year working relationship that I could remember her carrying a tray, serving me like a waitress at an expensive restaurant.

Then I noticed the cup.

It was a mug with a small Texas flag painted on it and the inscription "Senator Sam Davis."

She placed a napkin on my desk. Then with a nervous flourish, she set the mug on the napkin. "Congratulations," she said. And as she stepped back, she blushed, a reaction totally foreign to her usual demeanor. For an awkward moment, our eyes met.

"Thank you," I said, thinking how inadequate the two words were.

She started to speak, then stopped.

"Mrs. Hughes, I don't know what to say." I smiled and picked up the mug.

"I'm very happy for you," she whispered, her voice barely audible.

"I'm overwhelmed," I said and held the mug out at eye level to display the flag and the inscription. "Thank you."

"You're welcome," she said, her voice returning crisp and firm, the old straight-laced persona I knew and expected. She stepped back and turned to leave.

I stood and in a commanding voice said, "Rebecca, wait."

She had her hand on the doorknob, and I thought she might continue on through the doorway. But she stopped and partially turned toward me.

"How about a hug?"

She opened her mouth to speak, but nothing came out.

PUPPET POLITICS

I opened my arms.

She stood there, frozen, an appalled look on her face.

I wrapped my arms around her and squeezed.

She lifted her left hand and lightly touched my back. Not exactly a hug, but the most responsive gesture I'd ever received from her.

"Thanks," I said. Then I stepped back to find her face beet red.

With her right hand still on the doorknob, she bolted.

I went back to my desk chair. Sat. Put my feet on the desk. Picked up my new mug. And sipped the Rebecca's coffee.

Same old weak taste.

54

I hate ceremony. The swearing in of senators and representatives, in my opinion, is pure folderol, the sort of ssilliness that exemplifies government at its worst.

But I endured.

Next came resolutions honoring former senators, those who had passed away in the two years since the last legislative session. And I could handle those. But when the ceremonial voting progressed down a long list of resolutions that came to one commending the "beautiful roses grown in Tyler, Texas," I looked around for a way to sneak out.

Until I found they were taking roll-call votes.

Trapped.

No politician wants to be recorded as "absent" when a vote is taken to commend "Texas beef as the finest in world."

But even time-wasting, ceremonial nonsense has its limits, and when, two-hours later, Lieutenant Governor Homer "Whiskey" Williams

212

rapped his gavel ending the opening session, I bolted from the senate chamber like a parakeet who just noticed the door to the birdcage had been left open. Freedom exhilarates the spirit of any living being, even the most blasé of Texas state senators.

In the Texas State Capitol, senate offices are assigned by seniority. And since I ranked thirty-first among the thirty-one senators, I received the smallest office, the one farthest from the senate chamber. Which met my needs. In fact I rather enjoyed being off the beaten track, away from the mainstream of lobbyists and other political traffic that squander a legislator's time.

With the required work of the session's first day completed, I settled comfortably into my desk chair and started work on a stack of pink phone messages. Most were from well-wishers who had called to congratulate me on the beginning of my term of office. Many carried a hidden meaning—a subtle reminder of my obligation to support their special interests. Some brought questions about the forthcoming session and specific requests for legislation. I separated the slips—those that required a response and those that didn't. I tossed the "no response" pile.

Then I counted the slips that needed a reply—twenty-three.

Two were personal.

I called Sylvia—my chief of staff—and asked her to take all the others.

The first of my two pink slips was to call the lieutenant governor. He came on the line with a cheerful, upbeat, boisterous voice.

"Dinner at seven?" he asked.

"Sure." I remembered our dinner engagement. "Where're we going?"

"Texas Land and Cattle."

I frowned. "Is that a restaurant?"

"Senator Samuel Davis, where've you been?" His voice took a

practiced timber of condescension. "It's the 'in' place for upscale dining in Austin."

"Never heard of it."

"Out on North Highway 183. Built like a big ranch house with a huge fireplace and hand-peeled split logs. They have the best mesquite-grilled steaks in Texas."

"Sounds expensive."

"Or we could take you and your wife to McDonald's."

I laughed. "Exactly what I had in mind. Make a big hit with Suzanne."

"I'm sending you a copy of Senate Bill 107. And I'd consider it a personal favor if you'd sign on as co-author."

"Tell me about it."

"S.B. 107: West Texas Investment Incentive for Economic Development and Quality of Life Enhancement."

"Why me?"

He chuckled—the sound of a kindergarten teacher answering the question of a five-year-old student. "Well to start with, you're one of the senators from West Texas."

"Do I get to look it over before I say yes?"

"Of course. I'll send a runner to your office. You should have your copy in a few minutes."

"Thank you."

"And seven o'clock, I'll pick you up."

"We'll be ready."

I dialed up the phone number of my other pink slip, got their answering machine, and was just finishing my "sorry I missed you" message when Sylvia brought in a big bulky manuscript. Printed on legal sized paper, it looked thicker than the Houston phone book. With a ceremonious flourish, she held it about a foot high and dropped it on my desk. It landed with a loud thud.

"Whiskey Williams sent this to you."

"What is it?"

"Senate Bill 107," she said. "And there's a note. He wants you to co-sponsor."

I looked at the cover, SB 107, and shook my head at the twelve-word title. Everything about it hit me as excessive.

Sylvia smiled knowingly. "Ain't it great to be the senator from West Texas? You're so privileged you get to be one of the first to peruse a document like this."

I thumbed the pages. The reading of a massive tome like this would take days. "Sylvia, I would think Whiskey would consult me about writing a bill before he asks me to sign on as its co-sponsor."

"That's what he's now doing." Sylvia rolled her eyes. "He's asking you to help write the bill."

I used both hands to lift it. It must have weighed twenty pounds. "Looks to me like he's already written it."

She shook her head and said, "I just work here." Then she smiled her condescending smile, the one where her lips just barely lift at the corners, enough to communicate a "you poor slob" message. Sylvia turned and left.

I lifted the cover of the monster bill and started reading.

In 1836 when The Republic of Texas won its independence and established itself as a viable political entity, less than 1 percent of the population resided in the vast area now known as West Texas.

I read on for another dozen pages about early Texas, up to 1845 when the Republic joined the United States as the twenty-eighth state. The writer, or writers, had laced the story with constant reference to West Texas, its sparse population, its lack of development, its problems with the Indians, and the neglect accorded to it by Sam Houston and other early political leaders.

I looked at my watch—5:30. And I wondered when I'd find the time to study a bill that read like an eighth-grade history book.

55

The Texas Land & Cattle Steak House, Austin

There's something about the smell of piñon. For me it never fails to strike an emotional chord of pleasant memories, of comfort, or of respite from the cold. Combine it with the crackle of a huge fireplace, add a whiff of beef smoked on a nearby grill, and you have the sights, sounds, and aromas of welcome offered by this restaurant. A chilly, rainy January night in the Texas state capitol—I loved it.

Whiskey carried the conversation. And his expansive mood focused on coming legislative issues. It didn't matter what Suzie or I wanted to talk about. Our attempts to discuss food, weather, or people always came back to the same topic. Whiskey's monolithic mindset could only think of our questions or statements in terms of how they related to government and law-making.

Finally I gave up. And I fell into the role of interlocutor for his version of the Texas Senate.

"What do you think about water legislation?" I asked.

"It'll be contentious," Whiskey replied.

The waitress came to take our orders. Suzie ordered the six-ounce filet—medium, I asked for a ten-ounce rib eye—medium rare, Whiskey selected the sixteen-ounce prime rib—rare.

"Water will dominate the political scene for the next decade," Whiskey said.

I pictured us on the stage of an old-time minstrel show, where the person in my position would say, *And Mr. Bones, what can you tell us about 'da water?* I paraphrased. "Why is water going to dominate?"

"Throughout the United States underground water rights have mostly been subject to an unwritten law called the 'right of capture,' which basically says that landowners may pump as much water as they can from their land."

"Sounds simple to me."

"It may sound simple, but there are huge problems. First, it's difficult, if not impossible, to determine exactly how much water is there. And second, aquifer water is constantly moving, flowing under the surface."

"So?"

"So let me give you an example of why we need legislation. Take two landowners, side by side—farmer A and farmer B. But farmer A has a bigger pump and pulls all the water out from under both lands. He might get by with it if he's using it only to water his crops. But when he puts some of it into a retaining pond, farmer B sues. Farmer A says, "I can't be held liable if I just happen to pump water out from under a neighbor's land."

"This actually happened?" Suzie asked.

"Yep," Whiskey answered.

"Who won?" I asked.

"The case is still working its way up through the courts. Meanwhile,

I have more examples."

I chuckled and said, "I'm not sure I want to hear this." I meant it as a joke, a statement to lighten our conversation.

If Whiskey heard me, he didn't react. Instead, he just plowed ahead. "I see four major points of conflict." He leaned forward, his eyes lit up, and his voice projected a new intensity. "First, you have the agricultural community that needs water for watering crops. Second, you have municipalities that need water for their people. And third, you have industries—like a cheese factory—that need water for manufacturing."

Suzie goaded him on. "There's not enough to do all of these things, so the legislature will have to pass laws to regulate water?"

Whiskey smiled and started to continue, but the waitress brought our salads.

After she left, Suzie turned to Whiskey and asked, "You said four points?"

"The ranchers," Whiskey replied. "They, and other big landowners, have water beneath their land. They want to sell water rights."

"Sounds okay to me," I said. "Why not let them sell to the highest bidder?"

"Because of people like Bryan Fence."

"The oil tycoon?"

"Right. He's buying water rights like crazy and has plans to build huge pipelines to ship water downstate to cities like San Antonio and Austin. He thinks manufacturers in the Dallas/Ft. Worth metroplex will need his water in future decades."

"I'll bet this scares people in West Texas," Suzie said.

"There's an old saying in the Texas Senate," the lieutenant governor continued. "Whiskey's for drinking. Water's for fighting. That's how I got my nickname."

We all had a good laugh.

The waitress brought our steaks. Mine was bloody red in the middle, just the way I like it. I forked a big bite and savored it.

Conversation stopped momentarily, but my mind raced with the conflicts over water rights. As big as Whiskey made them sound, I had the feeling that they paled in comparison to the conflicts we faced over oil and gas.

I took another bite of steak.

56

I arrived at my capitol office at 7:00 a.m., energized and ready to go to work serving the people of senate district thirty-one. At eight o'clock the staff arrived, and we gathered around the table in our conference room.

With my budget of $35,000 per month, I could afford to hire five staff members. Isabel Vickers, Abner Stone's old secretary continued to run the Midland office. That left four positions to man the office in Austin.

Sylvia Newsom, Stone's chief of staff, stayed on to supervise our work in the state capitol. That gave me three slots for legislative workers. Sylvia wanted to keep Paul O'Hara and Ursula Jones, aides from the Stone era whom Sylvia knew and trusted. That left one position to be filled. I offered it to Harriet Wong, my favorite of the campaign workers, and she accepted. So on a cool, crisp January morning, Sylvia, Paul, Ursula, and Harriet gathered for the first time to organize our work for the coming legislative session, a period of 140 days that would end on May 28th.

"For the past several years, we've divided the staff into four categories," Sylvia said.

"How's that?" I asked.

"The three biggies are education, agriculture, and oil/gas. The fourth grouping is 'everything else,' or what's left."

"I've had agriculture," Paul said.

"And I've taken education," Ursula said.

"It works best for me to take the 'everything else' category," Sylvia said, "since I usually end up with all the bits and pieces anyway."

I looked at Harriet, "Guess that means you've inherited the oil-and-gas committee work."

"Fine with me." She smiled. "I worked with a lot of oil-patch folks in the campaign."

Sylvia passed out big, black, three-ring notebooks—four-inch binders that appeared to be mostly empty. She had them labeled agriculture, education, oil/gas, and everything-else. I watched as each staff member thumbed through the small number of pages that related to their assigned categories. "Not much so far, but over the next five months we'll see about six thousand bills and resolutions." She turned to me, and our eyes met. "Some will never make it out of committee, so you'll probably only have to cast a vote on a thousand or so."

"Wow, I'm going to have to become familiar with a thousand bills?"

"And resolutions."

I shook my head. It seemed impossible.

"Some are tough, and you'll struggle to find your way," Sylvia said. "But not all are going to require study." She passed out copies of a single-page resolution. "Here's an easy one."

PUPPET POLITICS

I read the title. "A Resolution to Name Friona, Texas as the CHEESEBURGER CAPITAL OF TEXAS." Then I scanned the paragraph that followed.

> *Whereas, the beautiful community of Friona, Texas, has for many years been recognized as the source of large, succulent cheeseburgers that have become famous throughout the country as unequaled in quality, nutrition, attractiveness, and tantalizing aroma . . . ,*
>
> *And furthermore, because the good people of Friona, Texas, have promoted the cheeseburger with their "Annual Cheeseburger Day," which has spread the fame of Friona cheeseburgers throughout the state (and even to surrounding states) . . . ,*
>
> *Be it hereby proclaimed that Friona, Texas, shall be recognized as the CHEESEBURGER CAPITAL OF TEXAS by the Texas State Senate and the Texas House of Representatives and entitled to all the rights and privileges pertaining thereto.*

At the bottom I found four spaces for signatures. Representatives had already signed three of the lines. The fourth had my name listed just below it.

"The house members from West Texas have invited you to join them as a co-author of the resolution," Sylvia said.

"Golly-gosh, uh, I don't know if I can support this." With a deadpan expression I lowered my voice. "It's going to upset some people and cause me to lose votes."

Sylvia's facial expression fell to a look of consternation. She bought my reluctance, hook, line, and sinker, "Who's it going to upset?"

"All the folks in Bovina, for sure, will be jealous. And Wayne Cope, who owns the Burger Shack in Canyon, will be furious because I didn't do this for him."

Sylvia smiled, realizing she'd been had. "Not all the voters in Bovina will be jealous."

"What's the population of Friona?" I asked.

Harriet called it up on her laptop. "The latest census reports 3,854."

"You lose Wayne Cope's vote and all the other owners of hamburger places . . . ," Paul said.

"But you gain 3,854 votes from Friona residents?" Ursula asked.

"Win some, lose some," I said. "Consuelo Hernandez could've used this against me in the debate."

"Who's Consuelo Hernandez?" Paul asked.

"Reporter for the *Austin American-Statesman*," Harriet replied. "She moderated the TV debate last summer."

"And almost caused us to lose the run-off election," Sylvia added.

"But no longer a threat," I said.

The meeting broke up. Everyone went his or her separate ways. I signed as co-sponsor of the Friona resolution.

A representative of the Texas Pecan Growers Association called on me, asking for my vote for a bill to support Texas pecans. He left a plastic package of shelled pecans and a gunnysack full of unshelled ones. After he left I stared at the huge sack and wondered what I could do with twenty-five pounds of unshelled nuts.

Sylvia buzzed me. "You remember Consuelo Hernandez?"

"Of course. We talked about her this morning."

"She's dead."

57

I felt conflicted as I read the headline story. Consuelo Hernandez, in death as in life, caused a ruckus. The *Austin American-Statesman*—always on the alert for news with controversy—gave the story far more ink than seemed reasonable. But I read it, word for word, in its entirety.

The newspaper divided the story into three segments, each written by different reporters.

The first gave facts. Hernandez had been found in her apartment by a co-worker who was investigating the victim's failure to report for work. Authorities estimated she had been dead for at least twenty-four hours. The medical examiner's preliminary report gave drug overdose as the cause of death.

The second article focused on the deceased's ten-year career as an investigative reporter for the *Statesman*. As I read the account, which glowed with high praise for Hernandez's journalistic ability, it amazed me that the writer of the article slanted the report to portray the dearly departed as a saint, a hard-working woman almost ready for the Pulitzer Prize. Only toward the end of the long story did I find a short paragraph about her efforts to sabotage the Midland TV debate. It seemed to me that the newspaper went far beyond any expectation of honoring the deceased. *C'est la vie.*

The third segment of the coverage was the biggie. Newspapers know that readers want controversy, so this writer took the circumstances of Hernandez's death and infused enough political rhetoric to change it from "probable suicide" into "murder mystery of the year." Austin police initially had listed cause of death as self-inflicted drug overdose. However, subsequent information from the medical examiner suggested that the cocaine was probably only lethal because it was combined with the "date-rape" drug rohypnol. The ratchet effect of this development caused Austin PD to bring in a CSI unit of the Texas Rangers to confirm the cause of death.

Reading between the lines, it seemed obvious to me that Austin Police were probably including the Rangers as a "CYA" move. The newspaper saw it as much more and interviewed the CSI team. The story included a quote from Lieutenant Charles Fuller: "The ruling of suicide is currently under investigation."

Charlie Fuller.

I wondered if he was still investigating me for the death of Abner Stone.

One thing I'd learned in my law practice about ratchet effect—whether it applied to wages, prices, or murder investigations—the facts being investigated rarely, if ever, returned to their previous level once the pressure subsided.

I decided to call Charlie. Might as well get bad news from the horse's mouth. I still had his number on my cell phone, and he answered on the first ring.

"Charlie. Sam Davis. Long time no see."

"*Senator* Davis. Yes, it has been a while. How're you doing?"

"You want me to address you as *Lieutenant* Fuller?"

"Naw, Charlie's fine."

"Then you've got to call me Sam."

"Okay, Sam. What's up?"

"Saw your name in the paper this morning. I'm sure you know that I'm interested in the Hernandez death, and I'm wondering what you can tell me."

"All I know is what I read in the paper. We've not received anything yet from Austin PD."

"Doesn't read that way in this morning's *Statesman*."

He chuckled. "They're trying to sell newspapers."

"Come on, Charlie. Surely you can give me a hint."

This time he laughed, a hearty reaction that came across as genuine. "Have you heard about the squirrel that lost its grip and fell from a tree? Poor thing was killed in the fall."

"No. Guess I haven't heard."

"Newspaper reported it as the precursor to a wave of endangered wildlife incidents. Global warming is causing the death of squirrels across the nation."

"Guess I'm out of it. I haven't heard of any other squirrels falling out of trees."

"Neither have I."

I held the phone for a long pause, four or five seconds, waiting for him to continue. Finally, I broke the silence. "So?"

227

"So, if a lone little squirrel falls and kills himself, that ain't news. But a newspaper has to have something to fill its pages."

This time, I was the one who hesitated and let the silence goad him into continuing.

After a long pause, he said, "So the newspaper *speculates* that there might be more than one squirrel. It's not exactly a lie, and the possibility turns an incident that ain't news, into one that might be."

"And?"

"And bingo, the newspaper now has something to fill its pages."

"Charlie, you're full of shit."

"No, just trying to answer your question about Hernandez."

"You're telling me that there's nothing to this stuff about her death being murder? That the *Austin American-Statesman* is raising doubt so they can sell more newspapers."

"I didn't say that."

"What exactly are you saying?"

"Like Sergeant Schultz, 'I know nothing.'"

"Thanks, Charlie," I said. "I'll do you a favor sometime."

"You're welcome, Sam."

I started to ring off, but at the last second, I blurted out another question. "How's your investigation into the death of Abner Stone?"

He didn't answer immediately. And sometimes it's a hesitation that conveys the message. After the brief pause he said, "Schultz number two, I know nothing."

"Charlie, I don't think the state is paying you that big fat salary for nothing."

"There must be some mistake."

"Oh?"

"My salary from the State of Texas is neither big nor fat."

We both laughed.

I heard a click, and the line went dead.

And I didn't believe him when he said he knew nothing about the investigation into the deaths of either Abner Stone or Consuelo Hernandez.

58

At 8:30 Sylvia came in with the representative of the Texas Pecan Growers Association. They seated themselves in the two chairs in front of my desk. He opened his briefcase and started unloading pecan candy.

"Your assistant has told me we have to limit this to fifteen minutes," he said.

Sylvia interrupted. "Senator, you have your committee meeting on Senate Bill 107 at nine o'clock, and Harriet is coming at 8:45 for a last-minute briefing."

Mr. Pecan Grower made a show of pushing up his left sleeve and displaying his wristwatch. "We can do it in half that time."

"How can I help the pecan growers?" I asked.

He placed an item named Texas Pecan Turtle in front of me. It was wrapped in mostly-clear cellophane with a cartoon turtle pictured on top. I picked it up with my good hand and examined it. The ingredients

230

were detailed on the back along with the standard, USFDA analysis of ingredients. It listed 485 calories for the small package. "We're starting our marketing plan for next Christmas and we're looking for an endorsement from the state."

I shook my head and frowned at his news. "It's only January."

He placed another item on the desk, a two-pound piece of candy called Texas Pecan Log. It, too, was wrapped in cellophane, but this one featured Santa, reindeer, and green holly leaves. "We have to start early," he said. "Takes almost a year from marketing to delivery."

I started to look up the calories. Then decided not to.

He produced a small paper plate, knife, and plastic gloves. With practiced movements and blinding speed, he ripped open the wrapping and cut some of the log into slices. Along with a stack of napkins, he placed the plateful of candy between Sylvia and me. "Have some."

Sylvia took a slice. I couldn't gracefully decline, so I did too.

Candy is candy, and I don't remember ever eating any that wasn't good. But this pecan log was the best I'd ever tasted. Without much encouragement, I could have snarfed down the entire log. I wondered how many thousand calories.

"What can I do to help you this morning?" I asked

"Put in a good word for the pecan growers." He pulled out two copies of a "suggested" endorsement. "A letter to the Texas Commission for Tourism and Commerce would be most appreciated."

Sylvia rolled her eyes.

I smiled. "We'll see what we can do to help you."

He pulled out a dozen pecan logs, closed his briefcase, stood, and, unlike most people, extended his left hand.

I shook it.

"Thank you, senator," he said. He looked at his watch. "I believe that only took seven minutes?"

I smiled.

He left.

"Sylvia, before I gain fifteen pounds, would you get rid of all this candy?"

"You like fat administrative assistants?"

A voice came at us from the doorway. "I'll take one."

Sylvia and I looked up to see Harriet Wong standing in the entrance to my office. I don't know much about women's dress sizes, but she had a tiny waist, narrow hips, and I guessed she shopped the petite racks.

"I hate people with high metabolism," Sylvia muttered.

I thought she was kidding, but I wasn't sure.

She looked at her watch. "Don't forget your meeting at nine o'clock." Then she gathered up all the pecan samples but one, and left, closing the door behind her.

"Coffee?" I looked at my watch. "We have about twenty minutes."

Harriet shook her head. "We need to take care of business." She plopped a massive copy on my desk. "SB107, not today's example of brevity."

"I've only read the first hundred pages," I said.

"That's okay," she answered. "You haven't missed anything, and I've more or less plowed through the entire tome."

I looked again at the title and read it aloud. "SB107: West Texas Investment Incentive for Economic Development and Quality of Life Enhancement."

"That's Texas political-speak for BS."

"Yeah, I thought it was bullshit when I tried to read it."

"Sam, I can't figure out why you're co-authoring."

"Because Whiskey asked me."

"Why is he messing with this?"

"Damned if I know," I said. "I guess it's somewhat like the Cheeseburger Resolution. We do it to win favor with a certain constituency."

She shook her head. "That was a resolution. Even when passed it was 100 percent BS. This is a bill. When passed it becomes law."

I looked at my watch. "We don't have time to talk about it this morning. Where's the bill stand?"

"It's been voted out of committee. It now needs twenty-one votes, out of the thirty-one senators, to reach the floor."

"And if it doesn't muster the twenty-one votes?"

"That's the end of it. It dies."

"And who cares?" I asked.

"Sam, I've only been on this job a week. But so far, I haven't found anyone."

I smiled and thought for a moment about whether or not to offer my opinion. I caved. Nothing wrong with expressing the truth.

"Except the lieutenant governor," I said.

59

The next morning, Denny's Restaurant on I-35

I have a morning routine of rising early, driving to Denny's, and reading the *Austin American-Statesman* with breakfast. With a forkful of pancakes poised momentarily on the way to their target, I felt my stomach tighten as I read the headline.

AUTHORITIES PROBE REPORTER'S DEATH

That was when I decided to change my routine. At the very least, I vowed to switch my breakfast reading to other newspapers. Obviously I needed the *New York Times*, *USA Today*, or some other publication to get me away from the *Statesman's* angry reporting of Consuelo Hernandez's death. I saw the local newspaper's day-after-day headlines as a blatant attempt to woo readers to their bias—a slanted view of local law enforcement failure. It infuriated me. Even Betty, the waitress, reacted to my foul mood.

"You okay?" she asked.

"I'm fine," I replied.

"You've barely touched your breakfast."

"The food is fine."

"Coffee?" She gestured with the carafe.

I handed her my cup, which was full. "I'm afraid I've let it get cold."

"That I can fix." She took my coffee, returned a few seconds later with hot moisture visibly steaming from the cup.

I forced a smile. "Thanks."

"See, you look better already."

I folded the newspaper and shoved it to the far corner of the table. When even the waitress recognized how the *Statesman* affected me, it was time for a change.

I ate about half on my breakfast, walked to the cashier's station, and had just finished paying when Texas Ranger Charles Fuller came into the restaurant.

"I need to talk with you," he said.

I looked back at the corner to see that Betty was clearing my old booth. "Follow me," I said.

Betty looked surprised. Not many customers return so soon. "Two coffees, please."

Charlie and I sat. "How'd you find me?" I asked.

"Sylvia was at the office. She thought you'd be here."

Betty brought our coffee.

"What's happening?" I asked.

"Have you read the headline story in this morning's *Statesman*?

I bit my tongue and mentally promised not to let my anger show. "Half of it," I said, "Enough to get the gist of the newspaper's editorial bias."

"They're breathing down my neck."

"Last time you and I talked, I think you characterized their reporting as 'trying to sell newspapers'."

"That was then. Now I think they may be on to something."

"Really?"

"There's new evidence that suggests foul play."

"What can you share with me?"

Betty came with the coffee pot. "Warm-up?"

Charlie held out his cup. "Yes, please."

I shook my head. "I'm fine."

Betty left.

I looked at Charlie, expecting him to answer my question.

He lowered his head and spoke in a whisper. "Sam, I want to tell you everything I know about Hernandez's death, but . . ." He stopped, sipped his coffee.

"That's okay. I understand."

"No. I don't think you do." He paused. "You're a suspect."

I chuckled. "What else is new?"

He set his cup down and leaned forward in his chair. "The *leading* suspect."

I laughed. "Here we go again . . . shades of Abner Stone."

Charlie reacted. He shifted his 300 pounds, and a scowl came over his face. "This ain't funny. Last night the DA's office talked about arresting you."

"Why don't they?"

"For one thing, I told them they didn't have enough evidence."

"Thanks."

Charlie picked up his cup, slumped back against the booth, and sipped his coffee. Then he held the cup close to his lips and stared at me.

I stared back.

He lowered his cup. "I shouldn't be here. When word gets out that I've told you this, I'll probably lose my job."

"Nobody's gonna hear it from me."

"Somehow, it'll get out. It always does."

"Okay, let's cut to the chase. Why *did* you come?"

He set his cup on the table in front of him. "You said it yourself. It's like the Abner Stone scenario. Last summer when Consuelo Hernandez pushed to have you indicted . . ."

"And the Midland County Sheriff had his handcuffs ready?"

"I thought they didn't have a case. Still don't."

"Yet you haven't charged anyone."

"Yeah. That's what the captain keeps telling me."

"Back to Hernandez. Can you tell me about your new evidence? What changed your mind from suicide to murder?"

"The autopsy found traces of Rohypnol."

"What's that?"

"The street name is roofie. Sometimes people refer to it as Roche, the name of a Mexican pharmaceutical company that manufactures it. When you see the pill, it often has Roche printed on it."

"So?"

"So roofie is the most powerful of the date-rape drugs. If you combine it with cocaine, it kills you."

"When Austin PD found the body, they ruled it as a drug overdose—a suicide?" I asked.

"Yep."

"But then the autopsy showed traces of roofie, and they called it murder?"

"You got it."

"Looks like someone gave her the roofie first, then gave her the injection of cocaine, trying to make it look like a drug overdose—a suicide."

"That's the scenario as we see it."

"That was dumb."

Charlie smiled for the first time. "One of the reasons I'm convinced it wasn't you."

60

At home in Midland

There's no place like home. Nothing beats the sounds, sights, and interaction of family— the sense of things familiar.

And sex.

I don't know if it was Suzie or me. Maybe both. But returning home after a four-day absence triggered a new passion in our marriage. On Thursday night I forgot about Austin, about legislative issues, about everything associated with Senate District Thirty-One, and concentrated on making love to my wife.

Life was good.

Until, at the breakfast table, I read the Friday morning headline in *The Midland Telegraph Reporter.*

REPORTER'S DEATH
REVIVES INVESTIGATION

I read the first couple of paragraphs, enough to learn that Consuelo Hernandez's death had caused the Midland County Sheriff's Office to reopen the Abner Stone case. Much of the story repeated—almost word for word—what I had been reading in the *Austin American-Statesman* the past couple of days.

"Daddy, can we practice barrel racing after school?" Emily asked.

"I asked him last night," Tim said. "He's too busy."

"How about Saturday or Sunday?"

"Saturday I have scouts. Sunday he flies back to Austin."

"Daddy, on Saturday could Tim go to scouts and you help me with barrel racing?"

"No," Tim said, before I could answer. "You know the horses don't like it when only one of us rides."

"Sometimes you go when I don't."

"No," Tim said, louder. "That's not true."

"Last summer," Emily yelled, "when I twisted my ankle."

Suzie's voice cut in. "Okay, you two. That's enough."

"He always gets his way." In a fit of temper, Emily threw her spoon down, hard. It bounced and landed in her cereal bowl. Milk and cereal splashed out on the table.

Suzie stood. "I said, that's enough." She reached for a dishcloth.

I folded my newspaper and laid it on the table, away from the mess. "Emily, in the Davis family, we don't throw things when we get mad."

"But he always gets his way."

"Not so," Tim said.

"Tim," I said. "Why don't you go brush your teeth?"

"She acts like this is my fault."

"Please." I nodded with my head toward the hallway.

He jutted out his lower jaw but made no move to leave.

"Go." This time I said it like a command.

He picked up his dishes, loaded them into the dishwasher, and sulked off toward his room.

Suzie handed the dishtowel to Emily.

Emily put her dishes in the dishwasher, came back and wiped up the mess. A tear rolled down her cheek.

"Good job," Suzie said. She took the towel and held out her arms. "Hug?"

Mother and daughter embraced.

I stood and held out my arms. "Me, too?"

Emily and I hugged. She left to brush her teeth and get ready for school.

"I think I'd better leave the office early this afternoon," I said. "Can you make arrangements for us to take the kids barrel racing?"

"And go for pizza afterward?"

"You bet."

When Suzie told the kids, she made it sound like I was a hero.

We got the kids off to school. As soon as they were out the door, Suzie came on to me. "I've really missed you this week."

We kissed. She unzipped my fly and in seconds had me fully aroused. By the time we made it back to the bedroom, our clothes were strewn from one end of the house to the other.

At the office two hours later, Mrs. Hughes gave me attitude. "It's almost ten o'clock," she said with a scowl as she handed me a stack of pink slips—telephone calls she had taken because I was late to work.

Some days you just don't have to please everybody.

61

Monday morning, Austin, breakfast at Denny's

The weekend at home recharged my batteries. Friday had been a day to remember. I got a ton of work done at the office. Barrel racing at Art's stable brought the family together. And pizza on a cold January night topped off a perfect day. Even our seven-year-old and ten-year-old laughed at their differences and acted like best of friends.

Saturday I took Tim to his Boy Scout Bivouac. Troop 148 won the camping skills contest, and his Beaver Patrol led the way with a first place in campfire building.

Sunday was our first time to attend church together since Christmas. After the service we joined three other families for dinner at Furr's Cafeteria. When Suzie and the kids dropped me off at the Midland airport, I felt ready for battle in the Texas State Senate.

Then, alone at my usual Monday morning breakfast, I wasn't so sure. Like an ostrich, I figuratively buried my head in the sand and chose to

242

avoid an unpleasant situation by refusing to acknowledge that it existed. Instead of reading about the Hernandez investigation in the *Austin American-Statesman*, I studied the nation's economic woes in the *Wall Street Journal*.

Until I got to the office.

I arrived at my usual seven o'clock to find Sylvia already there.

"You bucking for a raise?" I asked. I thought she might smile at my question. We both knew—with this year's tight budget—staff salaries were frozen.

"Not exactly," she replied, her face taut with a look of worry.

"What's up?"

"You read the headline in this morning's *Statesman*?"

My turn to smile. "I've decided to get my news from other newspapers."

Sylvia shook her head, and her look of worry deepened into an angry scowl. "Sam, I think they're coming to arrest you this morning."

"Who is?"

"Austin PD," she said. "And probably the Texas Rangers."

"You're telling me this was in the paper?"

"Not you by name, but—"

The door opened, and three men came into the office—Charles Fuller led two others who wore Austin Police uniforms.

"Senator Davis," Charlie said. "We'd like you to come with us."

"Sure," I said. "But may I ask a question?"

Fuller looked at the cops. One of them nodded.

"What's the question?"

"Am I under arrest?"

"We've contacted the district judge, and he's agreed to issue a warrant." He held up a cell phone. "I can have the warrant here in ten

243

minutes, but I was hoping you'd come voluntarily."

"And the warrant is for—"

"For the murder of Consuelo Hernandez."

I turned to Sylvia. "Call Art McComas."

She picked up her phone.

I shuddered. The involuntary muscle spasm rippled down my spine, and, for a moment, I felt paralyzed with fear. I decided to put up a front. With false bravado, I turned to Charlie and held out my wrists. "Handcuffs?"

"Sam, don't make this worse than it is," Charlie said. "If you're coming with us voluntarily, you're not under arrest. No cuffs."

Working to maintain my false front, I chuckled. "Lead on."

The tall policeman reacted. "This is no joke, sir." He moved in front of the door. "Fuller, you're making a mistake. We should read him his rights and slap the cuffs on him."

"He's a state senator," Charlie replied. "Trust me. When you get back to headquarters, you'll be glad you let the brass take the heat."

"This SOB's a smart aleck. He's making fun of the law."

"He's a *senator*. He writes the law. He's a political hot potato, and if you're not careful you're gonna get burned."

"He killed that reporter, and now he's laughing about it."

I held up my good hand, a gesture asking for a pause. "Lieutenant Fuller, I apologize for that quip, and I promise, no more levity."

"Levity?" the policeman snarled. "See, he's using big words as an insult. A put-down to us, to this arrest, and to police procedure."

"Officer, I didn't mean any disrespect. And I promise not to say anything more."

"Let's go," Fuller said. He grabbed my arm and pulled me toward the door.

PUPPET POLITICS

The other policeman held the door open.

Fuller led me down the hallway.

The tall, angry officer followed.

Thirty minutes later they led me into an interrogation room at Austin Police Headquarters.

This was no joke.

62

Interrogation Room #2 reminded me of the set for a TV detective show. Small, gray, and plain—very plain—this drab little room with a big mirror at one end barely had space for a table and four chairs.

Charlie introduced Eduardo Rodriquez, head of Austin PD homicide, and Norman Peters, Travis County District Attorney. Charlie and I sat side-by-side facing Rodriquez and Peters. I guessed there were two reasons for the seating arrangement. First, they wanted Charlie to sit by me, a token person who was on my side. Second, they wanted Peters to face me because, as I soon learned, he was the designated questioner.

"Senator, thank you for coming in voluntarily," Peters said.

I nodded. In truth I didn't feel I had a choice. But I didn't voice my opinion.

"I'm sure we all agree on the purpose of this meeting," Peters continued.

As he uttered those words, my brain flashed an answer to me

246

silently—*to nail Sam Davis for the murder of Consuelo Hernandez.*

Peters had a different answer, and he announced it with a loud flourish. "We're after the truth." He looked at me. "Don't you agree?"

"Of course," I said.

Peters shifted his gaze to Charlie.

"Yes," Charlie replied.

"Absolutely," Rodriquez said.

"Each of us knew Consuelo Hernandez in a different way. It seems obvious that by sharing our knowledge—by a full, open exchange of information—we can arrive at the truth and bring to justice those responsible for her death." Norman Peters paused.

I waited.

"Don't you agree?" he asked.

"Yes, full, open information," I said.

"Everything," Charlie said.

"Absolutely," Rodriquez said.

"We're not trying to convict a particular person. We're looking for the truth."

In a way, Norman Peters reminded me of Colombo, the mumbling, bumbling character played by Peter Falk. Since neither Charles Fuller nor Ed Rodriquez were suspects, his repetitious, muddled questioning appeared to be for my benefit. I decided to speak out.

"I think we're all in agreement about seeking truth," I said.

"Thank you, Senator. Uh, it's an established fact that the murder took place last Tuesday evening, January 12. Would you mind telling us where you were between seven and ten o'clock on that date?"

I thought about it before answering. Mentally, I worked through the exact details before speaking.

"Last Tuesday?" Peters prompted, his voice sharp.

"Last Tuesday," I said, speaking slowly and with exaggerated diction, "was the swearing-in ceremony for newly elected legislators. That evening my wife and I were dinner guests of Lieutenant Governor Homer Williams. He sent a limo to pick us up at seven o'clock at the Omni Hotel. Dinner was at the Texas Land and Cattle Restaurant out on North Highway 183. We got back to the hotel a little after ten."

"You remember the name of the limo service?"

"No, but you can ask Lieutenant Governor Williams. I'm sure he or his staff can give you that information."

I noticed Ed Rodriquez carefully taking notes. It seemed obvious that he would be checking both the limo service and the restaurant to confirm the credibility of my alibi for last Tuesday evening.

"Senator Davis." Peters lowered his voice to indicate a change in the mood of his questions. "Do you remember, as a child, having Thanksgiving dinner at your grandmother's?"

The question confused me for a moment, and I thought, *what does this have to do with the murder of Consuelo Hernandez?* "Yes," I said.

"Do you remember how the pumpkin pie smelled?"

"Sure."

"Describe it to me."

"Uh, may I ask a question?"

"Of course."

"What does the aroma of pumpkin pie have to do with your investigation into the death of Consuelo Hernandez?"

Charlie Fuller laughed.

Norman Peters gave him a sharp look. And for a moment, Peters lost his composure.

"Sorry," Charlie said. "It just slipped out."

I looked at Eduardo Rodriquez, expecting him to say *absolutely*. But

248

he didn't. Instead he looked away, and I thought he snickered.

Peters struggled to regain his equanimity, took a big breath, and spoke in a louder voice. "Sir, are you right-handed or left-handed?"

The sudden increase in volume startled Fuller and Rodriquez, and they flinched. It was as though Colombo had transformed himself into a Gestapo interrogator.

Peters's switch also caused me to react. Only I didn't flinch . . . I got mad. Inside me a voice said *that's enough.*

"Left," I said. And I held up my right hand. "As you can see, I have to work around this."

Human reaction to deformity is universal. We expect ten fingers, ten toes, and perfection in their size, shape and color—in the limbs as well as all parts of the body. We abhor even a minor, temporary disfigurement, such as a mashed fingernail turned black or a fever blister on the face. I learned in the first grade that my misshapen hand evoked discomfort in those who viewed it, and, for that reason, I kept it mostly hidden. But now, for the first time in my life, I capitalized on its shock value, and I literally stuck it in Peters's face.

Peters reacted. The sight of my deformity caused him to move back in his chair, away from the table. It wasn't revulsion exactly, but I could see in his facial expression a look of distaste—he was momentarily at a loss for words.

I took advantage of the moment.

"Gentlemen, I have a big day today at my senate office."

The mood of the meeting shifted.

I stood.

"Charlie, could you arrange a ride for me back to the Capitol?"

The other three stood.

Peters made one last attempt. "Senator, I'm not finished. I have additional questions."

I stepped away from the table, toward the door. "Fine. Send them in writing to my attorney, Arthur McComas."

I opened the door and walked out of the room.

Charlie followed.

63

In Charles Fuller's car, driving back to the Texas Capitol

"What was all that horseshit about my grandmother's pumpkin pie?" I asked.

"It's an interrogation technique," Charlie replied. "Peters wanted to see which direction you'd look away after a sensory question."

"Look away?"

"In an interrogation, most people pause for a moment after a question," Charlie said. "And before they speak their eyes dart away from the interrogator."

"So?"

"So it has to do with the right or left hemisphere of the brain. In a right-handed person, the left hemisphere controls the senses. When asked a question that requires a sensory response, like the aroma of a pumpkin pie at Thanksgiving dinner, the responder's eyes will dart to the left as the brain describes the delicious smell."

"What if the eyes dart to the right?"

"In all probability the person is thinking. Thinking or scheming about something. Like, how can I lie about my answer?"

"And that's why Peters wanted to know if I was right or left handed?"

Charlie nodded. "It's the same principle as a lie detector test."

"Hell, if you guys wanted me to take a lie detector test, why didn't you just ask?'

"Would you?"

"Of course," I said. "I've got nothing to hide."

Charlie lapsed into a prolonged silence.

I let him think.

We pulled to a stop near the capitol, and he turned to me with a serious look. "I'm assuming your alibi for that Tuesday night is rock solid."

"Damn right."

"So the next question is, did you hire someone to kill the reporter?"

"Same as the Abner Stone question?"

"Pardon?"

"That's where you and the Midland County Sheriff hit a dead end. You both knew my alibi for the oil well fire—the one that killed Stone—was airtight. The sheriff tried for months to find the arsonists, and, more importantly, to find a link to me. Finally, after a year, he gave up."

Charlie smiled. It was a benign smile, one that says *I know something you don't.*

"What?"

"He hasn't given up, Sam. He's still looking."

"Goddamn it, Charlie, how long is this going to continue?"

"There is no statute of limitations on murder."

"You mean this is a shadow that's going to hang over me forever?"

"Well, you could help us end it."

"How?"

"Two things. Help us find the bad guys, the perps who killed Stone and Hernandez."

"I'd like nothing better," I said. "Somehow, this has to end. But you said two things."

"And who hired the killers."

"Hired killers?"

"I'll stake my reputation on it," Charlie said. "It's the only way to explain the connection when we rule out Sam Davis as the perpetrator."

I lifted my hand off the car's door handle. Thoughts raced through my brain a mile a minute. Of the thousand or more that muddled my thinking, one stood out. I turned to Charlie, and our eyes locked.

"There's never been anything mentioned about hired killers."

He stared right back. "You'll never know how hard it's been to keep it out of the news."

I looked away and shook my head. "You want me to believe it's the *only* explanation, yet you won't tell anyone?"

"Abner Stone was a difficult, high-profile murder," Charlie said. "And now it's grown into a double homicide case. Whoever's behind this is a strongly motivated, ruthless criminal. Our best chance to break the case is to lull that bastard into thinking we've zeroed in on Sam Davis, that we've never even considered hired killers."

"Lucky me."

"Hey, you've got big shoulders." He chuckled. "I remember the TV series in the week before the primary election—the minister, the PTA president, and the scoutmaster."

I laughed with him. "Everyone said it was Gretel, our dachshund, and the vet. Those two convinced the voters I was innocent."

"You won the election."

"Correction, it got me into the runoff."

"Sam, the bottom line is—" He paused, exhaled a heavy breath . . . a sigh of exasperation.

"Is what?"

"Is that we've been working damn hard on this case for almost a year. Only a tiny handful of law enforcement officers are privy to the theory of hired killers. Even Norman Peters doesn't know."

"You can count on me." I pulled a make-believe zipper across my lips.

"Won't be much longer," he said. "I think the Hernandez murder will eventually break the case."

I opened the door and stepped out. "God, I hope so."

64

My office in the Texas State Capitol

"What happened?" Sylvia asked.

"Nothing," I said. "Everything's fine."

She frowned and gave me a look of displeasure. It was an expression I'd not seen before on the face of my always-genial chief of staff. "That tells me so much," she said.

"Hey, everything's okay. You asked how it went. It went fine."

"Headline story in the morning paper all but accuses you of murder. Police haul you off for questioning, and you give me a one-word answer. There must be more to it than just *fine*."

I paused to consider her words.

"Sam, I'm on your side." Her voice took a lower tone, one that reminded me of my mother. "But if I'm going to be effective as your chief of staff, there has to be totally open communication."

"Sylvia, I'll tell you everything. What d'you want to know?"

"How about some details?"

255

"Sure. But let's do it over a cup of coffee." I went into my office and poured two scoops into the coffeemaker.

Sylvia followed me in with her steno pad. "And I have a message from Arthur McComas."

"Good," I said. "What does Art have to say?"

I pushed the button to start the coffeemaker, and a whiff of Colombian Dark floated out into the room.

"He said under absolutely no circumstance should you go for questioning without a lawyer. And he gave me the name of Austin's top criminal law firm."

I chuckled. "Little late for that now."

She handed me a slip with the name and phone number of Art's recommendation. "He was very insistent that you do this."

"Thanks," I said. "I'll certainly consider his recommendation."

She shook her head and heaved a big sigh. "You going to tell me about the interrogation?"

I gave her a five-minute summary. Just as I described the end of Peters's questioning and my exit with Charlie, the coffeemaker gurgled and fell silent. I pulled the glass pot and filled two cups.

We each sipped our coffee in a moment of quiet meditation.

Finally I broke the silence. "High finance, I'll give you a penny for—"

She shook her head and said, "My thoughts aren't worth that much."

"Okay. Then for free, tell me what you're thinking."

"I'm thinking Austin PD is going to get that warrant and arrest you. And you'd better get busy and lawyer-up."

"Maybe, maybe not."

"Sam!"

"Think about it," I said. "Why didn't they get their warrant this morning and arrest me?"

She looked away for a second and then asked, "The newspaper story said they've established the time of death as last Tuesday evening—is that right?"

"Yes."

"Hey. I know where you were Tuesday evening."

I smiled.

"You have an airtight alibi."

My grin went ear to ear. I nodded my head for a moment and then let my grin fade into a sip of coffee.

She eased back into her chair and lifted her cup to her lips. A moment later, she finished her coffee, set the empty cup on the desk in front of her, and pulled out her steno pad. "Ready to go over the schedule for today?"

I set my cup by hers. "Go."

"Your committee on equine standards is meeting at ten in room 20E20, the Betty King Conference Room." She handed me a file folder. "Should be a short meeting. You're asking for suggestions for changes before next week's committee vote."

I nodded.

"At two o'clock Harriet's going with you to the meeting on SB 107. The senate vote is slated for February 4. You know you need twenty-one votes to move it out of committee."

"How many votes do we now have?"

"Counting you, Harriet says you have only five."

"Wow. Where're we going to get sixteen votes?"

"That's what the meeting at two o'clock is all about—rounding up votes."

"Who's going to be there?"

"We think there will be eleven people. You and Harriet, the other four senators who are supporting the bill, along with their aides—that's a total of ten."

"You said eleven."

"And the lieutenant governor."

I let the impact of her words linger for a moment, and then I reached for the coffee pot. "Second cup?"

She stood. "No, thanks. Now that your arrest is no longer imminent, I've got to get back to legislation." She gathered the empty coffee cups and turned to leave.

I thought about sharing Charles Fuller's information about hired killers. I trusted Sylvia. And she'd just given me the lecture about no secrets. She opened the door.

"Sylvia, wait."

She stopped.

"Better close the door," I said.

She did and turned to face me, her face blank, but with an unmistakable air of expectation.

"Charles Fuller is trying to help me. He told me some confidential information—the reason he's taking my name off the suspect list."

"So—"

"So, I gave my word to Charlie. I promised not to share his data with anyone.

"I understand," she said.

"I'm not sure you do," I replied. "I can't break my word. And another thing, it would probably destroy my relationship with him."

"Sam." She gave me *the look*. It was the same look my mother used to give me when she wanted me to shut up. "I understand."

Sylvia left and closed the door.

65

The Texas State Capitol

Sylvia was right. The ten o'clock meeting on equine standards passed without so much as a question. Even committee members from Dallas and Houston love horses.

Lunch was an apple and a cup of coffee in my office.

At two o'clock, ten people—Harriet and I, the other four senators who were members of the committee and their legislative aides—assembled in room 20E20, the Betty King Room, to discuss SB 107. In the first order of business, the others chose me as chairman pro tem. Railroaded was more apt than elected. I didn't want the responsibility.

"Whiskey reminded us that you're the senator for West Texas," one of the others proclaimed. "He said you should be the point man."

The vote was unanimous.

I called on Harriet for a status report.

"I've polled the chief of staff for every senator," she said. "The votes simply aren't there."

"What do they have against it?" I asked.

"Nothing," she said. "But they don't have any reason to support it either."

"We're scheduled for a vote next week. How many votes do we have?"

"Just the five of you."

The door opened, and Whiskey burst into the room. Everyone stood to shake his hand. I was last. He took my left with his right, smoothly, with a practiced familiarity.

We sat.

"I have some good news," Whiskey said.

He passed out copies of a single sheet of paper.

"Looks like we now have the twenty-one votes."

I scanned the sheet to see the names of senators. He listed my name at the top, followed by the other four seated in the room. Then, in alphabetical order, came sixteen more names.

An emotional silence fell over the room. No one said anything, but I sensed a tangible feeling of awe that pervaded the meeting. We had just been hit with political power, and everyone knew it. Our consensus of failure now reversed itself in the form of a piece of paper with twenty-one names.

Harriet broke the silence. "Uh, Governor, I just completed a survey. The sixteen new names you have listed . . . when I contacted their offices, all gave me a negative response."

Whiskey smiled. "When did you talk to them?"

"I didn't speak with any senators. But I did go to each office and personally visit with the chief of staff for each of these names within the past week."

"I called them this morning," Whiskey said, his smile broadening. "I guess they all changed their minds."

It wasn't funny, but everyone in the room joined him in a brief moment of amusement.

"Maybe we'd better call for a vote tomorrow before they change their minds . . . again," I said.

Everyone laughed, this time a much more robust round of mirth.

"Any more questions?" he asked.

No one spoke. Harriet shook her head.

Whiskey stood. "Thanks. I know the people in West Texas will be appreciative of your good work."

Again, we all stood for a handshake.

We took our seats.

"Meeting adjourned," I said.

Everyone started filing out of the room.

Harriet and I were the last to leave. We headed back to my office, together.

"I thought 107 was a dead duck," she said.

"You'll get all the credit," she said.

"Hey, I didn't do anything."

"Yeah, but your name's on it. You're the senator from West Texas. And today they elected you as their leader."

"Yuck, I don't deserve this."

"Hey, you're the senator who gets things done."

"Hey," I said. "I'm just a lowly freshman senator who hasn't authored a single piece of legislation."

She smiled, a gesture that mocked my self-deprecating statement. "Sam, in case you haven't noticed, SB 107 is the biggest, thickest, most wordy piece of legislation to come before this session."

I shook my head as we entered the office.

"And it has your name on it."

I wanted to protest.

Sylvia spoke up. "Whiskey called and wants you to go to Friona with him." She handed me a pink slip.

I read the message. "Friona, Saturday, April 18."

"What is this?" I asked.

"The Cheeseburger Festival," Sylvia replied. "He'll fly to Midland and pick you up."

I shook my head.

"After the senate passes the resolution naming Friona as the 'Cheeseburger Capitol of Texas,' he wants the two of you to fly there and deliver the resolution in person."

"Why me?"

"It's your district."

"So?"

"So he's had you named as author of the resolution."

For the next moment, I stood there trying to think of the implications. Sylvia spelled it out for me.

"And now it's listed as your bill," she said. "You're the man of the hour—a hero to all the folks in Friona."

66

"Call Whiskey, and tell him I'll go," I said.

"Already did," Sylvia replied.

I pulled out my smart phone and found that the third Saturday in April was the eighteenth. I typed in "Cheeseburger Festival-Friona." Then I took a minute to look over the calendar—January to April, over ninety days—it seemed like forever. I shelved any more thoughts about a trip to a small town in the Texas Panhandle.

But with my hectic schedule—of living in Midland and working in Austin—the weeks zipped by. Endless committee meetings, legislative hearings, delegations from the Permian Basin, delegations from the Texas Panhandle, and delegations from special interest groups . . . it seemed that each of the 500,000 citizens in the Thirty-First District wanted the special attention of their senator.

Of me.

The worst were the telephone messages, memos that Sylvia kept piling on my desk. Little three-inch square pink slips that wanted—demanded was more like it—a return call or some action on their behalf.

Some were reminders.

And it came as a shock when, one morning in mid-April, I read a pink slip *reminding* me that Whiskey would pick me up at the Midland Airport on the following Saturday morning at nine-thirty to fly me to the Friona Cheeseburger Festival. I had forgotten all about it. But when I opened my cellphone and looked up the date, April 18, there it was. Along with a note to bring the official resolution. I sent an e-mail to the lieutenant governor's office confirming that I'd meet him as planned.

Whiskey's sleek little Lear Jet made the trip from Midland to Friona in less than thirty minutes. The mayor of Friona and the executive director of the chamber of commerce met our plane and drove us into the city. Good thing. Parking was non-existent.

"What's the population of Friona?" Whiskey asked.

"Census reported 3,854 last count," the mayor replied.

We passed cars parked outside the city limits on Highway 60.

"How many do you expect for today's event?"

"Last year we had 6,000 visitors. Probably more this year."

I wondered how many cities could boast a tourist event that tripled the size of their population.

Traffic slowed to a crawl, but the mayor waved at a policeman who moved a barricade and allowed us to drive down an alley and park behind city hall. We walked a short distance to Friona City Park where the aroma of hamburgers cooking on charcoal grills filled the air. The park was beautiful, about the size of a football field, professionally landscaped, and with an old Santa Fe Depot in the center. The crowd milled, elbow-to-elbow, thousands of people jammed into an area filled with hundreds of card tables and chairs.

PUPPET POLITICS

"The Festival is a contest to see who can come up with the most delicious cheeseburger," the chamber director said.

"Smells wonderful," Whiskey said. "Explain your contest."

"We limit it to twenty teams." She pointed to a nearby tent with a sign, Team #1, First National Bank.

We walked along the east side of the park, where we found a row of tent tops, each about fifteen by fifteen, each with a charcoal grill and a crew of people busy cooking. The next tent's sign read, "Team #2, First Baptist Church." Smoke from their charcoal grill wafted out toward me with a tantalizing smell of beef seasoning. I made my way from tent to tent, reading the signs.

Team #3, Hillmar Dairy

Team #4, First United Methodist Church of Friona

Team #5, Diamond Cattle Feeders

Team #6, Friona Tastee Freeze

Team #7, Panhandle Trucking Company

Team #8, Clovis VFW

I looked along the south side of the park to see another row of tent tops with similar operations.

"We have eight judges, and they're seated inside the old depot," the mayor said. "Each team submits two cheeseburgers. First they're judged on appearance, then they're quartered for tasting by the judges."

The chamber director looked at her watch. "The first burgers are sent for judging at 11:00. Then every five minutes another team submits. Takes an hour and forty minutes to run the contest. We'll announce the winners at one o'clock."

"Do we get to taste?" I asked.

"Of course." She handed each of us a red plastic wrist bracelet with four tabs that were perforated so that they could be easily removed.

265

"We'll have 8,000 or more samples to distribute. Each of those tabs will get you one-fourth of a cheeseburger."

A country western band started playing.

Whiskey and I mingled, picked up the first of our quarter-cheeseburger samples, and found an empty table. I had a Hawaiian burger made by the Tastee Freeze team #5. He had a Worcestershire burger made by the First Methodist team #4. We each sliced off a bite and exchanged samples—both were delicious. I could see that judges would have a near impossible task of choosing a winner.

Whiskey reveled in the opportunity to work the crowd. He didn't wait for them to come to him. He took the initiative, introducing himself and shaking hands. If there were 10,000 people at the festival, he was hell-bent on greeting every single one.

At first I tried to keep up, but with my problematic right hand, there was no way. So I tucked it inside my pocket and did the best I could with my left—slower progress, but a sincere effort.

At one o'clock we assembled at the speakers' stand for the awards ceremony. It was a politician's bonanza.

"We're mighty proud to have two of Texas's most famous leaders with us today," the mayor said, his voice booming out over the loud speakers. "Help me welcome Senator Sam Davis."

I've had big ovations before, but none as wild and enthusiastic as that one. And I knew that I was just the first in a long program, so in less than ninety seconds, I congratulated the City of Friona and twenty of the finest cooking teams in Texas for producing the best cheeseburgers in the world.

They gave me a cheeseburger-shaped lapel pin and thunderous applause.

When the mayor introduced the lieutenant governor, I thought the crowd might turn into a riot. The explosion of clapping and cheering surpassed anything I'd ever witnessed. Whiskey struggled to gain control. When he did, I handed him the resolution.

Watching Homer "Whiskey" Williams present the official document was like a short course in political science. He knew just the right words to use and how to frame them with elegance and brevity. For his close, he read from the resolution— "The Cheeseburger Capital of Texas."

I remembered the old saw K.I.S.S.—keep it short stupid.

Whiskey did.

And the ovation was memorable.

In the plane on the way home I thought about the title of Senate Bill 107—West Texas Investment Incentive for Economic Development and Quality of Life Enhancement.

"After we pass SB107, or at the end of the legislative session, what would you think about having a presentation in Midland?" I asked.

Whiskey looked at me with a sardonic smile, sipped his Scotch on the rocks, and said. "Damn, you're starting to think like a politician."

67

Suzanne quizzed me.

"You should have gone," I said.

"Just tell me. What did you do?" she asked.

"I watched Whiskey—master politician—work the crowd."

"Well, what did you expect?"

"I thought we'd eat cheeseburgers."

"You didn't?"

"Not much. I had one-fourth of one burger."

"What did you do with the rest of your day?" She looked at her watch. "You've been gone almost ten hours."

"Like I said, I watched the most powerful man in Texas politics demonstrate how he got to be that way."

"I'm all ears."

"He doesn't just sit at a table and eat cheeseburgers."

"So?"

"So he eats a sample, just enough to let the crowd see him participating."

"And?"

"And then he tries to shake 10,000 hands."

Suzie shook her head, as though she didn't believe me. "That's a lot of handshaking."

"Whiskey's aggressive," I said. "He doesn't wait for people to approach. He goes after them."

"And what did you do?"

"I tried to do the same," I said. "But I couldn't keep up."

"Did you work the crowd and shake a lot of hands?"

"You're looking at the champion lefty hand shaker of West Texas."

Suzie hugged me. "And I'll bet they remember you at election time."

I pulled away. "Hey, we had a one-term deal, remember?"

"You could always change your mind."

"No way. When these four years are over, I'm done."

She kissed me. A long, slow meeting of the lips, filled with passion, and—I thought—with hidden motives. She liked being a senator's wife.

We heard Tim and Emily come in the back door.

"Daddy's home," Suzie called out.

The kids rushed into the room, full of energy. "Did you bring us a cheeseburger?" Tim asked.

"As a matter of fact, I did." I held up a small, white Styrofoam box. "I only have one. We'll have to split it into fourths."

Suzie took it into the kitchen, opened the box, and placed the sandwich on a wooden cutting board.

"It's called a *Hawaiian Cheeseburger*," I said. "It was judged the first place winner."

"Hawaiian?" Emily made a face. "What's that?"

Never one to miss the opportunity for an opposing view, Tim jumped in. "Can I have her share?"

"*May* I have her share," his mother corrected.

"May I?" Tim responded.

"Wait a minute," Emily said. "I didn't say I didn't want it. I just asked a question."

"Okay, Dad," Suzie said. "Tell us about the fixings for a Hawaiian cheeseburger."

I lifted the top of the bun. "It has pineapple and guacamole. And it's basted with a sauce of teriyaki and brown sugar."

Emily frowned.

"I love teriyaki sauce," Tim said. "I'll take her share."

"No," Emily said. "I want it."

"How do you know?" Tim laughed. "You've never tasted teriyaki."

"Mama, make him quit making fun of me."

I decided to step in. "Okay, you two. Take your chairs at the table. Mama's going to serve us each one-fourth of the cheeseburger. You can taste it, see if you like it, and then either eat it or leave the table."

We each tasted our quarter sandwich.

A minute later, not a crumb remained.

The kids left to watch television.

"That was delicious," Suzie said.

"First prize," I said.

"Tell me more about Whiskey. What's it like to spend the day with him?"

"You should see him work the crowd. I've heard people in Austin say he outdoes Lyndon Johnson. He grabs your hand, pats you on the back, gives you this big smile, and feeds you a line that makes you feel like a million dollars."

"Folks in Friona loved him?"

"You should've heard the response when they introduced him at the awards ceremony."

"Did they introduce you?"

"Of course."

"And?"

"And what?"

"And did people clap for you?" Suzie asked.

"Yes, dear. I'm their senator."

"But not as much as they did for Whiskey?"

I stood, held out my arms. "How about a hug?"

She came into my arms. Then she kissed me. And we hugged again.

"Whiskey Williams doesn't get hugs and kisses like that," I said.

"Maybe I need to go with you the next time and see for myself who gets the biggest and best ovation?"

"I think the next one's going to be here in Midland."

She released me and stepped back. "A Cheeseburger Festival here in Midland?"

"No, silly," I said. "For SB107."

"What's that?"

I heaved a big sigh as I realized we'd never talked about it. "Senate Bill 107, West Texas Investment Incentive for Economic Development and Quality of Life Enhancement. We call it SB107 for short. I'm the author."

"You wrote the bill?"

"No, Whiskey wrote it," I said. "But he asked me to sign on as author, to work it through the senate. On the plane this evening, we talked about having a public ceremony here in Midland after we pass the bill. It would be like today's event in Friona."

"Tell me about your bill. What's in it?"

"For starters, it's thicker than the Houston phone book."

"Okay, just tell me the main points."

"Well, I've only read the first hundred pages. But I've assigned it to Harriet Wong, and she tells me it's like the Cheeseburger Resolution— it's a public relations document."

"You're the bill's author. It's your bill. And you haven't read it?"

68

Monday morning, my office in the Texas State Capitol

I poured coffee for Harriet Wong and for myself. A copy of Senate Bill 107 lay on my desk. She pulled another copy from her briefcase and plopped it down.

"I'm getting tired of lugging this around," she said. "I think it weighs twenty pounds."

"You've scheduled the second reading?" I asked.

"Yes, tomorrow morning," Harriet replied. "I checked with the secretary of the senate. It's first on the list."

"Is that good or bad?"

"Probably good news."

"Fill me in. Why is it good to be at the top of the list?"

"Well, you know it's required to have three readings of a bill."

I nodded. I'm new in the senate, but every senator expects to have a bill presented three times. "What's our schedule for 107?"

"The first reading was January 22, the day after the committee met

273

and Whiskey presented us with his bombshell—he had the twenty-one votes. You wanted to introduce the bill before anyone changed their mind."

"That was the first reading," I said. "It seems like ages ago."

"Yes," she said. "Tomorrow will be the second reading. And I hope it will slip through without much discussion. That's why it's good to go first."

"Do we have a date for the third and final reading?" I asked.

"Whiskey called me and suggested we schedule it for May 28."

I pulled out my calendar and looked up the date. "That's the last day of the legislative session."

"Yes, I know," Harriet said. "But that's the date he wanted, so I called the secretary of the senate and scheduled it."

"From the war stories I've heard, the last day is a scramble."

"Yep. Everyone knows that it's *sine die.* Any bill that doesn't get voted on dies."

I shook my head. "I guess I don't understand Whiskey's strategy. Why are we having the second reading tomorrow?"

"Could be he doesn't want any changes."

"So?"

"So on the third reading, senate rules require an 80 percent vote to make any changes in a bill," Harriet said. "In the four months I've been working here, I've found that it's almost impossible to get an 80 percent vote on anything."

"I'll bet it's an *absolute* impossibility to get 80 percent on the last day of the legislative session," I said.

Harriet nodded.

We paused, both of us thinking, looking down at the two huge copies.

Finally, I broke the silence with a question. "Have you heard of any changes from any of the other legislative aides?"

"No. I think they're like us—intimidated by the size of the document."

"Have you found anything I might want to change?"

She shook her head. "I've only scanned it, but I'm planning to spend every available minute between now and tomorrow morning studying it."

"Don't forget, we have that luncheon with the Panhandle Producers and Royalty Owners Association."

She looked at her cellphone. "Ouch, I'd forgotten about that. What time and where?"

"It's at the Hotel Omni, 12:00 noon. They've chartered an entire Boeing 737 from Southwest Airlines. I think that's 150 people."

With a look of distress, she entered a note in her smart phone.

"Harriet, I'd offer to cover for you, but most of their questions are about oil and gas legislation."

"I know. You need me."

"Could you prepare a legislative summary sheet to hand out at the meeting?"

She rolled her eyes, and a weary look came over her face. I read the expression as resignation—too much work. "Of course."

"And then, whatever time is left this afternoon . . ."

"And tonight."

"Hey, there's never enough time to study all the legislation," I said. "We both know that."

She picked up her copy of SB107, and then she dropped it. When it struck my desk, it hit with a loud, dull whack. "Especially a senate bill like this one, a tome that's filled with BS."

"And I'll try to give it a good read tonight," I said.

The phone rang. "The lieutenant governor's on line two," Sylvia said.

HARRY HAINES

I punched the button. "Good morning, Sir."

"Good morning, Senator. Just wanted to touch base with you about the PPROA."

I thought hard, trying to remember the acronym. "Say again?"

"The Panhandle Producers and Royalty Owners Association. Today's luncheon at the Omni."

Duh. I kicked myself, mentally. "Sure. I'll be there with bells on."

"I'd like you to give a brief endorsement for SB107. Tell everyone the second reading is tomorrow and that we expect it'll slide right through."

"Sure. That's exactly what's going to happen."

"Thanks, Sam. See you at noon."

"You bet."

After he hung up, I turned to Harriet. "Wonder why he's calling me? And why make such a fuss with oil and gas producers over SB107?"

She smiled. "Sam, it's like Friona and the cheeseburger resolution."

"How's that?"

She stood to leave and made a show of lugging the big heavy bill. "Everyone loves PR legislation when it's about themselves." She closed the door behind her.

And I started thinking, maybe we should have *two* rallies when we pass SB107—one in Midland and one in Amarillo.

69

In the Senate Chamber, The Texas State Capitol

The lieutenant governor rapped the gavel. "The Senate of the State of Texas will now come to order," he said. Homer "Whiskey" Williams rarely presided over the senate. In fact, other than the opening ceremonies in January, I couldn't remember any other time he'd taken the chair.

Flabbergasted, I looked around and counted only five other senators at their desks.

"This morning we'll start with Senate Bill 107," Whiskey said. "West Texas Investment Incentive for Economic Development and Quality of Life Enhancement."

Three more senators ambled in and took their places.

"Senator Davis, will you speak for SB107?"

"Yes, I will."

"This is the second reading for 107. Do you have any changes?"

An hour ago, Harriet met me and apologized for taking almost the entire day, yesterday, with the PPROA. Then last night her cat was ill. She had spent the evening at a veterinary hospital, leaving less than three hours to devote to SB107. Which was more than I'd done. Bottom line, neither of us had had time to thoroughly vet the enormous manuscript.

"No, sir, no changes to present at this time," I said.

"You realize the implications for second reading?"

"Yes, sir."

"And that for the third reading, it takes an 80 percent vote to make any changes."

"Yes, sir, I understand."

"Very well, you have five minutes."

"Mr. Lieutenant Governor, the bill speaks for itself. I yield such time as is requested by other senators to speak for, or to raise questions about, SB107."

Several more senators came in and sat at their desks. It appeared we had more than a quorum of sixteen.

"Any comments?" Whiskey asked.

He paused. There were none.

"Do I hear a motion that SB107 be approved for its second reading?"

"So move," I said.

"Second," someone said.

"All in favor say aye."

"Aye."

"Those opposed, say nay."

No one spoke.

Whiskey rapped his gavel. "The second reading is hereby approved."

A few moments passed while the president pro-tem of the senate conferred with the lieutenant governor. Whiskey handed him the gavel and left.

The president pro-tem took over. "We'll now take up agenda item number two. The secretary will read SB157."

"Senate Bill 157, The Crime Victims' Compensation Act."

Three more senators came in and took their places.

"Senator Jones, will you speak for SB157?"

"Yes, I will."

I left and met Harriet in the hallway.

"That was easy," she said.

"What do you make of Whiskey's appearance?" I asked.

"Hey, it's his bill. You and I both know he wrote it. Maybe he just wanted to be presiding in case something came up."

"Harriet, I have an uneasy feeling about 107."

"Me, too."

"And I have a special request."

"Yessir, boss." She clicked her heels.

I smiled at her military parody. "We can talk on the way." I started down the hall toward the office.

She walked beside me.

"I want you to find time between now and May 28 to study 107 thoroughly."

"Yes, sir."

"Before the third reading, if there's anything more than fluff in the bill, I want to know about it."

"I don't think there is."

We stopped, and I looked her in the eye. "Harriet, *think* doesn't cut it. I want you to go over the damned bill with a microscope. Read every word. Twice if you have to." I didn't mean it to sound like a reprimand. But she took it that way.

"You want someone else to take over?"

HARRY HAINES

"No, of course not."
I gestured toward the office and resumed walking.
She joined me.
"I'm just a little paranoid about this bill."
She smiled. "Obviously."

70

Monday morning, May 26, Denny's Restaurant on I-35

The last three days of the legislative session, I started the week with my usual routine of breakfast and a quick read of *USA Today*. Betty, the waitress, brought me coffee and asked, "Have you checked out the headline story in this morning's *Austin American-Statesman?* It's all about the Hernandez murder and a senator from West Texas."

"Really?"

"It doesn't mention you by name, but—"

"But you think they're accusing me?"

"You want to look at my copy?"

I didn't, but I was afraid not to. "Sure."

She handed me the newspaper. The headline ruined my appetite.

TWO MURDERS: NO ACTION AGAINST SENATOR

HARRY HAINES

The lead story carried a byline that I didn't recognize. Apparently the newspaper had a new investigative reporter who was hell-bent to make a name for himself by impugning an unnamed senator.

I read it carefully with an eye toward a possible lawsuit.

Apparently the newspaper's lawyers had done the same.

I'm a lawyer, and I think I have a good nose for libel. But this article was so skillfully written it didn't come close to mentioning me by name. However, the inference that a certain Texas state senator should be indicted for the murders of Abner Stone and Consuelo Hernandez came through loud and clear. The writer excoriated Austin PD and the Texas Rangers for their failure to arrest and file charges against their leading suspect. One paragraph in particular really bothered me.

> More than a year has now passed since The Texas Rangers changed the legal status of Abner Stone's death from accidental to murder. Consuelo Hernandez's death was changed to murder over a month ago. The leading suspect in both cases has been a state senator, and law enforcement has failed to act. With only three days left in this legislative session, this unnamed senator will be leaving Austin and the case could easily be forgotten. Does this mean a Texas state senator can use his office—to get away with murder?

I picked at my breakfast and marveled at the inflammatory article. Nothing piques reader interest like a scandal in government, especially one about murder. This one was twice as juicy because it had two. The likely increase in circulation must be in double digits.

I drove to the office with a heavy heart. Convicted in the court of public opinion, I didn't know what to do. My life as a small-town, relatively unknown lawyer had been much happier. The job of senator had brought nothing but grief and trouble. I wished it to end. One thing for sure, I would absolutely, positively, unconditionally refuse to run for reelection.

At the office I found Charlie Fuller waiting, his Texas Ranger uniform crisp and his Stetson neatly creased. I checked my watch—7:05 a.m.

"You're up early," I said as I unlocked the door and gestured for him to enter.

"You read this morning's *Statesman*?"

I nodded. "Unfortunately."

"I had a phone call at six o'clock this morning from the DA, Norman Peters. He asked me to set up another meeting with you."

I laughed. "You've become his appointments secretary?"

Charlie didn't respond to my attempt at humor. If anything, his facial expression became more tense. "Norman's in the hot seat. He's desperate for something to ease media pressure. If he interviews you, he can appear to be working the case."

"Or he could get a warrant for my arrest. That's what the *Statesman* wants."

"Norman's no dummy. He knows he could never win a conviction with flimsy circumstantial evidence."

"He should tell that to the newspaper."

"He has. Several times."

I thought back to a year ago, to the primary election, to a reporter named Hernandez and her attempts to *point the finger* at me for the murder of Abner Stone. It seemed ironic that the newspaper was now using her death in their renewed attempts to discredit me.

"Sam, I've taken your side in both the Stone and the Hernandez murders."

"Yes, and I appreciate your support."

"Now, as a person who believes in you and your innocence, I'm asking you to meet again with Peters and Rodriquez."

"Why?"

"Because I think we're close. And I think if we keep the publicity on you, we'll nail the killers and the one who hired them."

"What do you want me to do?"

"Meet with Peters, Rodriquez, and me. Make a statement."

"Okay, how about next week?"

He shook his head. "Too late. Has to be today. This must be seen as a response to the headline story in this morning's *Statesman*."

"Charlie, you don't know what you're asking. These are the last three days of the session. I don't have time for meetings."

"One hour. Sixty minutes to help me help you clear your name?"

I heaved a big breath. Shook my head. "What's the alternative?"

He leaned forward, his nose barely six inches from mine. His breath smelled like Coalgate toothpaste. "More articles like this morning's."

"Okay, how about two o'clock this afternoon, my office?"

He smiled. Clasped me on the shoulder. And left.

I called Arthur McComas at his home in Midland.

"Art, I need a lawyer."

71

Two o'clock, the Texas State Capitol Building

Five of us crowded around the table in my office. Art and I sat at one end. We were the good guys. The long arm of the law—Norman Peters, Travis County DA; Eduardo Rodriquez, head of homicide for Austin PD; and Lieutenant Charles Fuller, Texas Rangers CSI Lab chief—sat on the other three sides. While I knew Charlie was, ostensibly, on my side, there was no question about Peters and Rodriquez. They were adversaries looking for any possible slip, for the tiniest bit of evidence that could be used against me.

"Thanks for meeting with us," Peters said. He placed a small digital recorder in the center of the table. "Okay if we record this?"

Art placed a similar recorder beside Peters's. "And we'll do the same."

The two electronic devices loomed like a line in the sand—physical symbols of the enormous chasm that separated us. I began to have second thoughts about the meeting. Why had I agreed to meet with these guys?

The next hour proceeded like a fencing match. Peters would ask a

285

question—a thrust. Art would set parameters for my answer—a parry. The DA attempted to commit me to incriminating facts about the deaths of Abner Stone and Consuelo Hernandez. Art advised me on how to respond to the question with nebulous words that danced around the query without actually answering it.

Charlie nodded his approval at every question, then sat impassively as I rattled on with my obfuscating responses.

After an hour of cat and mouse, I looked at my watch and decided to end it. "The legislative session ends tomorrow. People are waiting on me." I stood.

Charlie also rose, and for the first time he spoke. "Senator, we appreciate your time. Thank you for making yourself available."

The others stood, Peters and Rodriquez obviously unhappy to end the meeting. But we exchanged handshakes and parting remarks.

Peters, Rodriquez, and Fuller left.

"Whew," I said. "Thank God that's over."

"You did good," Art said. He started packing his things.

"Thanks for coming," I said. "I really appreciate your help today."

His smile grew larger. "You owe me a steak."

"Sure. And one for Linda, too."

"Fourth of July, in your backyard. We'll watch the fireworks."

"You're on."

Art left.

I asked Sylvia to come in and go over pending legislation. We went down the list and let the answering machine take calls. With only two days left, I wanted to be sure I didn't miss any of my legislative promises.

Five o'clock came and went. The phone quit ringing. We plowed on through the long list of bills that I would have to debate and vote on.

Another hour went by.

286

Then the phone rang, the first and only call since 5:00. Sylvia rose to answer it. "Let the answering machine take it," I said. "I really don't want to talk to anyone."

She sat back down.

A voice came on the phone's recorder. "Senator Davis, this is Boris Zerbanski. I'm the chief investigative reporter for the *Statesman*. I've read page 313 of your SB107 and plan to release a story about it in tomorrow morning's edition. I'm calling to give you a chance to comment. If you get this call, you can reach me at the newspaper's main number, 555-5000, or at the direct line to my desk at 555-5036. Hope you'll call, as I'd really like to hear your side of the story before we release—what seems to be—some very negative information about your bill."

Sylvia and I stopped our work.

I reached for my copy of SB107. "What was that page number?"

"Page 313," she said.

I found the page and set it between us so that we both could read.

> *This bill hereby changes the spacing requirement for oil wells in the state of Texas, from four to sixteen per section of 640 acres. It also changes the oil depletion allowance (the ODA) to double the figures established by the Revenue Act of 1926, the original "Spindletop Bill." And it removes all restrictions that limit Induced Hydraulic Fracturing (commonly known as fracking). These changes shall become effective immediately.*

"Wow," Sylvia said.

My stomach dropped to the floor. I felt sick.

72

Five minutes later

I counted the words—only 69—that really mattered. In our massive document of over 500 pages, if there were 350 words per page, I estimated a total of 175,000 words in the bill. This little bombshell amounted to about .03% of the verbage. Less than three one-hundredths of one percent—it seemed unbelievable that such an infintesimal number of words could wreak damage of this scale.

"You gonna call?" Sylvia asked.

"I'm thinking."

Obviously SB107 had been written to sneak in these changes to provide financial incentives and tax breaks for oil and gas interests.

"What are you going to say?" Sylvia pushed.

"I don't know."

"There's nothing illegal about submitting legislative changes that favor the oil and gas industry."

"Sylvia, I don't think that's the statement I want printed in the *Austin*

PUPPET POLITICS

American-Statesman."

We sat silently for what seemed like a very long time—probably several minutes.

"You want to call it quits for tonight?" she asked.

I came to a decision—it would be futile to call the newspaper. "Might as well."

That night I tossed and turned. If I slept any, it wasn't much. Finally, I gave up, went through my morning ablutions, and drove to Denny's at 5:30 a.m. The *Statesman's* headline featured me by name.

DAVIS BILL CARRIES
HIDDEN AGENDA

I stood outside under a streetlight and read the entire article. Twice.

Betty, the waitress, passed me on her way to work. "If you want to read inside, I'll get you a cup of coffee."

"Thanks." I followed her into the restaurant.

As promised, she brought me a cup of hot coffee. "You want to order breakfast?"

"I'm not sure."

She left a menu. "Let me know when you decide."

I read the article a third time. The reporter who wrote the story, Boris Yerbanski, accused me of burying "outrageous" oil and gas legislation in a mass of public relations verbiage.

Which was true.

Except that I wasn't the bill's author. It wasn't my bill.

But it had my name on it, and I didn't know if I could ever convince Yerbanski, or the newspaper, that Whiskey was the true author.

Betty brought the coffee pot. "More?"

I nodded. "How about scrambled eggs, ham, and wheat toast?"

"You got it."

An hour later, with some food in my system, I felt a semblance of rational thinking return. A confrontation with Whiskey loomed as unavoidable—sooner the better. I drove to the capitol and went straight to his office. I found him at his desk, reading the newspaper.

"Morning, Senator." He waved his hand toward a chair in front of his desk.

I thought he might immediately apologize for putting me in a politically embarrassing position. Instead he laughed.

I sat and tried to gather my thoughts.

"Damn," he said, his face lighted with a big smile. "They found us out."

"Whiskey." I struggled to control my mounting anger. "There's no *us*."

"Yeah," he chuckled. "I guess it's your name on the bill."

Rage came over me, and a surge of adrenaline shot through my brain. "I want you to stand up for me. Tell everyone that you wrote it."

Again he laughed, an even more robust outburst. "Hell, Sam, you know I can't do that."

"Why not?" I yelled. "It's the truth."

His demeanor changed. "It's politics," he said. He stopped laughing. The look of mirth drained from his face, and he leaned forward in his chair. "If people learn I wrote it, it'll undermine my leadership. Whereas, if an inexperienced senator from West Texas is recognized as author, everyone chuckles at an inept attempt to help constituents."

It was all I could do to keep from punching him in the face. I stood, and the words poured out. "Whiskey, I demand that you issue a statement absolving me as the writer of this charade."

A hard, sinister appearance came over his face. He stood and gave me a look of rage that I had never before seen from him. "Get out, you unappreciative son of a bitch."

For the next moment, I stood there, my brain muddled with fury, trying to think of what to say or do.

"I made you," he said, his voice hard as blue steel. "I handpicked you. I put out over four million to finance your campaign. And this is the thanks I get."

"And you set me up to take the fall for SB107."

He laughed at my words. "We'll just have to find another way to make our changes to oil and gas legislation. Now get out before I call Capitol Security."

I left, slamming the door so hard it should have broken the glass.

But it didn't.

Everyone in the hallway turned and looked.

Normally, I would have felt embarrassed—even mortified—to have all those people staring at me. However, at that moment, I was thinking so hard about how I could turn the tables on Homer "Whiskey" Williams . . . nothing else mattered.

73

My office, the Texas State Capitol

Sylvia met me with a worried look. She handed me a cup of coffee and, in a whispered voice, she asked, "Seen this morning's *Statesman?*"

"Yeah."

"Harriet's in her room with the door closed. She wants to see you."

"Give me a moment."

I went into my office and closed the door. I held my head in my hands and tried to gather my thoughts.

I heard a knock on the door. Harriet stuck her head in. "Got a minute?"

"Sure."

She came in, closed the door, and took one of the two chairs in front of my desk. When she looked up, I could see red eyes and smudged mascara.

"Here's my letter of resignation," she said. She laid an envelope on my desk.

I stood, picked up the letter, and made a show of tearing it up and throwing it into the trash. Then I came around the desk and took the chair next to her. "I'm not going to let you walk out on me. I need you."

"I missed the oil and gas stuff on page 313." Tears flowed. "It's my fault. I should have caught it."

I grabbed a box of Kleenex from my credenza and set it on the desk in front of her. "If you want to criticize anyone for failing to find it, you'll have to start with me."

"But it's my job." She reached for the tissue box and pulled three. Her sobs came in waves.

"Harriet, what about all the members of the committee? They missed it. Their legislative aides missed it. Hell, the whole senate missed it." I reached over and placed my hand on her back.

Gradually her distress eased. She pulled more Kleenex.

"We both need to get back to work," I said.

"I'm so embarrassed—"

"Good. That'll motivate you to go back to your desk and get busy."

She stood.

I walked her to the door. "How about a hug?"

We embraced.

She turned and went into the outer office.

Sylvia and I watched, silently, as Harriet walked across the room with a Kleenex to her face, headed down the hallway, went into her office, and closed the door.

Sylvia shook her head. "What're we going to do?"

"We're gonna work harder and try to get ready for this afternoon and tomorrow. Bring the legislative agenda and come in."

We sat at the table in my office and went over the schedule. One by one we reviewed each bill. We could both see that, starting at noon, I would have to be in the senate chambers for the remainder of the day. And all the next day—the last day of the legislative session—I'd have to be at my senate desk until the agenda worked its way to the end.

"When is SB107 scheduled?" I asked.

She shuffled through the list of legislation. "It's first on the agenda for tomorrow morning." She pointed to the schedule. "Starts at ten a.m."

I read the listing. SB107 had my name by it.

"Anything else you want me to do?" she asked.

"Thanks, Sylvia," I said. "Guess it's now up to me."

She left.

I studied my watch and realized that only a couple of hours remained before the inexorable march to the end began its process. Once it started, I'd be chained to my desk in the senate chambers. The 140 days that started last January now came down to minutes. I went over the list of bills one last time.

Senate Bill 107 glared at me.

Obviously, every member of the senate expected me to address it—to lead the discussion. I thought about reciting facts, about how the lieutenant governor had brought the bill to me, and about how I had ended up as its author. I took a yellow legal pad and started writing my speech.

The truth, the whole truth, and nothing but.

I took a calendar and tried my best to recreate dates—the committee's passage, the date we got twenty-one votes, the second reading and its unanimous passage. And especially the role of Homer "Whiskey" Williams.

But who would believe me?

Probably nobody. Even before the newspaper found the incriminating changes in oil and gas legislation, no one would have listened to my denials.

But now. Since the exposé—

Forget it.

Any accusations against the lieutenant governor by me would sound like the last gasps of a drowning politician.

74

The Senate Chambers

Yesterday's marathon session had lasted into the wee hours. Heated discussion prolonged a crowded agenda, repeatedly bringing tempers to the boiling point. One particularly contentious bill— SB321, legislation to increase the waiting period for divorce from ninety days to two years—had been debated for hours. The co-authors of the bill had taken turns repeatedly pressuring me to vote for it.

"We'll even support your bill if you help us," said one.

"You'll support what?" I asked. I meant it as a joke. He took me seriously.

"Your bill to sneak through increases for oil and gas."

"I don't know what you're talking about," I replied, egging him on.

His face scrunched up in anger as he looked at the legislative agenda. "SB107, the 500-page monster about West Texas."

"You'd vote for that?" I chuckled, trying to give him a clue that I was kidding him. He tuned me out and continued to take my banter

"Hey, we're desperate. Just three more votes and SB321 becomes law."

"Who cares?"

"Divorce lawyers. If we increase the waiting period to two years, attorney fees will triple, maybe even quadruple."

I shook my head. "Sorry."

"Hey, you're a lawyer, aren't you?" He grabbed my arm. "You should be helping us to pass this bill."

I smiled at him. "Easy." Then, gently, I used my good hand to disengage, one finger at a time, his grip on my arm.

He gave up. And moved across the aisle to hassle another poor soul.

Finally, due mostly to fatigue, the bill had failed, and the senate moved on.

Now this morning, the last day of the legislative session, our president pro tem rapped his gavel and called my name. "Senator Davis, we're ready to hear from you on SB107."

"Mr. President, I urge my senate colleagues to vote against this bill."

The room came alive with reaction to my statement. Senators never spoke against their own bills. The leader rapped his gavel repeatedly until, finally, the chamber quieted.

"Did I hear you right? Did you say you want us to vote *against* SB107?"

"Yes, Mr. President."

"Well, I, for one, would like to hear your reasons."

"No reasons, just my position. I'm against the bill."

Again the room came alive with chatter followed by the gavel calling for quiet.

297

"Discussion?" the president pro-tem called out.

"It's too late," said a gruff voice from the front row.

I recognized the voice. He was the leader of the group pushing the divorce bill, the very same senator who saw his mission as representing lawyers.

"Senator Davis tried to pull a fast one but—thanks to a sharp-eyed reporter at the *Statesman*—got caught. Davis is a disgrace to the senate, to the ideals of principled governance, and to the legacy of the state of Texas."

The senate chambers, which only moments before buzzed with chatter, now grew deathly quiet.

"If Sam Davis thinks that, by speaking against his own bill, he can excuse his unspeakably dishonorable actions, he has grossly misjudged me and, I think, every other senator seated here today."

I thought it interesting that this guy had no ethical problems with a bill designed to help attorneys increase their legal fees.

"I agree," said someone from across the aisle.

"Is it any wonder that voters view politicians with apprehension?" the voice in the front asked.

I felt lower than a snake's belly. If there were a hole anywhere in the capitol, I would have crawled into it.

"We, as senators, as elected holders of the public trust, must stand for fair and just government. We should—"

"Question," I said.

"The question has been called," the president pro tem said. He paused for a moment to look around the chamber. "Those in favor of Senate Bill 107 say aye."

No one spoke.

"Those against say nay."

"Nay," came a roar from virtually every senator.

"SB107 fails. You got your wish, Senator Davis."

A wave of relief washed over me.

The president pro tem called the next bill. "SB252, Senator Jones, you're on."

I leaned back in my seat and half-listened to the spokeswoman for the next bill drone on about the need to increase funding for dental schools.

I looked over to the seats reserved for media and saw a number of people leaving.

Here it was, barely five minutes into the most dynamic legislative day of the session, and journalists were packing. That told me, and presumably every person in the room, that SB107 was the "biggie." It was to have been the newsmaker of the session, the bill that symbolized graft, sleaze, and dirty politics.

The hot news was now stone cold.

However, I could see a guy pointing a camera—one with a telescopic lens—in my direction. He no longer had SB107, but he still had *me*. And it didn't take much imagination to guess what the next morning's headline story would be.

75

Southwest Airlines, Flight 35, Austin to Midland

I had false hopes that, with the failure of SB107, public interest in me and in my work as a senator might fade. No such luck. The Texas media—the *Austin American-Statesman* in particular—thought otherwise. After I saw the *Statesman's* headline, I made a point of not reading the paper. However, other people on the plane had copies, and the big, bold Austin newspaper's headline became unavoidable.

Flight 35 stopped in Dallas. I felt a sense of relief as most passengers with Austin newspapers left. Temporary relief was replaced by depression, however, when people with copies of the *Dallas Morning News* and the *Ft. Worth Star-Telegram* boarded the plane, different folks with different newspapers but with similar headlines. I tried not to look.

When we landed in Midland, things got worse. Reporters and photographers from both the *Midland Reporter-Telegram* and the *Odessa American* were at the airport looking for me. Kaye Kelly from KMID-TV elbowed her way to the front with a microphone.

PUPPET POLITICS

"Senator Davis, tell us about your failed attempt to change the spacing for oil and gas wells."

"Kaye, there's nothing to tell," I replied. I started walking down the hall toward the baggage claim area.

Kelly and her microphone walked with me. Reporters and photographers followed.

"Is it true that you asked other senators to vote against your bill?" she asked.

"It's public record. You don't have to ask."

"But why? That's not part of the record."

"Because I'm against changing the spacing. And, for the record, I'm against changing the Oil Depletion Allowance."

"Then why did you hide all of this in your bill and try to sneak it through the senate?"

The escalator forced our entourage into single file. At the bottom, I ducked into the men's room.

Ten minutes later, when I made my way back out into the baggage area, the reporters and photographers were waiting for me. So was Suzanne. She and I embraced and kissed. The paparazzi had a field day.

I left Suzie and the media to retrieve my bags.

On the way to our car, I was peppered with questions, most of which I ignored.

Finally, we made an escape.

"Whew," Suzie said. "You've become quite a celebrity."

"Chump would be more like it."

She laughed. "The *Midland Reporter-Telegram* called you a sleaze, and the *Odessa American* referred to you as a scumbag, dishonest politician."

"I love them, too."

"I don't care what they call you." She scooted over close and squeezed my arm. "You're still my knight in shining armor."

"Better get out your brush. The armor needs some polish."

When we walked into the house our dachshund gave me a royal welcome.

"See, Gretel still loves you," Suzie said.

I bent down and picked up the little dog. As I tried to hold her close, she wiggled and did her best to lick my face.

"Give it some time," Suzie continued. "People will forgive and forget."

"I don't think so." I plopped down on the sofa, still holding the dog. "The political arena has pegged me with two infamous headline stories."

"Good grief, surely this will die down and go away." She sat beside me, close.

"President Johnson's dead and gone. Yet people still remember the Landslide Lyndon story."

For the next few moments, Suzie nestled beside me quietly, reached over and joined in petting Gretel. Then in a very soft voice she asked, "What're you going to do?"

76

The next morning, at home, 3648 Everglade

I t started before the kids left for school. Three TV trucks parked on the street. Reporters and photographers gathered—waiting. As I peeked out the window, the image of a Bugs Bunny cartoon, one with vultures waiting, came to me. Only this wasn't funny. The vultures were real.

"I think I'd better drive the kids to school this morning," Suzie said.

"No, I'll leave," I said. "When I go to the office, the media circus will follow."

"What's going on?" Tim asked. "I thought your legislature ended two days ago."

"Daddy, how long will TV people keep coming to our house?" Emily asked.

I looked at my ten-year old son and my seven-year old daughter and thought about how best to answer. "Not much longer," I said. "Let's hope today will be the last time."

I went to brush my teeth. Then I grabbed my briefcase and walked out the front door to face the mob.

Kaye Kelly, as usual, asked the first question. "Senator Davis, how about a statement?"

"The legislative session is over. I'm back in Midland trying to take care of my law practice."

"Is your law practice exclusively with oil and gas investors?" a reporter asked.

"No. In fact I have very few clients who ask me for legal services relating to the oil and gas business."

A ripple of laughter swept through the crowd.

"Senator, Midland's an oil town," the reporter replied. "You don't expect us to believe that."

"Is there an indictment coming from the two murders?" another reporter asked.

"Yeah, you have another statement that you don't expect us to believe?" a third voice called out.

I looked around at the unruly mob as their combined questions increased to an undecipherable cacophony of sound. I raised my hand, gesturing for quiet.

"Kaye, one more question, then I've got to go to work."

"Senator Davis, there are too many unanswered questions. People want to know about your attempts to change regulations for the oil and gas industry and your involvement with the Stone/Hernandez murders. Why do you think all of these reporters are here this morning?"

"I don't know why you're here. And I don't have any new information for you about regulations or murders."

"Senator, you can't stiff us," she insisted. "It won't work. May I offer a suggestion?"

"Go ahead," I said.

"Set up a press conference. Give the media a chance to ask questions. Otherwise we have to keep hanging out, bothering you and your family."

"Okay. What do you suggest?"

"Sooner is better. How about the conference room at your law office?"

I thought about it for a second. "Five o'clock this afternoon?"

She smiled. "That would be great."

"Pass the word." I got in my car and drove to the office.

At seven a.m., I arrived to find the office dark. After turning on some lights and settling in, I started the coffee and looked over the piles of paperwork Mrs. Hughes had neatly stacked on my desk. Most daunting was the pile of pink slips, messages asking me to return calls. I sat and looked through them. Almost all were from the media.

A little before eight o'clock, Art poked his head in, "Do I smell coffee?"

"Have a seat. We need to talk."

He took a chair in front of my desk. I poured the coffee.

"Yesterday the phone rang off the wall," he said. "Mrs. Hughes is not too happy with you."

I related the details about the scene at my house that morning and the promise of a press conference at five o'clock. "Would you help me? I don't know what I'm going to say."

"When all else fails, why not give them the facts?"

"That Whiskey wrote SB107?"

"Why not? It's the truth."

"I tried. They won't believe me."

"You have any proof to back up your accusation?"

"No. Unfortunately, it's just my word against his."

Art sipped his coffee and turned away to stare out the window—

his thinking posture. I'd seen it many times over the years when we conferred about tough legal cases. It usually worked best for me to wait, to sit quietly and let him think. I reached for the coffee pot and poured us each a warm-up.

"They're gonna ask you about the murders," he said.

"Already have. It was the second question this morning."

"What did you say?"

"Nothing. I had no new information."

Art looked at me pensively. It seemed obvious that he wanted to say something—something critical of me.

"Go ahead," I said. "Let's hear it."

"It's probably nothing . . . but last week I caught a snatch of a conversation between the Texas Rangers and the Midland County Sheriff's Deputies."

"And—"

"And it had something to do with hired killers."

My heart did a flip-flop. I started to blurt out Charlie's name and all that he had told me. But before I could utter a sound, a tiny brainwave wormed its way into my subconcious—I had given my word to Charlie. It was one of those moments of classic indecision.

Art saved me. Unaware of my dilemma, he blabbed on and refocused the conversation. "Legal pads? Two—one for you, one for me."

Like we had done so often over the past ten years, Art led the discussion and we brainstormed together, trying to anticipate the questions and our best answers. McComas and Davis, law partners at our finest, bouncing ideas off one another. Two hours later I had three pages of handwritten notes.

"I'd like you to come to the press conference," I said.

He smiled, a wry expression I'd often seen when we faced a tough legal challenge together. "Wouldn't miss it."

He left.

Mrs. Hughes came in with her memo pad.

"There's a camera crew here from KMID-TV," she said, her face stern, eyes blazing with disfavor. "They want to set up equipment in the conference room."

"There's a press conference at five o'clock."

"I don't have it scheduled."

"Damn it Rebecca. Would you please make arrangements?"

She flinched. I could see the hackles rise.

"Excuse me," I said. "I didn't mean to snap at you. But I'm under attack, and I need your help."

"Yes, sir. I understand. Yesterday we had a number of calls."

"Thank you."

"Is there anything else I can do to help you?"

I looked down at my scribbled notes.

She waited, note pad in hand.

"Yes. I've got to get ready for this press conference at five o'clock. It would be an enormous help if you could handle my calls so that I can prepare."

She nodded. "I can do that."

She left and closed the door.

Rebecca Hughes was the best doorkeeper in the world. I felt completely sure I wouldn't be disturbed the rest of the day.

77

The law offices of McComas and Davis

The press conference was an unmitigated disaster. First, the site was too small. By four o'clock everyone knew it—we had over one hundred people who wanted to attend an event scheduled in a room that, at best, could barely accommodate twenty-five.

Art decided on a lottery. He explained the rules. Give each of the reporters, photographers, camera crews, etc., a number—then at 4:45 hold a drawing. The first twenty would be invited into the room with the provision that they "pool" their information and make it available to everyone present.

"That's the way they do it in Washington," he said.

I turned it over to Art.

The media bitched. Especially those who had traveled from Dallas and Houston and now felt left out. Even the twenty who joined me in the conference room griped because of the crowded conditions and limited camera angles.

You can't win.

But I plowed ahead and tried my best to give them the information they wanted. I expected the press conference would last thirty minutes and then we'd all go our separate ways.

Wrong again. They pummeled me with questions for an hour. But that didn't end the event. Fifty or more lingered outside on the street, waiting to catch me as I walked to the parking garage. Thinking it better to answer questions—and therefore get rid of them—than to try to "stiff" them and run away, I continued on the street for another thirty minutes, the same inane questions asked and answered in a dozen different ways.

I didn't make it home until after 8:00 p.m.

But, thank goodness, there were no reporters.

Suzie had saved a hamburger for me. I love Suzie.

We sat together at the kitchen table. Between bites I tried to give her a summary of the day.

"Art tried his best," I said.

"Do you think it's over?" Suzie asked. "No reporters tomorrow morning?"

"Who knows?" I took another bite of hamburger. It was delicious.

"Surely they'll get tired and go away."

I nodded, my mouth full.

"What kind of questions did they ask?"

"The usual." I took a drink. "But there was one new query. A reporter from the *Amarillo Globe-News* wanted to know who would benefit most from the two provisions in SB107."

"No one," Suzie replied. "It didn't pass."

"Yes, everyone knows that," I said. "However, his question was 'would.' Who *would* have benefited most if SB107 had passed?"

"Obviously, the oil and gas people—producers and royalty owners."

"Yes, but—"

"But, what?" Suzie asked.

"But, it got me to thinking—who are those people? This past year our law office has had a lot of traffic in oil and gas leasing."

"People selling leases in the Permian Basin?"

"Yep. Old stripper wells that hardly produce anything have been selling like hot cakes."

Suzie sat up, her face beaming with discovery. "You know, Consuelo Hernandez wrote an article about that. She tried to link it with the death of Abner Stone."

I put down my hamburger. "Say that again?"

"No one paid her the time of day," Suzie said. "I remember someone saying that stripper wells were worthless. And that paying money for worthless oil and gas leases was not a motive for murdering a state senator or anyone else."

"Unless—"

"Unless what?" she asked.

"Unless Texas changed the legislation for spacing and fracking." I smiled, the smile of enlightenment. "Those old leases would be like gold in Ft. Knox."

Suzie smiled back. "I don't really understand the Oil Depletion Allowance, but wouldn't that also sweeten the pot?"

I laughed as I thought about doubling the tax advantages of the ODA. "Yes, you could say that."

78

Midland County Courthouse

I went to see Barbara Burgess—the County Clerk of Midland County. Barb, as everyone called her, had been a fixture at the county courthouse long before I started practicing law.

She had taken me under her wing a decade ago when I was struggling to learn the ropes as a young, inexperienced lawyer. The sale of property almost always requires the services of an attorney, and many Midland lawyers derive a significant portion of their income from this revenue stream. I'd prepared the papers for many sales in Midland County. In the beginning, Barb had been a big help.

On this particular day, Barb was busy, and I knew how to search for a warranty deed for the sale of mineral rights, so I took a stool at one of the computers in the public area of the county clerk's office and went to work. However, using my normal approach of looking up a deed by location or by owner's name wouldn't work in this case. Instead, I tried using the computer's search engine for "recent sales" and got a listing of every property in the county that had been sold in the past month. It included houses and businesses, farms and ranches, everything that had a deed in Midland County. Of the several hundred sales listed, I found two for mineral rights. And this was only for the month of April.

After thirty minutes of tedious, mostly unproductive effort, I saw Barb coming over. She took the stool next to me and asked, "Why the big frown?"

"I'm trying to find the sale of mineral rights for the past couple of years." I showed her the results of my search—a stack of warranty deeds about two inches thick. "At this rate, I'm going to be here for weeks, maybe months."

She gave me a maternal smile, the same gesture I remembered from years ago when I was a young lawyer, just starting out. "Want some help?"

"Please." I slipped off the stool in front of the computer and offered it to her.

"You want only the sale of mineral rights?"

"Yes."

"You know you can limit your search to specified dates. For example, you can ask for the year 1945."

"Uh, how about the last two years?"

"No problem." She typed in the dates and the command for print. Immediately the printer started spitting out pages. Together we watched for several minutes. The printer stopped, and Barb went to refill the paper tray.

"Wow," she said. "I had no idea we'd recorded so many sales for minerals."

Finally the printer stopped. She picked up the stack and handed them to me. I guessed it to be five or more inches thick. Most warranty deeds require two or more sheets of paper, so I estimated we had paperwork representing at least four or five hundred transfers of ownership.

"How much do I owe you?" I asked.

She read the counter. "At ten cents a copy 1,122 sheets would be $112.20. I can put it on your tab and send you a bill."

"Thanks. And Barb, could we keep this quiet for a few weeks?"

She shook her head. "Sam, the sale of property is public information. If I try to hide it, I'll be breaking the law."

"I'm not asking you to break the law or hide anything."

"Then what is it you want me to do?"

I explained about Senate Bill 107, the proposed changes for well spacing, the increases for oil depletion allowance, and the new regulations for fracking. Immediately she put two and two together.

"If the bill had passed, whoever owned these leases stood to make a pile of dough," she said.

"People thought it was me."

"Weren't you the author of the bill?"

I shook my head. "Dumb me, I was just their puppet."

She smiled. "Sam Davis is anything but dumb."

I smiled back. "Barb, if I'm so smart, how is it that my name is the one in the headlines accused of sleaze and graft?"

She gestured to the stack of printouts. "The names of the people who've been buying these leases are the ones who stood to make all the money."

"That's why I'm asking you to give me a few days. I'll research the sales, compile a list of names, and call a press conference."

She smiled again, the same maternal smile of approval. "Sam, the whistle-blower."

"How about it? Can you help me?"

"These are public records."

"But you don't have to broadcast the news that I've been searching for names of buyers."

"True."

"And if the reporters want to search for names, you could let them look at deeds one at a time, like I was trying to do."

Barb gave me her biggest smile of the morning. "Yes, I could do that."

"And I have a big favor to ask."

"Okay. What can I do to help?"

"I need to do a search like this in all the counties in the Permian Basin. Could you contact the other county clerks?"

"Sure. We do favors for each other all the time."

"Think you could get them to do the searches quietly?"

"We'll call it Operation Night Before Christmas."

"Oh?"

"Not a creature was stirring, not even a mouse."

79

McComas and Davis Law Offices

The UPS delivery guy pulled a two-wheeler dolly into my office and unloaded a stack of seven boxes. I signed for them, and he left. As I lifted each parcel onto the conference table, I read the name of the sender:

County Clerk, Andrews County
County Clerk, Classcock County
County Clerk, Crane County
County Clerk, Ector County
County Clerk, Gaines County
County Clerk, Howard County
County Clerk, Martin County

I ripped open the first package and found photocopies of hundreds of warranty deeds for the sale of mineral rights. I spent fifteen minutes doing spot checks and did not find any date of sale to be older than two years. For the next hour, I opened the other parcels and found identical contents. As promised, Barbara Burgess had contacted her buddies, and each was sending me photocopies of warranty deeds of mineral rights that had been sold in their counties in the last two years.

From the number and sizes of the packages, it appeared obvious that there had been a huge volume of sales. If true, that fact alone would be an indication of massive malfeasance.

But the greater question was *who?* I could hardly wait to find the names of those who were doing the buying.

Anxiously, I arranged the warranty deeds in stacks by counties. Starting with Andrews County, the first deed listed the buyer as AE&A—Austin Energy and Associates. I also copied the address, 1203 Congress Avenue, Austin, TX 78714.

I went to the next deed and, not surprisingly, found the name of the buyer to be the same, AE&A. Same address.

The third deed listed the same buyer.

I laid down my pen and went through the next ten deeds. All listed the buyer as Austin Energy and Associates.

Thinking there would probably be different buyers in different counties, I shifted to Howard County. Wrong again. It didn't take long to find that AE&A had been buying most, if not all, the mineral rights in Howard County.

I spent the rest of the day going through the stacks of deeds only to find that 99 percent of all the warranty deeds for the sale of mineral rights in the Permian Basin in the past two years had been to the same buyer—AE&A.

Next step. I had to find the names of those who owned AE&A.

I had their address.

PUPPET POLITICS

The next morning I flew Southwest Airlines to Austin, rented a car, and drove to 1203 Congress Avenue. As a person familiar with downtown Austin, I recognized the location as part of the old downtown business district just south of the state capitol building. Once a thriving commercial area, most retail stores had closed and moved to suburban shopping malls. What was left was the "low rent" mixture of businesses typical of major cities throughout the country. I found pawnshops, used furniture stores, a few restaurants, and a number of offices related to state and local government.

The address 1203 was a doorway with steps leading to the second floor of a two-story office building. The stairway was located between the office of the Texas State Plumbers' Association and the TRM&CCA, the Texas Ready-Mix and Cement Contractors Association. I climbed the dingy old wooden stairs and found the door to AE&A locked.

Back downstairs, I interviewed the neighbors.

The plumbers maintained a two-person operation—a crusty, bald-headed guy who looked to be in his 60s or 70s and a petite blonde who might have been his granddaughter. Both came to the counter to greet me.

"I'm looking for the AE&A," I said. "I wonder if you could help me?"

"Upstairs," the man said.

"But you won't find anyone there," the blonde said. "There never is."

"Do you know anything about them?" I asked. "Have you ever seen anyone come or go?"

"No," the man said. He turned and went back to his desk.

The blonde shook her head. "Wish I could help you, but I've been here two years and never seen a single person. I do know this—they don't get much mail, so there's probably little or no need to come to the office. You might try the TRM&CCA."

"Who?"

"The cement people next door."

I thanked her and went to the Texas Ready-Mix and Cement Contractors Association where I found a dour, elderly, overweight woman at the front desk. "What do you want?" she growled.

I asked her the same questions about the AE&A office upstairs.

"I don't know nuthin' and I'm busy." She immediately went back to her computer.

I left.

All corporations in the state of Texas are required to file copies of their legal paperwork with the Corporation Division of the Texas Secretary of State. This includes the articles of incorporation, bylaws, and—most importantly—the names and addresses of the officers and board of directors. I decided to call on the Secretary of State.

Located near the capitol, the office was housed in the James E. Rudder Building on Brazos Street, an impressive structure with very little parking. I circled the block several times before finding a spot.

Inside I walked up to the counter and asked, "I'm trying to find information about a corporation called Austin Energy and Associates. Could you help me?"

"Fill out a request," the woman said. She handed me a form.

I filled it out and handed it back.

"Five dollars to cover Xeroxing and postage."

"I'd like to wait and pick up the copies."

"Sorry, we don't offer same-day service. We'll mail it to you, probably next week."

I pulled out my Texas State Senator ID. "This is for a senate committee. I'd like them while I wait."

"Senator Davis." She looked at her watch. "I'll do it myself. Give me ten minutes."

I took a seat.

In five minutes she was back with a manila envelope.

I thanked her and took the envelope to the car.

Seated alone, hands trembling, I pulled out the official papers of the Austin Energy and Associates Corporation. About ten pages into the stack, I found what I was looking for—the list of officers and board of directors.

Only three names.

Homer W. Williams was listed as president and majority stockholder.

A wave of emotion gripped me, and it took my breath away. I let my head fall back against the driver's headrest and tried to relax. As I thought about it for the next few seconds, my emotional equilibrium gradually returned and my breathing fell to normal. While I hadn't expected to find Whiskey's name, I guess I really wasn't surprised.

So I sat up to read the other two names, the members of the board of directors—Thomas Butler and Richard Klemkowski—the Tom and Dick of my "Tom, Dick, and Harriet" campaign trio.

I dropped the papers.

80

The Ballroom, Midland's Hilton Hotel

Art immediately called another press conference. "This time, can we find a place that's large enough?" I asked.

Art picked the Hilton Ballroom for two reasons. "It's plenty big," he said, "and it's just across the street."

We found a two-wheel dolly and took all the mineral deeds as exhibit A. Art displayed the stacks on a table by the speaker's lectern. I predicted it would create a sensation for the media.

What neither of us had counted on was the attendance.

No one came from Dallas, Houston, Amarillo or even Lubbock. We had the local newspapers—the *Midland Reporter-Telegram* and the *Odessa American*—one local TV station, and a couple of stringers who freelanced for radio stations and the news services.

I counted.

Including the cameraman from the TV station, we had a total of six people.

PUPPET POLITICS

Not much when you compared it with the more than a hundred who came to last week's press conference. And the irony that, last time we had no new news, whereas now we had a scoop—the stuff of which memorable headlines are made.

And virtually no coverage.

But you go with what you've got, so I did my best to reveal, what I thought to be, the top political news story of the year— Austin Energy and Associates, Inc.

I spoke with passion about Lieutenant Governor Homer "Whiskey" Williams, the president and majority stockholder in AE&A, the corporation that had recently purchased vast holdings in the Permian Basin. That was a fact. I invited the media to check it out and gave each an information sheet telling them how to do it.

I also passed around a sworn statement about Thomas Butler and Richard Klemkowski, former members of my campaign organization— who had been offered to me at no cost by Whiskey—and stating that, until two days ago, I had no knowledge of their involvement in AE&A.

And finally, I gave a detailed history of Senate Bill 107, how it was written by the lieutenant governor's office, how I had been asked to attach my name to the bill, how it had been guided through committee and the senate by Whiskey, and finally how he had maneuvered and left me as the sole author.

The little group who attended the press conference took my handouts and left, all except Kaye Kelly, the investigative reporter from KMID-TV. She lingered behind with her cameraman to ask a question.

"Senator Davis, do you see any link between this information and the two deaths?"

"What deaths?" We both knew, but I wanted her to be the one to say the names.

"Abner Stone and Consuelo Hernandez, of course."

"Yes," I said. "Hernandez even wrote a story about Abner Stone's plan to publicize the purchase of stripper wells in the Permian Basin. She thought the information provided a motive for murder."

"When was that?" Kaye asked.

"I believe it was published in the *Austin American-Statesman* the day before she was murdered."

"You can't give the exact date?"

"Wouldn't be hard for you to check it out."

"Do the Texas Rangers know this?"

"I believe so. But you could ask Lieutenant Charles Fuller."

"Sam," she said, calling me by my given name for the first time I could remember, "if all of what you're telling me is true, this will be the story of the year."

"Has Pulitzer written all over it."

"I doubt that." She stopped, her face aglow. "But wouldn't that be nice?"

"You have a way you can send this to the network?"

She paused again, thinking, and her eyes got big.

"Millions, maybe even billions, in oil money. Hidden political graft. Two murders—" I continued.

"Centered around a legend in Texas politics with a colorful name," she added.

I looked around the room and laughed. "Where are all the reporters?"

Her face turned serious. "This scares me. What if you're wrong about Williams being the instigator?"

"Someone has to connect the dots," I said. "Why not Kaye Kelly?"

"Why hasn't law enforcement done that?"

Good question. And I remembered my pledge to Charlie Fuller

about hired killers. Then, like a bolt of lightning, I thought of a way to convey this to Kay.

"Suppose the Texas Rangers suspect hired killers were responsible for the Stone and Hernandez murders?"

"I've never heard or seen reports about hired killers."

"Bare with me," I said. "Suppose that theory became something to investigate?"

"A theory is just a theory," Kaye replied.

"Hey, for the first time two names have surfaced as suspects."

"Names that have a connection to Whiskey?"

I gestured to the table and stacks of warranty deeds. "It's a *fact*, Richard Klemkowski and Thomas Butler are co-owners of those stripper wells."

"That's only motive. You have no evidence they are connected to the murders?"

"Kaye, you're a reporter. It's your job to report the facts. I'll bet the Texas Rangers would welcome this information."

She looked at me, silently, her eyebrows pulled together, obviously thinking over my advice.

"As Jack Webb would say on the old *Dragnet* TV series." I paused. "What?"

Grinning, I delivered my punch line. "Just the facts, ma'am."

Kaye, who was at least fifteen years younger than I, and had probably never watched *Dragnet,* gave me a blank look.

81

We gathered around the television. KMID showed my interview with Kaye Kelly as their lead story. I timed it— three minutes and twenty-five seconds. They had edited a blockbuster exposé down to a local news story.

Someone—Kaye, the news director, or perhaps the station's lawyer— was being super cautious about libelous statements. No aspersions, no suppositions, nothing the station nor I could be sued for. Kaye stuck to the facts, and she didn't quote me. It took the sizzle out of the story, but, thank goodness, the names were there. She gave Homer Williams as the president and majority stockholder of Austin Energy and Associates. And she named Richard Klemkowski and Thomas Butler as members of AE&A's board of directors.

The camera briefly panned my display of warranty deeds.

At least anyone watching the news now knew that, had SB107 passed, these three names were the ones who stood to make millions.

PUPPET POLITICS

Kaye credited me with two important aspects of her story—the research that uncovered purchase of all the mineral rights and the person who defeated SB107 in the Texas Senate. No question, she made me look like the proverbial "good guy."

The next morning, before the sun came up, I went out to get the morning paper in my pajamas, robe, and slippers. I couldn't wait to see how *The Midland Reporter-Telegram* would handle the story. I found it on the front page.

Yes, it was a featured news item with my picture plastered nearby—but only a shadow of last week's headline story about the end of the legislative session and my role in SB107. Still, I read it carefully, twice. And the good news was that I found nothing Whiskey and his cohorts could consider libelous.

Too bad the newspapers in Dallas, Austin, and Houston had missed out.

I went to the office feeling exonerated yet disappointed that the big metropolitan centers didn't have the story.

The day passed without incident.

The first inkling that something might change was a phone call the next morning from the Texas Rangers.

"Asshole. Why didn't you call me about AE&A?" Charlie Fuller asked.

"Wait just a goddamned minute," I said. "Why didn't the Texas Rangers go digging to find out who was buying all the stripper wells in the Permian Basin? If you'd been doing your job for the last couple of years, you'd have known about AE&A."

That stopped him. For the next few seconds he didn't know what to say. "Uh, we didn't put it together with SB107 until—"

"Save the mea culpa," I said. "I was gonna call you. I just hadn't gotten around to it."

"Exactly when did you plan to get around to it?"

"Soon."

"Listen, you SOB, I've been working on this case for almost two years. I've defended you, helped you, and done everything I could to protect you and your reputation."

"Yes, and I appreciate it."

"Hell, I don't need appreciation. I need a call when you get a break in the case."

"I know. And I was going to."

"Tell me what you know."

For the next half-hour I gave him everything I had. Eventually he settled down and his anger dissipated. Finally, as our conversation drew to a close, I changed the subject from content to communication.

"How did you learn about AE&A?" I asked.

"There was an article in the *Austin American-Statesman* this morning."

"Really?"

"They quoted a TV reporter in Midland. And the Austin TV stations now have it. They're all sending camera crews to interview me. Sam, this is big."

I relaxed. Kaye had gotten the story out.

"Damn it," Charlie continued. "I wish you'd called me two days ago."

"Hey, I wish you'd have caught this when Abner died almost two years ago."

Again, that stopped him. This time he changed the subject. "Have you heard from the lieutenant governor?"

His question caught me off guard. I hadn't thought about any reaction from Whiskey.

"No. And I don't expect to."

"Sam, how about a little advice from me?"

"Sure."

"He's not going to like this."

"Yeah," I said. "Obviously."

"I can't prove it, but I think he's already murdered two people who got in his way."

I knew that. But until Charlie put it into words, I hadn't thought about the implications of what happened to people who *got in Whiskey's way*. A chill trickled down my spine as I contemplated what Charlie was trying to tell me. It was a good thing I was sitting down.

"You still there?" he asked.

"Yes."

"If I were you, I'd take precautions."

"Thanks, Charlie. I appreciate your concern."

We said our goodbyes. I got a cup of hot coffee and tried to think about what to do.

I went to see Art. He shrugged off my concerns. "It's too late. The information's out. Don't worry about it."

I didn't get a lick of work done for the rest of the day. At four o'clock, I decided to call it quits and go home early. Just as I was about to walk out the door, Mrs. Hughes buzzed me.

"Lieutenant Governor Williams on line one," she said.

For a moment, I thought about not taking it. Then I said, "Okay. Tell him I'll be with him in a minute."

Then I took Art's little digital recorder and attached it to the phone.

"Hello," I said.

"Senator Davis," came the familiar voice, dripping with sarcasm. "I've been reading about you in the *Statesman*." He paused.

I waited, silently.

"All the Austin television stations are hounding me about interviews."

"That's your business. I have nothing to do with it."

"Oh, but they're quoting you, your research—some private information about my investments. And there's a rumor you're blaming me for SB107."

"Whiskey, I asked you to take responsibility for authoring the bill. You laughed at me."

"Senator, have you checked at home this afternoon?"

He hung up.

I was left with a dial tone.

82

My Office

Immediately I called home. Suzanne answered. "Hello," she said.

"You okay?" I asked.

"Of course. Why do you ask?"

"Are the kids okay?"

"They're not home yet. And it's only four o'clock." She paused. "You know they usually don't get home until 4:30 or so. What's with all the questions?"

"Anything unusual happen today?"

"No."

I heard the doorbell.

"Hang on, someone's at the front door."

Before I could caution her, I heard the clunk of the phone being put down and then the sound of her footsteps on the kitchen's wood floor.

A minute passed. I could hear voices, but they were too far away to distinguish words. I assumed Suzie was talking with whomever was at the front door.

Again footsteps.

"Sam, this is Dick Klemkowski."

I recognized the voice. It so surprised me, my mouth went dry and I couldn't speak.

"Are you there?" he asked.

"Y . . . yes," I stammered.

"Tom's at school. He's picking up Tim and Emily to give them a ride."

"You bastard," I yelled. "Leave my family alone."

"Easy, Sam. Nothing's going to happen to Suzie or the kids."

"I'm calling the police."

"No need. Your family's perfectly safe."

"I'm hanging up to call Midland County Sheriff and the Texas Rangers."

"Before you call, you should know we have Whiskey's Lear at the airport."

"You just said my family's safe."

"Yes, they are safe if—"

"If what?"

"If you'll just play it cool and settle down. However, that ride I was telling you about— Tom now has the kids on the Lear and, unless you forget about calling the police, they're heading for Mexico."

His words hit me like a thunderbolt. "You'll never get away with this," I yelled. "I'm calling the cops."

"Sam. Sam, don't do anything foolish. Hear me out."

"What is it you want?" I asked.

"Not much. Just a little help."

"I'm not doing anything to help you or Whiskey until my kids are safely home."

"Okay."

Of all the things he could say, that was the least expected. For a moment I didn't know how to respond. Then I asked, "How do I know I can trust you?"

"Give me your word that you will not call the police."

I hesitated. What else is going through his mind? Perspiration trickled off my forehead and rolled down my face. I needed to make a decision. "Give me your word that you will have Tim and Emily back home?"

"Yes," he said. "I give you my word."

"When?"

"Tom can have them at the house in less than thirty minutes."

Again, I thought about it, this time longer, several seconds. I used my sleeve to wipe my forehead. "Okay. I give you my word. But if you don't have my children safely home in thirty minutes, I'm calling every law enforcement authority in Midland County and we're gonna nail your ass."

I heard him breathe—a sigh of relief. "Deal."

"Deal," I replied.

"You coming home?"

"I'll be there in ten minutes."

"Sam, trust me. You'll see. We can work this out."

"I want my family safe. Then I want you, Tom, and Whiskey to leave us alone."

"We worked together to win an election," he said. "We can work together again. You'll see."

I hung up.

As I slammed the phone down, it surprised me to feel the wires. I stopped, looked at the receiver, and saw that the digital recorder was still attached. I pushed the play button and heard Whiskey's voice. Then I skipped ahead and listened to the conversation with Dick Klemkowski.

I had everything recorded.

I went to see Art.

I gave him the recorder and a brief summary of the situation. Then I arranged for us to call each other in thirty minutes and for him to notify the police unless everything worked out. We'd use the kids' names as secret code. If I said "Tim and Emily," things were okay—don't call police. If I reversed the names and said "Emily and Tim," he should call for help and send the police immediately to my house.

Hands sweating, heart racing, I drove home.

83

At home

I kept looking at my watch. And my jaws hurt. Then I realized that, as I watched events unfold in front of me I'd been clenching my teeth so tightly that they now ached.

If I had a gun, I'd kill Tom Butler and Dick Klemkowski. Then I'd go after Whiskey. These bastards violated every moral law known to mankind by taking my innocent children and involving them in their perversion of the law.

With a minute to spare, a black SUV pulled into the driveway and my two children jumped out. They looked happy and carefree, as though nothing were wrong.

Tom Butler opened the driver's door and stepped out. He followed the kids into the living room.

"Mama, take the children to the kitchen," I said.

"Come on kids, you heard your father," Suzie said. "Time for an after-school snack."

Suzie whisked the kids into the kitchen. Tom, Dick, and I said our first words.

"See, the kids are fine," Dick said.

"We went up to traffic-pattern altitude and circled the airport," Tom said. "They loved it."

"I want you to leave me and my family alone," I said, my voice hushed but hard. "Now get out." The phone rang. "That's Art McComas. I'll have to talk to him or he'll call the police."

"You gave me your word you wouldn't do that," Dick said.

"And I haven't."

"Sam, you need to get Art to do the right thing."

"Get out."

"It depends on you," Dick said.

Suzie came to the doorway. "Art wants to speak to you."

I went to the phone, furiously thinking about how to say the kids' names.

"Everything okay?" Art asked.

Speaking slowly and carefully, I said, "Tim and Emily are fine."

"Will you call me again in thirty minutes?"

"Yes."

"And when you do, I'll . . . ask . . . again . . . about . . . the . . . children." He said the last words slowly and with emphasis. I got the implication. He wanted me to use the code.

"I understand."

"Call sooner if you can."

"I will."

"Good luck."

"Thanks."

I hung up and went back into the living room. Tension hung among the three of us like an invisible fog. I could feel it, and I could see it in their facial expressions.

"We need to do this quickly," Dick said.

"Go," I said.

"Whiskey wants you to quit making waves about SB107," Dick said.

"If you just cool it and let everyone think you wrote the bill, we'll leave you and your family alone," Tom said.

I thought about the press release I'd handed out two days ago. "It may be too late for that."

"That's what Stone and Hernandez said," Dick continued.

At first I didn't react..

"Don't back us into a corner like *Stone* and *Hernandez*," Tom said the two names slowly and with careful articulation.

Then I realized the implication. Both men stared at me while the names of a senator and a reporter—both now deceased—hung in the air like death threats.

Which they were.

I felt paralyzed. I didn't say anything—I couldn't speak if I'd wanted to.

Richard Klemkowski and Thomas Butler stood and walked to the door.

Tom turned to me, and our eyes met. In all the time he and I had worked together in the campaign, I'd never before seen the sinister look he gave me. "Two nice kids," he said, his voice so soft I could barely hear him. "Sam, don't make us do it."

They got in the black SUV and drove away.

84

In the kitchen

The last thing I wanted was to alarm my family, so I tried to make my words sound casual. "I want you and the kids to go away for a few days," I said. "How about visiting your aunt in Oklahoma City?"

Suzanne looked at me with big eyes.

"Tom and Dick took the kids, didn't they?" she asked.

Tim and Emily, sitting at the kitchen table with peanut butter sandwiches, looked at me. Tim put his half-eaten sandwich on his plate.

I made a quick decision—the less said in front of the children, the better. "I don't know, but it may not be safe for you and the kids."

"What about you?"

"I have information that must be turned over to the authorities. They'll protect me."

She put her arms around me. "I don't like this. If we're going to leave, I want you to come with us."

I hugged her tight. "I'll be careful."

"Dad, what's going on?" Tim asked.

I took a chair between my two children.

"There are some bad guys who are very angry at me," I said. "They are so mad, I think they may try to hurt y'all."

"Is Mr. Butler one of the bad guys?" Emily asked.

My throat tightened as I thought about how to answer her. I stood, bent over, held out my arms to my children, and whispered, "How about a hug?"

They came, and we wrapped our arms around each other. Suzie joined us. For a long time we embraced as a family, a special feeling of togetherness.

When we broke, I knelt before Emily and took her hands. "I think it's better not to talk about the bad guys. Sometimes, the less you know, the better." I kissed her on the forehead. "Okay?"

She peered at me with a look of trust, a sort of half-smile, the expression of faith that tears your heart out. "Okay."

I kissed her again, stood, and then turned to Suzie. "I think everyone should pack enough clothes for a week."

"Tim, Emily, you heard your father. Let's go pack."

In twenty minutes we had the car loaded. Suzie and the kids drove to a convenience store on I-20. I followed in our old pickup. I gassed the car while Suzie called her Aunt Phyllis in Oklahoma City.

"Let's call each other every night at seven o'clock," I said.

"I hate this," Suzie said.

"We'll use the kids' names as a code. If you say 'Tim and Emily,' that means everyone's safe."

She nodded. "And if I say 'Emily and Tim,' that means to call the cops."

I could see moisture in her eyes as I took her in my arms. She held me tight, so tight it felt like she was holding onto me for dear life. Gently I eased my embrace, and, as we separated enough for me to view her face, a big tear rolled down her cheek.

"When you say their names you'll have to be careful and not get mixed up."

She made a fist and punched me, her blow landing harmlessly on my arm. "Listen, you bozo, this is the safety of our children we're talking about. I won't get mixed up."

We embraced again.

Then she and the kids headed east.

As I watched the car disappear among I-20 traffic, a wave of fear fell over me, and I shivered. Then thoughts of anger seeped into my brain, and gradually the muscles in my upper torso tightened. A sense of rage came over me, and I wanted to lash out at those who threatened my family. I kicked the tire of my old pickup, hard. It felt good.

A man at a nearby pump looked at me. "Are you okay?" he asked.

I relaxed, tried my best to look normal, and replied, "It's been a tough day."

He nodded. "Some days are like that."

I got into my truck and pulled about fifty feet over to the corner of the lot. Then I called Southwest Airlines and booked a seat on the last flight to Austin.

Next I called Charles Fuller of the Texas Rangers. He had given me his cellphone number with the understanding that I could use it for emergencies. When I punched in his number, he answered after the first ring.

"Sam, where are you?"

"In Midland," I said. "I need to talk with you."

"Okay. You want me to come to Midland?"

"I'm flying to Austin this evening. Southwest Flight #1195 arrives at 9:30. Could you meet my plane?"

"Sure."

I paused to take a deep breath, realizing that I was about to step into a world of conflict with my next statement. "I have the names of the hired killers who murdered Abner Stone and Consuelo Hernandez."

"Really."

"Thomas Butler and Richard Klemkowski."

"Wow."

"You want to guess the name of the person who hired them?"

"Homer Williams?"

"Bingo."

"But Sam, a guess is no good. We need evidence."

"I have it in spades on my digital recorder." Then, for the next five minutes I gave him a detailed report of what I had. At the end we paused. For at least ten seconds, neither he nor I spoke.

Finally, I asked, "Charlie, you still there?"

"Yeah," he said. "Sam, I'm worried about you and your family. We've already had two murders because Whiskey and his cohorts thought someone was about to leak information."

"My family's okay. I've sent them away where they'll be safe."

"Good. Do you want me to assign law enforcement officers for their protection?"

I thought about it for a second. "No one knows where they are. I think they're safer if we keep it that way."

"Okay. Then I want you to drive to the Midland County Sheriff's Office. I'll call and tell them you're coming."

"Why not just drive to the airport and get on the plane?"

"Because," he said, the steel in his voice startling me, "I don't want anything to happen to you."

The threat had been against my children.

Duh.

His harsh words caused me to think about who was next.

85

Bergstrom International Airport, Austin, Texas

Midland County sent two sheriff's deputies with me and the three of us boarded Southwest Flight #1195 at 8:30 p.m. for the one-hour, non-stop flight from Midland to Austin. People gawked, but that was nothing compared to our arrival in Austin.

When we came through the jet way and stepped into the Austin terminal, the Texas Rangers were there to meet us—six of them, all in uniform. With their Stetsons and side arms, they looked like an army of law enforcement.

People stared, especially deplaning passengers. I heard the man behind me whisper to his wife, "Probably a drug bust."

I wanted to turn around and say, *No, worse—it's crooked politicians.*

The couple walked on.

The Midland deputies turned me over to Lieutenant Charles Fuller. He introduced me to the other five. Then with two in front, two behind, and one on either side, the seven of us walked outside to a line of Texas Ranger vehicles—six gleaming white SUVs with flashing lights and an officer in each. A crowd gathered.

"Wow," I said.

"We have a judge standing by," Charlie said. "I want him to hear your recordings and your testimony. I think he'll issue indictments immediately. If so, I'll drop you off, and we'll make the arrests."

I started to protest. I didn't want to be *dropped off*. But in the hustle and tussle of high-speed travel, testifying for a judge, and gathering indictments, Charlie had his attention focused on organizational details. I could see he wouldn't be sympathetic to a mundane request about letting me tag along.

After we had legal authority to make the arrests, Charlie assembled his force of twelve rangers and six vehicles. "We're gonna split," he said. Then Charlie proceeded to divide the group into thirds—two vehicles and four officers in each. One group would go after Tom Butler. Another was assigned to Dick Klemkowski. The third, which Charlie commanded personally, would arrest Whiskey.

I saw my chance. Charlie took the driver's seat, his sidekick in front beside him. I hopped in the back seat.

"Charlie, I think I might be able to help with Whiskey," I said. "I know his home and his office."

"Sorry, Sam," Charlie replied. "This is police work, and it'll be dangerous—"

"Unit 601," the radio crackled.

Charlie picked up the microphone. "Unit 601. Go ahead."

"Lieutenant Governor Williams has just been sighted in a general aviation hangar at Bergstrom Airport. He and his pilots are rolling out a Lear Jet for takeoff."

"Contact the tower," Charlie replied, his voice rising in pitch and in volume. "Order them to hold the jet."

"Unit 601, you want us to try and stop the takeoff?"

"Yes, damn it. We have a warrant for his arrest. Don't let him get away."

"Roger, 601. We'll try."

Charlie burned rubber as he took off and quickly increased our speed into triple digits—lights flashing and sirens screaming.

"I know where Whiskey's hangar is," I said.

"Good. And Sam, since we don't have time to drop you off, for God's sake, try to stay out of the way, and don't get yourself shot."

I started to say, *I've got this T-shirt with a bull's-eye painted on the back*, but I decided Charlie's receptivity for humor was limited, so I changed the subject. "You know where the general aviation gate is?"

"Yes. But I don't know Whiskey's plane. What's it look like?"

"It's a Lear. All white. Small, with a needle nose and high tail. It's the only one I've ever seen with both a Texas flag and an American flag painted on the tail."

Charlie picked up the mike. "Unit 601 to dispatcher."

"Unit 601, go ahead," the radio crackled.

"Call Bergstrom Airport. Ask them to clear me at the general aviation gate for an emergency, high-speed entrance. See if you can find out anything about the status of Williams's Lear Jet."

"Roger, will do."

Charlie raced ahead, passing other cars at breathtaking speed, the second SUV right behind us. I could see the airport's rotating beacon ahead.

"Unit 601," the radio called.

"Go ahead," Charlie replied.

HARRY HAINES

"Bergstrom Security reports that you are cleared at the general aviation gate. They understand the emergency and have the gate open. Williams's Lear is taxiing out to runway 35. They've ordered him to turn around and return to his hangar, but so far he has not responded. The tower thinks he may try to takeoff without clearance. They're in the process of clearing the airspace just in case."

"Unit 601, roger. We're approaching the gate now."

I could see that the gate was open. Charlie slowed just enough to make the turn then barreled through.

"Straight ahead another hundred yards, then veer left," I said.

Seconds later we could see the runway. At eleven p.m., only one plane was in sight. At night it was impossible to tell, but I thought it was probably Whiskey's Lear. It was just starting its turn onto runway 35.

Charlie floorboarded our SUV. We raced toward the runway, making the turn on two wheels, just behind and slightly to the left of the plane.

At first we were traveling faster, and for a moment we pulled ahead. For sure, anyone on the jet could see us and our flashing blue and red strobes. Any normal plane would abort its takeoff under those circumstances. But immediately the jet's intentions became clear. Its engines roared and it started to surge away.

"Duck," Charlie yelled.

He swerved to the right, toward the plane.

I rolled down onto the floor of the back seat as I heard the sickening crash of metal.

The next few seconds were a mixture of panic, of g-forces shoving me upside down, of loud explosive sounds, and most of all, of bright, yellow-orange flames.

86

Bergstrom International Airport, Austin

Confusion and disorder dominated my senses. I couldn't see, hear, or even think. Through a blurred world, I struggled to hold on to something.

Then we stopped, and the first rational thought that came to my muddled brain was one of heat—intense, scorching, burning temperature. And for some reason I thought I was back in the horse barn with my son Tim.

I tried my right arm. It moved. In these circumstances, my deformed right hand didn't matter, and I used it to shift position. In so doing I realized Tim wasn't there, and I didn't have to worry about his safety.

Someone shouted. "Don't move. Stay down."

Second by second, rational thinking returned. I remembered that I was in Charlie's SUV and at the airport. I blinked, and my vision returned enough to see that the flames now moved away from us.

HARRY HAINES

At the same time, my hearing communicated with my brain and I recognized Charlie's voice. "The jet is continuing down the runway," he said. "It's safest to hunker down."

He didn't need to convince me.

I tried to take stock of our situation. Apparently we had crashed into the tail of the Lear, then rolled, and ended up on the left side of our vehicle. I sensed that the right front and right rear wheels must be in the air and still spinning. I could hear the two Texas Rangers in the front seat talking.

"You okay?" Charlie asked.

"Yeah, I think so," the other replied.

"Sam, how're you doing?"

"I'm okay," I said.

In the distance, the sound of sirens grew louder.

A voice came over the radio. "Unit 601, are you there?"

"Where's the damn mike?" Charlie said.

The next few minutes came as a blur of good news. Fire trucks and ambulances surrounded us. Firemen pried open the right-hand doors—which were now the roof of the overturned vehicle—and lifted us out of the SUV. EMTs put the three of us on gurneys, loaded us into ambulances, and rushed us to the ER at Seton Hospital. I felt shaken but otherwise okay. An hour later they released me.

I found Charlie in the hallway conferring with the two Rangers who were following us in the other SUV. They had escaped injury but experienced a ringside view of the accident.

"When we saw you swerve to the right, we went left," the driver of the second SUV said. "We bounced out onto the grass and rolled to a stop. We thought you were goners."

"Describe the accident as you saw it," Charlie said.

346

"As you know, you veered right just as the jet rotated for lift-off. You hit the tail, causing the left wing to come down. When the wingtip caught the ground, the plane cartwheeled. Fuel spilled, ignited, and it was all over."

"Any survivors?"

"Are you kidding? You saw the fireball. No way anyone could live through that."

"Do we have a manifest?" Charlie asked. "Do we have names of those on board?"

"First thing we did was check with the ground crew that rolled out the jet. They gave us sworn statements for five names."

"Five?"

"Two pilots, three passengers."

"Names of the passengers?"

"Butler, Klemkowski, and Williams."

"Tom, Dick, and Whiskey," Charlie said.

I called Southwest Airlines and booked a flight to Oklahoma City. Then I called my wife and gave her all the details. It took me a while to reassure her, to win her confidence that the danger was over, but by the time we came to the punch line, the reason for my call, she was laughing with joy.

"Can you and the kids pick me up at the Oklahoma City Airport? I need a ride to Midland, Texas."

"I don't know. We're really particular about who we give rides to."

"Southwest Flight 611, arrives at 10:55 this morning."

"You're sure a lot of trouble."

"But I love you."

She stopped laughing, and her voice grew serious. "And I love you,

HARRY HAINES

too, more than you'll ever know."

At Oklahoma City's Will Rogers World Airport, when I came through security I saw Emily at the head of the crowd waiting to greet passengers. She yelled "Daddy" and ran past the TSA security guard, breaking the rules to enter the restricted area and throw her arms around my neck.

I picked her up and walked in front of the guard, gave him a smile, and went to Suzie and Tim.

It was a family reunion I'll never forget.

The seven-hour drive from Oklahoma City to Midland gave us a renewal of family. The kids played "alphabet," a game where they search road signs to look for words that begin with the letters in alphabetical order. Suzie and I talked about Texas politics, about how much I hated it, and how glad we'd both be when my term of office was finished. When we drove past the "Midland City Limits" sign, Suzie and the kids clapped. And when we got to Everglade Street, we were amazed at all the cars. We pulled into our driveway only to find a banner hanging over the front porch. It read—

Welcome Home Senator Davis and Family

I opened the car door, and music wafted from the back of the house. It sounded like a party in full swing.

The kids ran ahead. Suzie and I took the path around the west side of the house to the backyard. I guessed there must have been a hundred or more people.

Art came to greet us.

The band switched to a loud, up-tempo arrangement of *For He's a Jolly Good Fellow*.

People started singing.

Art led me to an elevated platform with a microphone. "May I have your attention, please," he said.

The crowd quieted.

"It's my honor to introduce to you tonight that rare person in Texas history, an honest politician . . . our own Senator Sam Davis."

The crowd clapped and cheered.

I thought he would ask me to say a few words.

He didn't.

Instead he introduced the Midland County Republican Chairman.

"Sam," the chairman said, "we're mighty proud of you and what you've done to break open the ring of sleazy politicians who have dominated Austin."

Again, people clapped and cheered.

"And this afternoon the Midland County Republicans have drafted a petition. All of us here tonight have signed it."

He unrolled it and started to read.

"Whereas, Texas needs new, ethical leadership in state government, and whereas Senator Sam Davis has proven he has both the ethics and the leadership, we the undersigned do hereby offer our pledge of support to draft him for the office of . . .

. . . Lieutenant Governor.

Credits

I am indebted to a great many folks for their help in the researching and writing of this novel. While it's impossible to thank everyone, I want to recognize (what I believe to be) the five sources who contributed most.

First would be my long-time buddy Steve Mayes. He has designed the covers for all six of my novels, and he always insists on reading the manuscript before beginning his creative work. At the time he first saw this story, I had another, more prosaic title. Steve suggested I change to *Puppet Politics,* and it stuck. Thanks, Steve, for the title, for all the cover designs, and for your personal friendship over the years.

Second would be Pam Kessler, the lady with the blue pencil. She edited the gally-proofs and made numerous suggestions about improving the story. Thanks, Pam, for your eagle eye and catching all those mistakes.

Third would be Texas State Senator Kel Seliger and his Amarillo chief of staff, Christy Bertolino. Senator Seliger (who bears no resemblance to any of the politicians in this story) gave me an extraordinary amount of time for interviews, and he instructed his staff to help me with political details. Christy, especially, spent considerable effort in chasing facts and figures about the 31ˢᵗ district, about Austin, and about the lessor-known minutia of the Texas political process. If you like the "insider facts" of a political thriller, thank Senator Seliger and his staff.

This is a story about the Texas oil patch, and for information about the state's oil and gas economy I sought help from lots of people. Chief among them was Wayne Hughes, executive director of the PPROA, the Panhandle Producers and Royalty Owners Association. Thanks, Wayne, I couldn't have written this novel without your help.

And finally, I want to acknowledge Robert Redford and his movie *The Candidate*. Initially, it was this film, about running for senator, that started me thinking about an election story. If you haven't viewed it recently, I recommend it. It's a really good movie.

And once again, I want to thank the good people at Denny's on I-40 in Amarillo. Most of *Puppet Politics* was written in the restaurant between 5:00 and 10:00 a.m. with their white noise and food aroma providing a comfort zone that made the words flow. Someone once asked me, "How do you think up a story?" And (for me, at least) the answer is "caffeine." Special thanks to Diane McGinnis, the world's best waitress, who provided an untold number of cups of hot coffee to keep the writer's muse going.

Harry
Summer, 2013
Canyon, Texas